# The Games We Play

## Sicilian Mafia Wars
### Book 2

Meaghan Pierce

Pierced Soul Publishing

*For The Group Chat. Y'all make me better.*

Dear Reader,

Please be aware that *The Games We Play* contains content that may be triggering for some. For a list of triggers, please see the next page.

*The Games We Play* contains the following content: degradation kink, exhibtionist kink, threats of rape.

# Chapter One

She hated absolutely everything about her life.

Maybe not everything. She still had her camera. The one possession she'd refused to sell. It sat hidden in the back of her closet in a beat-up box under a pile of clothes. As much as she wanted to pull it out and frame the perfect shot, hear the click and whir of the shutter as it captured her vision, hiding it from prying eyes was the point.

There was no telling what her mother would say about such an expensive thing sitting unused. Not when it could be sold. But she'd worked hard to save up for that camera, and it was the only thing still tethering her to her old life, to the person she used to be. To the person she was giving up hope of ever becoming again.

Pulling even with the curb, she cut the engine and glanced up at the house that felt more like a prison than a home. She hated coming back to this place every day, to the people inside it. Or, rather, to her mother. She'd escaped to Rome and avoided relocating to Sicily ten years ago for a reason.

At least the house was paid off. One less bill to scrounge up the money for each month. Not that it was in great condition, with its yellowing stone and peeling paint. There was a hole hidden behind a picture frame in the kitchen. Her mother's half-hearted attempt to fix a leak before getting bored with it and leaving it for someone else to deal with.

Something ugly hidden behind something pretty while everyone went on pretending it didn't exist. The story of her fucking life. With a sigh, she shoved out of the car and trudged up the front walk to the shallow stoop. Letting herself in, she headed for the stairs. She needed a hot shower. Something to wash off the sweat and the disappointment.

"Emilia? Is that you?"

She squeezed her eyes shut at the sound of her mother's voice. She did not need another tense conversation with her mother that dissolved into an argument.

"Hey, Mama. I'm going to go up and grab a shower."

"Can you come here for a minute? Please."

Emilia's head swiveled toward her mother's voice. There was something about her tone and the way she'd used the word please. Turning from the base of the stairs, she walked down the short hallway to the living room, stopping dead in the archway. Shit.

Her mother was perched on the edge of one of the high-backed wing chairs at the far end of the room, and her sister was just as rigid on the couch, an untouched glass of iced tea in her hands. But Emilia's eyes were drawn to the man sitting in the other chair next to her mother. He smiled, but it was cold, an unspoken threat, and her heart began to pound.

"Good to see you, Emilia," he said. "Won't you join us?"

He gestured to the couch next to her sister, and she dropped her eyes to the empty spot, then looked back at his face. "What are you doing here?"

Her mother sucked in a sharp breath, but the man ignored her, leaning forward in his chair, eyes narrowing on Emilia's face. "It's Wednesday."

When her hands began to shake, she shoved them into her back pockets. It couldn't possibly be Wednesday. Yesterday was Monday. Wasn't it? She wasn't late. She hadn't been late in the six months since moving to this godforsaken island.

"Are you sure?"

"Emilia!" her mother hissed.

She swallowed past the panic rising in her throat when he fixed her with that sinister grin again. "I'm sure. I wouldn't be here wasting my time if you'd kept to our bargain."

"I have it. Just…wait there."

She flicked a glance at her sister's wide eyes and spun on her heel, sprinting up the steps and slamming into her bedroom. Stupid. She was stupid. Every Tuesday for half a year, she'd laid money in the palm of the man in her living room. Each time reminded her how far she'd fallen. How not in control of her own life she was.

Dropping to her knees, she pushed the rug back and used her fingernail to pry up the loose floorboard between her bed and the wall enough to grasp it and pull it free. While most of her mother's money went to day-to-day living expenses, every penny Emilia earned went to the man sipping iced tea with her family like they were old friends.

She pulled the money out and counted it, muttering to herself as she did. It was all there. Assuming he didn't get the wild idea to charge some kind of late fee. If he did, she'd be screwed. And fuck knew what would happen to them then.

Folding the money and clutching it in her fist, she made her way back downstairs. The man smiled when he saw her, but his eyes were lifeless, almost black. He pushed out of his seat and stopped in front of her, close enough that she could smell the overpowering scent of his cologne.

She held the wad of cash out to him, and he took it gently from her fingertips, counting it slowly without bothering to step away. When he was finished, he pocketed it and ran his finger across her cheek and down her jaw, lifting her chin to meet his gaze.

"Good girl. I'll let your tardiness go this time." He gripped her chin in his fingers, squeezing roughly. "But don't let it happen again, or there will be consequences. Maria."

He tossed her mother's name over his shoulder, and then he was gone. As the adrenaline slowly leeched out of her body, she trembled, squeezing her hands into fists to still them. There was relief on her sister's face now that the house was theirs again, but her mother looked…irritated.

"I can't believe you forgot," Maria said, gathering the tray and carrying it back to the kitchen. "He sat here terrorizing us for nearly thirty minutes because you were irresponsible."

"Because *I* was irresponsible?" She followed her mother into the kitchen. "Need I remind you that I am not the one who got us into this mess?"

Maria heaved a dramatic sigh, setting the tray down on the counter with an angry snap and dumping the still full glasses of tea down the sink. Emilia's anger kicked up a notch watching her mother waste something they could have saved. What else was fucking new?

"How could I possibly forget? You won't let me. I'm sorry, Emilia," Maria sneered. "Is that what you need to hear me say? Again?"

"It might help if you meant it," Emilia snapped. "If I thought for even a single second you cared about what you've done to this family, to your children, to our futures."

Something akin to guilt flashed in Maria's dark eyes, but it was gone again too quickly for Emilia to be sure. She doubted her mother was capable of such an emotion. Maria Sagona was too selfish to care about anyone but herself, which is exactly how they'd ended up here. Mired together in this hellhole, all of them wishing to escape.

"At some point, you're going to have to forgive me so we can move on together, Emilia."

Her mother's favorite line when anyone tried to hold her accountable for this nightmare they were in.

"At some point, you're going to have to feel genuine remorse for what you did. When that miraculous day comes, we can talk about forgiveness."

Leaving her mother alone to pout, Emilia climbed the stairs to her room and sank onto the edge of the bed. Dropping her head into her hands, she very nearly gave in to the urge to cry. But what good would that do?

She'd shed too many tears already after arriving in Sicily, assuming she'd be here for a few days, a week at most. She had no idea what she was walking into. No idea that walking back out would be impossible.

Part of her wished she'd stayed away. Kept her head buried in the sand and written her mother's problems off as just that—her mother's problems. She might have, if not for her brother and sister. Bella and Antonio deserved someone who was there to put their needs first. Something their mother wasn't capable of.

"Emmy?" Emilia looked up to see Bella framed in the doorway, her long thin fingers twisting the hem of her shirt. "You okay?"

"I'm fine." Bella didn't look convinced. "Really. The payment's made. It's done." Until next Tuesday. "How was school?"

Bella sighed, plopping down on the bed and collapsing flat on her back. Emilia mirrored her sister's pose, resting her hands on her stomach and staring up at the ceiling.

"It was fine. Boring. When am I ever going to need to know any of this stuff?"

"You won't," Emilia confessed, and Bella laughed.

"Finally. A grown-up who's honest. If I don't need any of it, why do I have to learn it?"

"I have no idea." She tried to remember the last time she ever needed to use one of those complicated math equations she'd memorized in school. "But school is your job, and we all have to do stupid things at our jobs so we can move on to the next thing we want to do."

"Like university."

Emilia looked over at something in her sister's tone, but Bella continued to stare at the ceiling. "Yeah. Like university. Don't you want to go?"

"I feel bad about leaving Mama."

"Don't." Bella turned to stare at Emilia's harsh command. "What I mean is, you're supposed to leave home and do better for yourself. You and Antonio. I want that for you. And Mama would too."

She said it, but Emilia had a sinking suspicion both she and Bella knew it wasn't true. If given the chance, Maria would prefer some kind of controlling stake in her children's lives until she took her last breath. How else could she live out her days as the victim of her own circumstances? It was no fun without an audience.

"Do you regret coming back?" Bella wondered in a small voice. "Do you hate that you had to give up your life to rescue us? That you're suffering?"

Emilia reached out and gripped her sister's hand, squeezing it tight. "Being here with you, with Antonio, isn't suffering."

"But not with Mama."

"Mama is..." Infuriating, selfish, irresponsible. "My relationship with Mama is complicated. It always has been. It has nothing to do with you or with this. It just is. And it isn't your fault."

Bella rolled onto her side and laid her head on Emilia's shoulder. "I'm glad you're here keeping the wolves away."

Emilia gave Bella's hand another squeeze and kissed the top of her head. "Me too."

Because someone had to. Emilia didn't care if she died in this shitty house in this tiny village in Sicily. Not anymore. She knew what it was to get out from under her mother's thumb, and she wanted that for Bella and Antonio. She wanted them to have the world. Even if it meant she had to sacrifice herself for them to get it.

# Chapter Two

"This month is already looking better than last after those changes we made."

"Good. Do we have estimates back for the renovations on the east side club yet?"

Dom tuned his brothers out as they continued to drone on about sales and profit margins and staffing changes. His younger brother had always been good with numbers and business plans. Luca could see years into the future, mapping out how a venture would go and what changes they'd need to implement to make it happen.

The patience to realize that kind of vision wasn't in Dom's nature. He didn't have it in him to sit in a boardroom going over business plans or in a back office crunching numbers and tallying up spreadsheets. He much preferred to be in the thick of things, with boots on the ground and blood on his knuckles.

Truthfully, he'd been grateful when Matteo came back to town after their father's death a few months ago. He'd never relished the idea of taking over the family while Matteo wandered to fuck knows where finding himself. The tedious details needed to maintain their territory didn't interest him.

He'd much rather be out there with his soldiers, enforcing their boundaries, collecting information on the other territories from his spies, and ensuring anyone who crossed them or tried to cheat them was dealt with swiftly and severely. The violence necessary to keep the family and their interests safe had always come naturally to him.

Which is why his older brother appearing out of nowhere for the funeral and then announcing his intention to stay were more a relief than anything else. The prodigal son home at last.

And Matteo returned with plans. Big plans. Plans Dom wanted to help him achieve—just not by sitting in endless meetings about the politics and the business of it. Matteo wanted to build a kingdom in Sicily and sit on its throne, and Dom was eager to use his skills to help get them there.

But those skills did not include sitting here going over the financials of the strip clubs they'd recently acquired from the Romanos. He didn't give a shit how well the only Romano they'd left alive was handling the transition.

He was already focused on their next target.

"Dom," Alexei said, and Dom could tell by his tone it wasn't the first time Alexei had tried to get his attention.

He glanced up at his sister's lover—or fiancé now, if the giant rock on her finger was any indication—only to realize everyone at the table was staring at him.

"What?"

Matteo muttered something under his breath about focus and shared a look with Luca. "I asked you what you thought about the men we have stationed in Romano territory. Are we good to pull them back, or should we leave them in place a little longer?"

There was a question he would happily answer. "Leave

them. It's only been two months since Elio was killed. Just because favor was waning with him before doesn't mean people were keen to have us swoop in and take over."

"So there are still rumblings about uprisings?" Alexei wondered.

Dom nodded. "I get fewer and fewer reports about them, but every once in a while one comes through." He turned to Matteo. "Keep paying them well and giving them work, and it'll be harder to forget who keeps roofs over their heads and food in their mouths."

"We'll do that then," Matteo agreed with a nod. "And we'll touch on it again in a month or two and see where we stand. Davide is holding steady," Matteo said of the new Romano Don, who was really a Bianchi puppet. "Any reports about him?"

"Not so far. People seem to be fine with him. I haven't heard about anyone planning a coup, if that's what you're asking."

Alexei chuckled, and Matteo shook his head. "I like that he's pliable. But it does make me suspicious," Matteo admitted.

"Not out of character, according to Carina," Alexei said.

"Another thing she was right about," Matteo muttered. "And don't tell her I said that."

Alexei held his hands up in surrender, but Dom imagined there wasn't much the two didn't share with each other—including their love of scalpels and torturing people for information. Carina had become quite the seasoned interrogator in the last few months. Though he wondered sometimes if it was her natural skill with a blade or the fact that she was a woman that loosened tongues.

Whatever it was, it worked. They'd gotten a ton of information out of the spies they'd captured within their borders and the men they captured in enemy territory too. It was why they were in a good position to finally ramp up their plans to the next level.

"What's the update on Varda?"

Dom grinned. This was where he shined. The strategy of war. "Losing out on Elio's loan hurt him. He's still got income coming in, but not as much as he was anticipating when he thought he was getting his seven hundred and fifty mil back. Sources say he's pressing his other loans harder to pay him. Upping their weekly payments."

"I heard he's extended beyond loans to extortion."

"He has," Dom confirmed. "I've gotten a few reports saying he's started going into smaller villages and forcing them to pay a protection fee. If they don't, he burns down their houses."

"Jesus," Luca murmured. "One way to make a living, I guess."

"He's gathering resources for something."

"An attack?" Alexei said.

"My thoughts." Dom leaned his elbows on the table. "I think we're done with data collection. Time to take action."

"Going after his capos."

Dom nodded at Matteo. "His most loyal ones, yeah. The old guard still stands staunchly by his side, but the younger ones not so much."

"And you trust them?"

"I trust their intel. But any spy can turn on a moment's notice. And I'm always watching my back for that shit. For now, their intel from deeper in Varda's inner circle corroborates what our own spies are able to pick up from the fringe. Varda is getting increasingly desperate to figure out how to get the upper hand. I'd like to make sure he never does."

"So far, we've avoided all-out war. We can't anymore once we start dropping bodies," Matteo reminded him.

"It was always going to come to this. There was only so

much intel we could gather before we would be forced to make a move."

"And it's better if we make it."

Matteo looked from Dom to Alexei and back, and irritation rose in Dom's chest. His brother's obsession with thinking every step through five different ways made for slow progress. But Varda couldn't be outmaneuvered with business the way Romano was.

Varda ran his territory old school. He didn't care about funneling money through legit businesses the way they did with the Bianchi casinos or Romano had with his strip clubs. Which meant they'd have to take him down the old-school way—by brute force. It was a mission Dom was looking forward to. Assuming he wasn't an old man by the time Matteo made up his goddamn mind.

All of it hinged on how badly Matteo wanted that throne. It would be harder to claim it for himself, to plant the Bianchi flag, if any family remained fully in control of their own territory. The easiest way to reach and topple Gallo and Antonetti was to first take down Varda.

Otherwise, he could lend his army to either or both at any time. Nothing brought feuding families together against a common enemy like a war. And that was a risk he wasn't willing to take. The Antonettis and Gallos were already in talks to link themselves by marriage. No need to give them another ally to guard their borders.

"Who would you take out first?"

"Cipriani," Dom said without hesitation.

"Why him?" Luca wanted to know.

"He's close to Varda, but he's not all the way in the inner circle. He is, however, a substantial link between Varda and some of the men sitting on the fence. Cipriani is the only thing holding those men in place. They're more likely to defect if we get rid of their tether."

Matteo nodded slowly, glancing at Alexei before looking back to Dom. "Is it worth bringing him in? Getting some answers out of him first?"

Dom shrugged, but he didn't miss the way Alexei's eyes lit up at the idea. It had been over a week since they'd brought him any fresh blood. "We could try, but I wouldn't advise risking men on the off chance you could get him to talk. I doubt he'd give us much."

"Because you doubt my skills or because he doesn't know anything?" Alexei asked.

"I've seen you in action. You and Carina," Dom added, ignoring Matteo's frown of disapproval. "So I'd never doubt your skills. I'm just not sure he has any information I can't get from somewhere else. But I'm happy to bring back a new toy for you to play with if I can."

"Let's at least attempt a live capture," Matteo said. "But don't risk any of our men to make it happen."

"Done," Dom agreed.

Matteo sent a look around the table. "Anything else?"

Dom debated bringing it up again. Matteo had shot the idea down twice already, but a southern stronghold would help, and right now they didn't have one. "Have you given any more thought to my proposal to buy that property on the southern border?"

Alexei and Luca paused in their rise from the table, but Matteo urged them off with a flick of his wrist and waited until they were gone to speak. "First Carina hauls Alexei off to Marsala so he's at least thirty minutes away whenever I need him, and now you want to live more than an hour away on the southern coast?"

"It's not like I'm taking a vacation," Dom replied, rolling his eyes. "It takes two hours to get from Palermo to Agrigento. On a good day. It would be better if I lived close to the action and housed soldiers with me too."

"I can buy a chopper."

"Yeah," Dom said, drawing out the word. "Because those are known for being real subtle."

Tapping his fingers on the edge of the table, Matteo considered. Dom had been scoping out this property for weeks. Ever since they'd lost a man in a skirmish because they were too far away to provide proper backup. A southern base of operations would be the perfect solution to make sure that didn't happen again.

"How big is it?"

Dom took a steadying breath for patience. He'd told Matteo the specs of this place at least four times now. Either his brother didn't listen, or something was wrong with his memory.

"Eight bedrooms in the main house. One in the pool house. Two staff cottages. Four men in each cottage and two men in each bedroom gives us enough space for two dozen men."

"And the pool house?"

"That's mine." He still wanted his privacy. "We'll hire local staff, so they don't have to live on the grounds. There are at least a couple loyal families down there. I'm sure we can find someone to come in to cook and clean."

Matteo stared off into the distance over Dom's shoulder but ultimately nodded. "Fine. But you're in charge of the running of it. The staffing, the scheduling, their training, everything. I have enough on my plate without having to manage that too."

"It's handled," Dom assured him. "If we make a generous enough cash offer, I imagine we can close on it pretty fast."

"I have contacts. I'll push it through." He shoved back from the table, and Dom stood with him. "Let me make some calls, and I'll let you know the timeline. In the meantime, set up that op for Cipriani, and we'll start there."

"Done."

Dom watched his brother disappear inside the house and turned toward the sea with a grin. They wouldn't really know what this war had in store for them. Not until they took their first shot. And he had Cipriani in his sights.

# Chapter Three

She walked the final two blocks to the café, greedily soaking up the last of the sun before fall descended in earnest and the rains with it. A gull called, and she glanced out to sea. She hadn't been able to afford to live near the water in Rome, and while she missed her apartment with its old-world charm and beautiful mosaic tile, she did appreciate the views here.

Dodging a family of tourists, she jogged across the street and let herself into the café through the side door. The kitchen was relatively quiet, although it wouldn't stay that way once it got busy, and she quickly stored her bag in the makeshift break room and clocked in.

It was a Friday afternoon, and she was scheduled to work the dinner shift. She liked working the weekends, even though she was usually dead on her feet by the time she got home. American tourists tipped well on bellies full of good food and local wine, even though they didn't need to. And she could use every penny she could get.

After her memory lapse on the last payment, she was

paranoid about missing another one. She didn't want to know what Varda or the enforcer he sent to the house would do if they were late again. She'd seen movies about people who failed to pay loan sharks on time and all the horrible things they'd do to them and their families.

That's what the last six months of her life had felt like. A movie. Or maybe a nightmare. One she couldn't wake up from. You read things about the Mafia in the papers, usually as an aside, buried in the middle pages. Some Mafioso arrested for racketeering or tax evasion or drugs. She had no idea it was still like this.

That there were still dangerous men running huge illegal empires right under the noses of normal, everyday people and the cops. That they could, would, and did kill without thought or remorse. None of that seemed real. It was a long-forgotten past, the stuff of legends.

Until Bella's desperate plea on the phone one afternoon. She remembered it with crystalline clarity, though she wasn't sure why that day stuck out to her. Maybe because it was the day everything changed. Even if she didn't know it yet.

She'd been sitting outside a little café enjoying an espresso and a scoop of gelato even though the weather was still chilly. But the sun was shining for the first time in a week, and it felt like cause for celebration after so much rain.

Then her phone rang. Her sister sobbed on the other end, mumbling incoherently about money and being scared and not knowing what to do. Their mother had intercepted, told Emilia it was nothing, and hung up. But Emilia couldn't get past how terrified Bella sounded.

With her most recent project at work wrapped and a little time before the next one began, she took a week off and flew down. She'd been sending her mother money to cover some debts she'd mentioned offhand at Christmas. A few credit cards that got out of control after Emilia's stepfather died two years before. It was so far beyond what her mother insinuated that it seemed laughable now.

It wasn't credit cards. She could have forgiven credit cards. It was tens of thousands of dollars borrowed from a man who shouldn't exist, but who very much did. He didn't just operate outside the law; in this part of Sicily, he *was* the law. There was no getting away from Aroldo Varda or his thugs.

She'd tried, albeit naively. When she found out her mother was behind on payments—choosing instead to spend the money Emilia had been sending on stupid shit like clothes and expensive meals—she'd tried to negotiate the loan down. Varda wasn't interested in negotiations. And if she wanted to keep her fingers and toes, if she wanted to keep her family alive, she'd have to figure out a way to get him his money.

There had been so many fights that first week. Emilia screamed at her mother for doing something so stupid, so reckless as to borrow money from the fucking Mafia and then not even being responsible enough to use the money she'd tricked her own daughter into sending to pay off the loan sharks.

It hadn't been any use. Each time Maria realized even a sliver of the gravity of her situation, she retreated into tears, eager to play the helpless victim. But Emilia knew her mother was smarter than that. She didn't want to have to do hard things like deny herself a new dress or a night out with friends. She didn't care about the consequences, but Emilia did.

Especially about the safety of Bella and Antonio. They were only sixteen. Still so young, even though they were starting to look like adults. She couldn't bear the thought of something happening to them because their mother was too selfish to do the right thing.

Before the week was out, she knew what she needed to do. She returned briefly to Rome and quit her job, then subleased her flat until her lease expired. It wasn't hard. She was in a beautiful spot. A spot where the church bells pealed every day and anything you might want was only a short walk away in any direction.

She packed up most of her clothes and a few important things she couldn't bear to part with, like her camera, and sold the rest. She bought a cheap car, packed everything she could fit inside it, and moved in with her mother to make sure the loan got paid and everyone stayed alive. Not that her mother appreciated it.

Maria acted like Emilia was an enemy combatant. They were always sparring about something. And there was never enough money. No matter how much she saved up, no matter how much she threw at Varda and his goon to make it go away, it felt never-ending.

At this rate, her children's children would be making payments to one of Varda's great-grandchildren or something. Assuming she ever got the chance to get married and have kids. Who would marry her with something like this hanging over her head? Who would willingly put themselves in that kind of danger for her?

A customer sat in her section, and she studied him. He didn't look American. He was too comfortable claiming his own seat, and his eyes weren't constantly straying to the beach in awe. But he was alone, so it was hard to tell if he had the telltale American twang.

His phone rang, and he answered. A series of tattoos covered the back of his hand and traveled up the length of his arm until they disappeared under the sleeve of his t-shirt. Moving closer with a pitcher of water, she kept her ears trained on his conversation.

His Italian was fluent, quite good if he wasn't a local, but that isn't what struck her. It was his voice. The deep, rich tone floated on the breeze while he asked whoever was on the other end about a house and details for an operation. Was he a doctor? Did doctors have tattoos on their hands?

She topped off the water of an American couple enjoying plates of ravioli, humoring their broken Italian even though she'd learned English in elementary school. When she turned away from the table, the man was staring at her.

His eyes were dark and intense, and he sent a little shiver down her spine. Something about him was dangerous, a clear warning to stay far away from him. But there was something alluring too.

Maybe it was the sweep of black hair that looked like he was always running his hands through it or the square cut of his jaw covered with a day's growth of beard. Or maybe it really was just his eyes. Eyes that skimmed down her body and back up without lingering in any particular spot. Just taking her in.

She drew closer, reaching down to flip his water glass over and fill it from the pitcher. "Is there anything I can get you?"

He tilted his head while she spoke, as if he was trying to decide what to make of her. "I'll take a glass of house red and your favorite plate."

"Mine?"

His lips twitched, and though he didn't smile, there was amusement in his eyes. "Yours. What's your favorite thing to eat here?"

"The tiramisu," she confessed, and he chuckled, low and deep. "Best in Sicily. Did you want a full meal? Or a single course?"

He checked the time on his watch, flashing another tattoo on his opposite forearm. "A single course."

"Then I'd have to say risotto with octopus. It's wonderful here."

"I'll have that then."

When she moved to brush past him, he closed his fingers around her wrist, holding it lightly. She wondered if he could feel the way her pulse sped up at his touch or the way her skin heated. His lips parted and her gaze dropped to them, but he didn't speak.

"Was there something else?"

"No," he said, the single word rumbling from his chest and hanging in the air between them. "Nothing else."

He released her, and she brushed away the momentary flare of disappointment. What in the hell was wrong with her today? She must still be on edge from that run-in with Varda's man earlier in the week.

"I'll be right back with your wine."

He was on the phone when she hurried back with it, but he spared her a glance and a small nod, waiting for her to leave before he resumed his call. Business picked up and she kept herself busy, constantly checking on American patrons who didn't know Italian dining customs.

She didn't understand why someone would want to be interrupted so often while having a meal. But the friendlier she was and the more she dropped by, the more money they left on the table, and she wasn't going to complain about that.

The Italian patrons were more laid back, signaling when they needed something rather than expecting you to stop and check on them. And every time she glanced over at him, he was watching her with those dark, mesmerizing eyes.

When he finally signaled for the bill, she went to set it on the table and leave, but he caught her wrist again, stroking it lightly with his fingertips before releasing her. "The risotto was delicious."

"I'm glad you enjoyed it."

He slipped far too much money into the folder and held it out to her. "I'll have to come back for the tiramisu."

"You will," she replied, a little breathless as she clutched the folder to her chest.

"Until next time, then."

She stood there, unable to do more than nod as he rose, his body brushing against hers when he moved out from behind the table. Then with one last look, he was gone. Something was definitely wrong with her. She rubbed her chest over her rapid heartbeat, sticking the folder in the pocket of her apron and clearing the dishes.

The table was filled by another group before she made it back to the kitchen, and she shook her head. Dumping the plates in the sink for the dishwasher, she peeked at the bill he'd left, her mouth dropping open. She quickly shoved it into her apron pocket with the rest of her American tips, glad her boss wasn't in the kitchen to ask her about it.

Forty and balding with bad breath, he was the owner's son, and from the moment she'd started this stupid job, she'd decided to stay as far away from him as possible. Not that he made it easy.

He was creepy, always making inappropriate jokes and rubbing up against her when there was plenty of room to get past in the kitchen or the dining room. And just last month, he'd asked her out for coffee. She politely declined, but he retaliated by docking her pay fifty euros, claiming she was chronically late.

It was bullshit, of course. She was ten minutes early most days. But she couldn't afford to lose this job. Finding it had been hard enough; it didn't matter that she was wildly overqualified. She needed the money. So she smiled and apologized and swore to be better about being on time.

He was no doubt working himself up to ask her out again, knowing he had the trump card because he held her paycheck in his hands. But she'd deal with that when the time came. Until then, she could think about the generous stranger with dark eyes and swirling tattoos and a touch that made her pulse soar.

23

# Chapter Four

Dom rolled the map flat on the table, securing it at the corners with some books and a gun, and studied it again. Their intel pegged Cipriani as a creature of habit. Stupid, all things considered. Predictability in their line of work often got you killed. But it would make his job easier.

He'd spent days putting the plan together while his spies gathered intel on Cipriani's whereabouts. Alexei suggested making it look like an accident. He was good at those, but Dom wanted to make a statement. This wasn't just about weakening Varda's stronghold in his own territory. This was about sending a message.

He didn't simply want to take Cipriani out. He wanted Varda to know who'd done it. They would at least try to get Cipriani out alive and deliver his body later. More information was always better than less. But Dom felt sure it wouldn't happen. Sometimes you could tell which men wouldn't go down without a fight.

Still, they would make the attempt. Even though he'd be more satisfied if things got a little bloody. He was looking forward to this war. The death and destruction of it. The power. This was the shit he was made for.

"Cipriani confirmed at his last stop before heading home."

Dom glanced up at Franco Rossi, one of his best capos, and nodded. After Cipriani stopped for a drink at a local bar, he'd head home to have dinner with his wife. They didn't appear to like each other much, and she would go upstairs to bed shortly after they finished eating.

Then Cipriani would sit downstairs, zoning out in front of the TV and occasionally taking calls. In the two weeks they'd been watching him, it didn't even appear he was getting laid. Not by his wife or a mistress or a prostitute. The man's life seemed torturously boring. He deserved to be put out of his misery.

They didn't care about the wife, and since Dom wasn't interested in terrorizing women, the plan was to intercept him between the bar and his house. His drive home cut through a pretty isolated stretch of road, and if Cipriani stuck to his usual timeline, he'd hit that stretch at just the right time.

Dom checked his watch. They had about thirty minutes to intercept him before they lost their window and would have to roll with the backup plan to follow him to his house and take out him and his wife.

Fixing the gun to his hip, he rolled the map back up and laid it neatly on top of the others he had of Varda's territory. They'd been infinitely useful over the last few months. He'd marked strongholds and safe houses and homes of some of Varda's top capos. He knew where their mistresses lived and how often they visited.

Once they took this first step and the war officially began, they could use their knowledge to systematically wipe out every loyal Varda capo and soldier. Then Matteo would be able to easily install new leadership. Leadership that, like

Davide Romano, would bend the knee to Matteo Bianchi and bring them one step closer to conquering Sicily. The possibility of it hummed in his blood.

"Let's load up and head out."

He locked the door to the cottage he was renting while he waited for the sale of the compound to go through. True to Matteo's word, he had connections, though Dom had no idea how he'd made them while jet-setting around the world for the last seven years. But the realtor on the property turned out to be a Bianchi man, and the whole process would no doubt be smooth sailing.

The property would be the perfect place to spread out and post up within less than an hour's drive from Varda's main villa and a stone's throw from the border between the territories. There was a risk of Varda's own spies finding out they were setting up a base so close, but he had plans to ensure the compound was heavily fortified and monitored.

The entire thing was built like a fortress, with several different security systems already in place. Apparently the expat American who'd built the thing was very paranoid. Something that worked in Dom's favor. It wouldn't take more than a few days to get it fully operational.

Plus, it didn't hurt that it was so close to the café he'd stumbled into the other day while in the area scoping out the property for weaknesses. The one with the pretty waitress with auburn hair and dark gray eyes. She was captivating. He hadn't been able to keep from touching her or watching her or fighting to catch the sound of her voice as she spoke to other guests.

He was most definitely going back there for a slice of tiramisu and the chance to talk her into his bed. The thought of the sounds she'd make with that lyrical, almost smoky quality to her voice while he moved inside her had been playing through his mind for days.

But he'd think about that later. Right now he needed to focus on the task at hand. The sky faded from blue to shades of purple and orange as the sun dropped toward the horizon. The tail on Cipriani reported he was still at the bar but nearly finished the one glass of wine he drank before going home to his frigid wife.

Traffic was thin, which was good for them. This part of Sicily rarely attracted tourists who preferred to keep to the coast, and the locals would be home preparing dinner rather than out and about. They were on a perfect path to intercept when they got the call that Cipriani had left the bar and was on his way to them.

"Silencers on," Dom said as he pulled even with the guardrail and slipped his gun from his hip. "Take him alive unless he doesn't give us any other choice."

A phone signaled in the car seconds before Rossi said, "Inbound."

Headlights slashed across the waiting SUV, and he glanced at his men in the rearview mirror. Placing his gun on the dash, Dom jerked the wheel and angled the car across both lanes of traffic, forcing Cipriani to slam on his brakes, his vehicle skidding to a halt.

When Dom jumped out, he could smell the faint scent of burned rubber. Cipriani shoved out of his car, waving his arms and gesturing between them.

"You fucking idiot! What's the matter with you? You could have gotten someone killed!"

Dom stopped inches in front of the man, finally bringing his gun level with the guy's chest, and grinned. "We're not after killing you yet."

Cipriani's hand went to his waist, and Dom shook his head. "Ah, ah. Don't do anything stupid. Take the gun off and put it on the hood of the car."

When the rest of his men moved in behind Cipriani, his

shoulders slumped in defeat. He removed the gun from its holster and set it on top of the car, holding his hands in the air, palms out. Rossi rushed forward, patting Cipriani down for more weapons, and removed a second gun from an ankle holster and a knife from his pocket.

"Clean," Rossi declared once all the weapons were accounted for.

"Good. Load him up."

"My wife's going to notice I'm missing."

Dom chuckled. "Will she?"

Cipriani jerked against Rossi's hold as he wound rope around his wrists and secured it, refusing to get into the SUV. "If you hurt a hair on her fucking head, I swear to God I'll—"

"You'll what?" Dom raised a brow. "Do tell." When Cipriani only glared, Dom waved a dismissive hand in the air. "I have no intention of doing anything to your wife unless you make me. Who knows, maybe once you're dead, she'll find a man who can actually give her some good dick instead of falling asleep in front of the TV every night."

Rossi laughed as he shoved a struggling and bound Cipriani into the backseat and climbed in behind him. Dom slammed the door and turned to the other two men with him.

"Get rid of the car. The chop shop's expecting you." Climbing behind the wheel, he took the phone Rossi offered him over the console.

"Wifey's been texted to say he's running late."

Dom glanced down at an incoming text. "Looks like she's not too happy about your tardiness." He tossed the phone on the passenger seat. "At least it means she won't call Varda to report you missing for a while. Maybe we'll even deliver your body to him before she gets the chance."

"What do you want?" Cipriani demanded. "You think this will be a strike against Varda? He won't even feel it."

"Already lying to me, and we've only just met." Dom

tsked. "Personally, I don't want anything from you. Other than your death, I guess. But I have an associate who's good with a blade, and he'd like to ask you some questions."

Cipriani spit on the headrest, and Dom pinned him with a look in the rearview mirror. "I'm not saying shit to you or any other Bianchi motherfucker."

"My associate is very persuasive."

The car lapsed into silence as they sped away from Varda territory back toward Palermo. The whole thing had gone off without a fucking hitch, and Dom was patting himself on the back for it. Eventually, Cipriani's wife would go to Varda—once she got over being mad at him.

He liked the idea of delivering Cipriani's body before the wife could raise the alarm. But that all depended on how long it took Alexei to work his magic and pull whatever answers he could from Cipriani's mind. Dom still didn't think he'd know much more than they already did, but who was he to deny Alexei and Carina their opportunity for fun?

"What the fuck are you doing?" Rossi inquired from behind him.

Dom glanced in the mirror and saw Cipriani convulsing. When white foam appeared around the edges of the man's mouth, he cursed under his breath and jerked the car to the side of the road. By the time he'd thrown it into park, gotten out, and wrenched open the rear door, Cipriani was dead.

"Jesus fucking Christ. A goddamn suicide pill? What century is this?"

"I'm sorry, boss," Rossi said, bracing his hand on Cipriani's chest to keep him from slumping over too far.

"Don't be." Dom watched the thin white foam drip down Cipriani's chin onto his chest. "This is an interesting development, though."

"How do you mean?"

"Is this a one-off? Or is Varda asking his men to hide

suicide pills in their teeth so they can't be taken alive? Because if he is, I might have to rethink our strategy on infiltrating Varda's inner circle."

"Alexei is going to be very disappointed," Rossi said.

"Yes. About this one and others he might not get to interrogate. I'll worry about him later. Right now I want to deliver this prick to his boss. But I want it to look like the death was our choice and not his."

"How do you plan to do that?"

Dom considered his options. "Grab me the tarp from the trunk."

As Rossi climbed out the other side of the SUV, Dom grabbed Cipriani by his shirt and hauled him onto the gravel shoulder, using the car to shield him from the road. He pried Cipriani's jaw open with his fingers and rinsed the foam from his mouth and face.

Rossi returned and helped him roll Cipriani onto the tarp. Rising, Dom drew his gun and fired six shots into Cipriani's lifeless body. It jerked with the force of the silenced bullets, and blood oozed from the wounds enough to look like he'd been murdered instead of committing suicide. It's not like Varda was going to call the cops and get an autopsy.

They rolled the body tightly in the tarp and shoved it into the trunk in silence. Then, as the stars winked to life against the backdrop of an inky blue and purple sky, they drove toward Varda's HQ. It was time to declare war.

# Chapter Five

It was Tuesday. Again. No matter how much she wished this day away, it stubbornly arrived every week. There would be no forgetting to make a payment today. Not after the screaming match she'd had with her mother once Bella and Antonio had left for school.

She wouldn't have forgotten. She came down the stairs with the money in her pocket. Like every other Tuesday, she was going to drop it off before she left for work. It was out of her way, about an hour in the opposite direction, but she couldn't help that. It's not like she got to choose when and where she paid. Although the stranger's generosity at work on Friday had helped her pad this week's payment considerably.

He hadn't been back since, but that didn't stop him from invading her thoughts. It was silly, really, how often she thought of him. But one of her old friends who worked as a therapist would probably say something like he's an escape from the hellhole of your life. Enjoy it while you can.

And even if her friend wouldn't say that, it was nicer to wonder what other tattoos he might have and where than to dwell on her current circumstances. Dwelling hadn't done her any good so far, and he was a very sexy distraction.

Standing over the sink eating a piece of toast, Emilia jumped when the doorbell rang. Who would be randomly knocking on doors at this time of day? Panicked, she grabbed for her phone, nearly knocking it onto the floor in her rush. Tuesday. The calendar said it was Tuesday. So this couldn't be Varda's man.

Shoving the last bit of toast in her mouth and tugging on the hem of her shirt to smooth it, she crossed to the door. Her heart plummeted into her stomach when she saw the figure waiting for her on the stoop.

"I-I'm not late," she stammered. "It's Tuesday. I was going to drop the money off before I went to work."

He held a finger up to his lips and grinned, and she snapped her mouth shut, gripping the doorknob with trembling fingers. "I'm not here about your payment. But I do need you to come with me."

Her mouth went dry, and her knees nearly buckled. "What? Why?"

"Because Varda wants to see you." He waited a beat, pinning her with a violent look. "And we don't want to keep the boss waiting."

She nodded, numb, and grabbed her purse off the table by the door. Locking the house behind her, she followed him down the narrow walk and climbed into the passenger side of a black sedan. The space was small, and she was too close to him, close enough for him to touch her if he wanted.

The urge to bolt, to run as far away from him as fast as she could, was overwhelming, and she had to remember she was doing this for Bella and Antonio. Doing this so they could be safe and happy without this hanging over their heads.

He pulled away from the house and drove in the direction she always went to deliver her payments. She realized for the first time that she didn't know his name. Somehow that felt ridiculous. She'd been meeting the man once a week for six months and had no idea what his name was. Not that she wanted to. The less she knew about this life and the men who lived it, the better. It would be easier to forget when this was all said and done.

There was no attempt at conversation, and she was grateful for that. She didn't think she'd have anything to say around the constricting lump in her throat. Rubbing her sweaty palms on her jeans, she went over and over what this could be about.

It had been months since she'd tried to negotiate. Varda couldn't be coming back to punish her for that. Could he? Anything was possible at this rate. If the Mafia had rules, she didn't know what they were, apart from silence. That one was unspoken, and she imagined the penalty for breaking it was death.

But she hadn't told a single person about any of this. Her friends in Rome hadn't understood her sudden desire to blow up her entire life, shut down a lucrative career she was good at, and sell all her shit. And she hadn't explained. Not really.

What was she going to say? That she had to move to Sicily to help her irresponsible mother stop blowing off a debt to Mafia loan sharks? Right. That would go over well. They probably would've accused her of needing more sleep or had her committed. No. She'd been on her own in this from the moment she made the decision.

Without the convenience of proximity, her friends had slowly fallen away until no one was left. And she hadn't made any new friends here. Some of the other waitresses were nice, but they didn't hang out. She might be Italian, but she wasn't Sicilian, and that mattered, apparently.

They drove past the pizza place that was really some kind of Mafia hangout where she normally stopped and made the payments, and she swiveled in her seat to look back at it with a frown.

"He prefers to meet at his villa," the man explained. "It's more secure."

And he wasn't kidding. It wasn't one of the villas you might see on the coast, Agrigento was too far inland for that, but it looked like four regular-sized row houses had been turned into one massive home and set apart from the rest on the street. There was a gate blocking a paved drive, and the man hit a button to open it.

When they pulled through and around to a hidden courtyard, she saw men standing around in small groups. Guards, no doubt. Protecting Varda and whoever else lived here.

The man opened her door, but she ignored his outstretched palm and climbed out of the car on her own. Trailing behind him through the courtyard, she clutched her purse tight to her chest and did her best to ignore the leering stares of the gathered men.

The gaudy decor might have made her laugh if she wasn't so terrified. All the gold and marble and statues of saints seemed ripped out of the set of a movie. Art really did imitate life in this case.

She followed the man down a maze of hallways to a dead end, stopping at a closed door. He opened it, gesturing for her to enter, but her feet were rooted to the floor, immovable. What if she went into that room and never came out?

"Emilia," he growled, spurring her into action. "Good girl," he murmured, amused, as she darted past him into the room.

It was empty save for one man sitting behind a large desk topped with more ugly gold statues. His hair was slicked back, and he wore a sea-green collared shirt with the first few buttons undone and white slacks. Rings adorned nearly every finger on each hand, and his skin was deeply tanned.

The man was a caricature. She almost felt embarrassed for him.

Almost. He still held her life in his hands.

"Emilia Sagona," he said, and she jolted at the sound of her name on his lips. "Come in and have a seat. We've not met, but my name is Aroldo."

"I know who you are."

He smiled, but it was all sharp edges and harsh angles. It looked unnatural on his round face.

"Good, good. You've done well making your payments. Did a fine job getting your mother off her knees, even if some of my men were disappointed by that turn of events."

Emilia gripped her purse in aching fingers. She didn't want to be reminded of the ways her mother had chosen to hold the Varda debt collectors at bay.

"I have this week's payment." She reached into her bag and pulled out the folded-up bills. "I'm not late."

Varda glanced at the man who'd brought her in, and he stepped forward to pluck the money out of her hand before fading into the shadows again. She swallowed hard. What in the hell was she doing here if this wasn't about the money?

"I have a proposition you might be interested in."

She blinked. "What kind of proposition?"

"There's some information I need. And I want you to get it for me."

"Information about what?"

Varda scowled, and her heart beat faster. "There's a man who wants to wage war against me. And I want to stop him."

War? No. She couldn't be involved with some Mafia war. Not with everything else going on. She was barely surviving as it was.

"I don't think I—"

"You're perfect. You're exactly his type." His eyes traveled lewdly over her body from head to toe, and he licked his lips.

"All you need to do is get close enough to your target to find out what he knows, what their plans are. Then report it back to me."

This was insane. She wasn't a spy. How was she supposed to get close enough to a man who was probably wary of strangers for him to spill all his secrets? Unless…

"You want me to sleep with him so you can win some stupid war?"

Varda sat forward, anger etched into every line of his face, and she shrank back against the chair. "You can seduce him on your back, your knees, or upside down for all I care. What I want is the information you can get from him. Whether a good suck on his cock loosens his lips or you poke through his things while he's asleep makes no difference to me."

"And what's in it for me?"

Sitting back, Varda grinned. "You're a clever girl. I like that about you. For every bit of useful information you bring me, I will forgive five thousand euros off your mother's debt. And if I win this war, you can consider her debt paid in full."

Emilia chewed the inside of her cheek. This was a stupid idea. What the hell kind of information would she even be able to get? She had no idea what you needed to know to win a war. Or how to outsmart a Mafioso dumb enough to wage one against someone like Aroldo Varda.

But the look in Varda's eyes made it clear saying no wasn't an option. And what did she care if another Mafia thug got caught in the crossfire?

"What do I have to do?" she asked at last.

Varda motioned his man forward, and he moved to hold his phone in front of her face. On the screen was a picture of a man with dark hair curling around the collar of his shirt. He was clean-shaven and broad-shouldered. He looked normal. Like any guy you might pass on the street. But no one in Sicily was who they seemed.

"This is Franco Rossi. He's in their inner circle, and he has a thing for redheads. They've been trolling my border a lot in recent weeks, and they've been spotted at a bar near the boundary multiple times."

"I doubt he'll share intimate details about all the ways he wants to kill you after a one-night stand."

Varda narrowed his eyes. "Then I guess you'll have to keep spreading your legs until you get what I need."

The idea of that nauseated her. "When am I supposed to start?"

"Immediately. It's not terribly far from where you work. You can stop there on your way home."

"How do you know where I work?"

Varda tilted his head to study her, like a predator sizing up prey. "I know everything about the people who owe me money. Don't forget that." He dismissed her with a wave, and his man came to grip her arm and haul her out of the chair. "I expect my first report by the weekend. Oh, and Emilia? There will be consequences if you disappoint me."

Of that, she had no doubt.

# Chapter Six

Dom walked the perimeter of the property, marking the location of each security camera on the roughly sketched map in his hand. Their Bianchi connections and the desperation of the American looking to get back to the States as quickly as possible meant they'd been able to take possession of the entire property before the deal officially worked its way through the banks.

He'd spent days making lists, buying supplies, loading trucks, and selecting the men for the job. And now everything was moved in, rooms were assigned, and the men were settling in and unpacking—something he still needed to do.

Later. After he finished cataloging all their security measures and seeing where the gaps were.

The villa was set on a fairly large piece of property, one side facing the Mediterranean and the other surrounded by rolling hills of grass and trees. This was a less populated part of the island, but Dom imagined the American who'd built this place had bought up and knocked down several houses to ensure he had the view and the privacy he wanted.

Which suited Dom just fine. The more open space, the easier it was to see the enemy coming.

The house was ringed on three sides by a stone wall, and the fourth side was guarded by sheer cliffs that fell down into the sea. State-of-the-art security cameras were perched at intervals along the wall, and there were cameras in nearly every area of the house save for the bedrooms and bathrooms.

The long drive was protected by a gate that required a numeric code and was also fitted with multiple cameras between the gate and the house. No one was getting into this place undetected. Dom hadn't heard any rumblings about Varda knowing he was establishing a base here, but that didn't mean he wouldn't figure it out eventually.

Circling back to the front, he darted out of the way of someone carrying in some boxes and let himself into what he'd dubbed the security room. Banks of monitors lined the walls, each showing the feed from a different camera. He used a keyboard to toggle between views, comparing each perimeter camera to the ones on his list, impressed when a view from a camera he hadn't noticed appeared.

The cameras were movable, the direction and angle of each one able to be manipulated with the press of a button. The level of security both impressed and aroused suspicion. He wanted to know what the hell an American living on his island needed so much goddamn security for. He'd have to ask Luca to look into that later. His little brother could find out almost anything about anyone if you gave him enough time.

Even with all the security precautions, Dom still wanted to make up guard rotations. Two or three men to monitor the cameras and three or four more to walk the grounds with guns. Just in case. It never hurt to be prepared. He figured he'd do six-hour shifts around the clock.

Then there were training schedules to figure out. Rossi would help with those, and he'd been toying with the idea of having Alexei come down to teach better knife skills. So add that to his ever-growing to-do list.

Abandoning the security room, he weaved his way through men wandering the house and let himself out the side door. Skirting the edge of the pool, he unlocked the pool house and stepped inside. Quiet enveloped him, and he took a deep breath.

It was about the size of one of the cottages, maybe a little larger. There was a generous living space, a large bedroom with a king-sized bed, and a full bathroom with an impressive shower. It didn't have a kitchen like the cottages, but he was close enough to the house to grab whatever food he might want.

The only thing he really cared about was that he wouldn't be sharing it with three other men. Aside from the fact that he deserved his own space as the one in command here, he needed the quiet to think and recharge. And this would give him plenty of that.

Picking up one of the boxes he'd left in the living room, he carried it into the bedroom and set it on the edge of the bed. He still needed to interview housekeepers and cooks. He had no desire to add a cooking and cleaning rotation schedule to his already full plate. Or stomach whatever god-awful thing someone might whip up in the kitchen.

Carina had offered to help with that, but he hadn't confirmed with her. He'd have to give her a call and set something up. Sooner rather than later, or they'd all end up eating microwave meals for the foreseeable future.

Emptying one box, he went back into the living room for another until all the clothes he'd thought to pack were shoved into drawers. He didn't know exactly how long he'd be here, and running back and forth to Palermo every time he needed more supplies didn't seem like an efficient use of his time.

Matteo was already insisting he travel for a weekly meeting. And while it wouldn't necessarily be a waste, Dom didn't relish driving an hour just to listen to his brothers drone on about profit margins and equity. Maybe he should have let Matteo buy the helicopter after all.

With the bedroom finished, he moved back into the living room to set up a sort of command center. He had plans to use the solarium on the second floor as a war room. It was big enough to put at least two large tables end to end. Then he could stretch out a blown-up map of Sicily, marked with the territory boundaries and all the intel he'd been collecting. It would be a damn sight better than the smaller ones he'd been stuck rolling and unrolling for weeks.

But he'd use this spot in the pool house to keep himself organized. Starting with those guard rotations. Grabbing a pad of paper, he sat at the small two-person table and made a list of names, pairing people up based on skill set and temperament.

He'd chosen only single men for this assignment, reminding them of what he expected of them and what this meant. They were the tip of the spear. More backup would come if needed, but it would be slow to arrive. If something needed doing, they would be the ones doing it. Not a single man had declined.

With twenty-four men, twenty-five if he counted himself, and six-hour shifts, he'd given them a good balance between guard duty, training, ops, and downtime. He wanted to make sure they had time to get out, stretch their legs, get laid. They might be here a while, and he didn't want them getting cabin fever.

Plus, it gave him the perfect excuse to go back to that little restaurant for some tiramisu and another look at that waitress. Something he had every intention of doing as soon as he could manage it.

Until then, he'd called a meeting to discuss ground rules and go over these schedules. Once that was done, he'd call Carina and see if she was available to come out tomorrow and chat with some housekeepers and cooks. Another thing crossed off his list.

"Hey." Rossi poked his head around the door. "All-hands meeting still in fifteen?"

Dom checked his watch. "Yeah. Then I figure I'll give the guys the night off. They can scrounge up dinner at one of the local restaurants or that bar you like."

"I thought you were hiring a cook?"

"I am." Dom gathered his papers and rose, securing the pool house door behind him. "But I haven't talked to Carina yet about coming out to do some interviews."

"Then why is she in the kitchen talking to women right now?"

"She's what? When did she get here?"

Rossi shrugged. "Couple hours ago. Was I supposed to turn her away? I didn't take her for a security risk."

Dom glared at Rossi's sarcastic grin and shoved the papers at his chest. "Take these into the great room. I'll be right there."

"Sure thing, boss."

Their paths diverged off the living room, Dom going left toward the kitchen and Rossi going right toward the larger great room at the back of the house. He stopped in the archway, and sure enough, his sister was perched on a stool at the sizable kitchen island, talking with a woman who looked to be in her late forties.

The woman made eye contact with him over Carina's shoulder and froze. She wouldn't do. He didn't want to deal with women in the house who were so afraid of him that they lost their train of thought, for fuck's sake. Carina glanced at him and must have come to the same conclusion because she thanked the woman for coming and showed her to the back door.

"What are you doing here?" Dom asked once they were alone.

She frowned at his tone. "Alexei said you needed help hiring staff."

"I do."

"Well, then." She picked up a piece of paper she'd been making notes on and scanned it. "That's what I'm doing here."

"But I didn't call you."

"I knew you were moving in today." Dom's brows went up, and she cocked a hip. "People do tell me stuff. Well, Alexei and Luca tell me stuff. Matteo only under duress. I'm working on that."

"What about me?"

"You, dear brother, have never told me anything about anything." She made two circles on the paper and handed it to him, her emerald engagement ring glinting in the light. "These are the women I'd recommend. Two housekeepers for a house this size. They're sisters, each married to men who work at the casino near here."

"Are they going to be afraid of me?"

She crossed her arms over her chest. "Do you want them to be?"

He lifted a shoulder. "Not if it interferes with them doing their job."

"I think they'll be fine. The woman who will cook for you is old enough to be our grandmother. I'm sure she's seen worse than the likes of you."

"Are you?"

Carina shook her head, but she was smiling. "She'll be

bringing two of her grandchildren to help with prep and cleanup since there are so many of you."

"This is a lot more staff than I was planning for."

"You brought a lot more people than Matteo assumed. I've cleared the expense with him. He's fine with it."

"I highly doubt he just nodded agreeably."

"I never said that." Carina grinned. "But he's agreed to it now, at any rate. So unless you have objections, I'll contact them all."

He handed the paper back to her. "No. No objections."

"Good." She plucked it from his fingers and picked up her phone from the counter. "The housekeepers can't start for a couple more days, so you'll have to pick up after yourselves and try not to make too many messes until then. But the cook can start tomorrow."

"What about tonight?"

Carina pressed the phone to her ear and raised a brow. "Try a local restaurant."

With a grin, Dom turned and left her to make her calls. It looked like he was going to get a taste of that tiramisu sooner than he thought. Hopefully the waitress wasn't far behind.

# Chapter Seven

S tanding in front of the fan in the corner of the kitchen, Emilia lifted her hair off her neck and sighed as the air dried the sweat. It was hot today, and she already regretted agreeing to switch her day off. She needed Saturday off to meet with Varda, but she'd much rather be at the beach right now.

Not that she had any information for him. She'd gone to the bar he gave her every night this week, and not once had Franco come in for a drink, alone or otherwise. She had no idea how Varda would react when she told him the only update she had was no update at all. But she'd find out tomorrow.

A family of six got up, the parents shepherding the children out the door with their big beach bags slung over their shoulders. They were all pink from the sun, and the youngest child was tucked in his father's arms, fast asleep on his shoulder.

With a sigh, she moved out of the path of the cooling air and cleared the table, wiping it down with a damp cloth and replacing the glasses before carrying the dishes to the sink. It was slow, so she took her time to unload the clean dishes, stacking the plates by size and lining up the glasses on the shelf.

It was unusual for a Friday evening to be this quiet, and she wondered if it was the sunshine or the heat keeping people down by the beach. Or maybe it was the restaurant that just opened a few miles away that offered live music.

Alessia, another waitress who started around the same time Emilia did, pushed into the kitchen through the swinging doors. "Table's up in your section. You're lucky I didn't steal it out from under you."

"Why? More Americans?"

"No." Alessia peered out through the small window into the dining room. "Bunch of very hot guys. But if you don't want them, I'll take them."

Emilia pushed onto her toes to see over Alessia's shoulder, and her eyes widened. He was back, those dark eyes sweeping the restaurant like he was looking for her.

"I'll take them," she assured Alessia, debating whether to toss her messy waves up or leave them be.

In the end, she settled for tying the strands off her face and leaving the rest down. Grabbing a sweating pitcher of water from the counter, she moved into the dining room. His eyes found her instantly, again traveling up and down her body in a way that felt more like a curious exploration than a leering stare. Something was really wrong with her.

"Gentleman. I'm Emilia." She flipped over their water glasses and filled them. "What can I get for you?"

"A bottle of house red," the man said, his voice the same deep rumble that haunted her dreams.

"And I'll have an Amaretto neat."

Emilia nodded at the man who'd spoken. Something about him was oddly familiar, but she couldn't place it. Leaving them for the bar, she turned his face over and over in her mind. She'd seen him somewhere before. She was sure of it.

Carrying their drinks back, she filled their glasses with wine and left the bottle in the middle of the table. The man smiled when she handed him his Amaretto, and it hit her. Franco Rossi. He had a beard now. Varda's photo must be old, but it was definitely him.

Her gaze swept the table, landing on the man with dark eyes who was still watching her. Mafia. If Franco was, they probably all were. Of fucking course. The first man she'd been attracted to in almost a year was a dangerous criminal.

She forced a smile, and his brow twitched in question before she pivoted her attention back to Franco. He was the one she was supposed to be flirting with and trying to get information from. He was the one who liked redheads. Not that his friend seemed entirely disinterested.

She ran her hand playfully along Franco's shoulder. The man's brow shot up even higher, but she ignored him. She had a job to do and debts to pay. She couldn't let something like her libido get in the way of that. No matter how much it might want to.

"Let me know when you're ready."

Someone whistled under their breath as she walked away, but she didn't risk glancing over her shoulder to see who. It didn't matter who. She only needed to entice Franco enough to get him to let his guard down. He hadn't been at the bar, but he was here now. And she was going to make the most of it. She needed to be able to give Varda something when she saw him tomorrow.

The restaurant finally, blissfully, began to fill as the sun faded and people left the beach. But even as she flitted from one table to another, she kept her eyes trained on him. It wasn't her fault her attention kept shifting from Franco to him. She didn't even know his name. Probably better that way. She didn't need a name to slip into her fantasies when her attention should be on Rossi.

As if sensing her eyes on them, Franco turned in his chair and lifted his glass to call her over. Her blood hummed as the man tracked her journey across the room. He either didn't notice Franco was also watching her, or he didn't care.

When she stepped up next to the table, Franco brushed her hip with his fingertips. She leaned into it and smiled shyly—she wasn't a totally hopeless case when it came to flirting—but it didn't have the electricity she'd felt when the man touched her wrist the week before.

"Ready for *primi*?"

They murmured their assent and ordered from the menu. She turned toward the man, Franco reaching up to idly draw circles over her hip when she shifted toward him. The man's gaze dropped to where Franco touched her and then slowly dragged back up to her face. His expression was hungry, possessive, and her heart fluttered. That look should not be sexy on a man as dangerous as he probably was.

"The risotto is good," she said, hoping he couldn't hear the slight tremble in her voice.

"With octopus?"

She shook her head. "Mushrooms today, I'm afraid."

"Risotto with mushrooms, then." He focused on Franco's fingers again until she stepped away and they fell from her body.

They were deep in conversation when she dropped off another bottle of wine and their food. It didn't stop Franco from touching her, and it didn't stop the man from looking like he wanted to rip Franco's fingers from his body. Again, something that should not warm her the way it did, but her body was acting of its own accord at this point.

As she cleared their dishes from the second course, she thought for sure one of the men called him boss, and she jerked, nearly dropping a plate. Was he higher up than Franco in whatever organization Varda was so afraid of? And would Varda consider that a good thing or a bad thing? Christ knew this man would be easier to flirt with than Franco.

Not that Franco was bad looking, it would be unfair to say that, but he was overshadowed by his boss in every way. She wouldn't say Franco was less dangerous either. She imagined you needed to be capable of pretty much anything to survive in the Mafia, but he was less intense about it. And apparently her sex-starved brain found the intensity very appealing.

They sat well into the night, after other patrons began to clear out for home or their hotels, and she finally gave up against the heat and tied her hair up in a messy bun to escape it and the sweat she could feel dripping down her neck. As much as she didn't want the rains, she was ready for the cooler temperatures of fall.

She checked the coffee while they chatted. Theirs was the only table left in the restaurant, making it harder and harder to avoid the man's constant gaze or the way it tingled down her spine. And still, she didn't know his name. Everyone at the table insisted on calling him boss.

"Dessert?"

Franco pushed his chair back from the table and hooked his arm around her waist, drawing her onto his lap. His lips found the back of her neck. "I could think of something I'd like to have for dessert," he murmured against her skin.

"I think my boss would frown on something like that in the middle of the restaurant," she said with a flirty wink over her shoulder. She didn't miss the way the man's jaw clenched at her response.

"Mine wouldn't," Franco replied, not glancing up at the man across the table. "Would you, Dom?"

Dom. It fit him. In more ways than one, she imagined. "Tempting. But some things are better without an audience."

Dom's hand curled into a fist on top of the table and his voice was rough when he said, "We should get out of here anyway. Early day tomorrow. And I believe you have the midnight shift, Rossi."

Rossi sighed, his breath fluttering against her neck, and loosened his grip. "So I do. Some other time, Emilia." He slipped a piece of paper with a phone number into her hand and closed her fingers around it, pressing another kiss to her skin.

She stood, and the rest of the men did the same. Only Dom remained seated, those dark eyes boring into hers.

"You coming, Bianchi?" someone called from the door.

"In a minute," he said without breaking eye contact.

He reached into his pocket and counted out more than enough bills to cover their check, tucking them between two glasses and rising to his feet. Moving in behind her, his chest pressing against her back and his breath warm on her cheek, he skimmed his fingertips down her forearm to her hand. Prying open her fist, he plucked the piece of paper from her palm with Franco's number on it and dropped it into a glass of water. She watched the ink slowly diffuse until the numbers were unrecognizable.

When she looked back at him, he shifted closer, wrapping his arm around her waist and pressing his hand flat against her stomach as he leaned down to whisper in her ear.

"You don't need that. I saw you first."

She opened her mouth to respond, but no words came out. He grinned, dragging his fingers over her stomach and around her hip when he moved past her toward the door. She stared after him long after he was gone, her skin tingling where he'd touched her and her brain screaming a warning.

Dom Bianchi was dangerous. And against her better judgment, she wanted to find out how much.

# Chapter Eight

He set the last marker on the map taking up most of the long table and stepped back to admire his work. On it was all the intel he'd gathered over the last few months. The placement of Bianchi soldiers in Varda territory, the homes of each of Varda's top capos, locations of properties Varda owned, places where Varda's enforcers collected payments from people who owed them money. All of it was marked.

Each time he got a new piece of intel, he added it to the map. And another report was due any minute. He'd been carefully and quietly building a network of spies in Varda's territory for months. Men who were able to join Varda ranks or befriend low-hanging fruit in the Varda army, even some of Varda's own men. All of them were on his payroll, and their information had proved solid so far.

Now that Matteo was back, they had someone with tech skills at their disposal. Matteo's assistant Maeve had been able to get them some surprisingly good information with her hacking skills. Still, Dom preferred his boots-on-the-ground reports. You couldn't look a machine in the eye and tell if it was lying to you.

"The latest."

Otto, the youngest son from one of their most loyal families, pressed a folder into his hand, and Dom dropped it on the table, leaning against the edge with one hand while he flipped it open. He scanned the shorthand, moving pieces around on the map to match the new information.

He'd moved men deeper into Varda territory, and they'd successfully set up a base undetected. Varda controlled a significant portion of the island. It was less populated, with lots of hills and farmland, but it was big. Which gave him lots of places to hide or store supplies if he wanted to.

So far, none of their intel included any mention of a weapons stockpile, not beyond what anyone in their line of work would consider normal, anyway. But that didn't mean Varda couldn't make one if he tried. Their warning shot with Cipriani wouldn't go unanswered.

Flipping the page to the next in the stack, he moved more markers around. Two more properties added to Varda's collection. Dom stood back to take in the whole map again. For someone with dwindling capital and influence, the man owned an unusually large number of homes and properties, even for a territory as large as his.

He glanced up at Otto. "How hard do you think it would be to get men into some of these homes Varda owns?"

"Depends on how deep they are."

"We got anybody in deep enough to give it a shot?"

Otto rubbed a hand over his beard and scratched his jaw. "Sforza, maybe. He usually brings us the best intel, and his meets have turned to drops so he doesn't get caught."

Dom nodded, looking down at the spread of properties. "Let's get a message to him. Have him start with these." He indicated the cluster of houses starting in the center of Agrigento and radiating in all directions. "Then he can move to the east, toward their border with Antonetti."

Otto scribbled the order in a little notebook he always kept in his back pocket. "Got it."

After one last look at the map, Dom flipped to the next page of the report. It looked like Varda was still actively terrorizing the smaller villages with extortion schemes. He'd burned down four houses in the last two weeks. The more he razed to the ground, the less he seemed to care who was inside it. The bastard was going to draw the suspicion of the cops if he didn't calm the fuck down.

Not that the Bianchis didn't have their share of Italian police in their pockets. Every family on the island did. You couldn't survive without a few cops on the payroll. Hell, Matteo had Interpol connections. But they couldn't look the other way forever if you were being reckless. There was an art to operating outside the law. It was obviously an art form Varda didn't appreciate.

"Jesus," Dom muttered at the next report. "He killed a toddler?"

Otto grimaced. He had young nieces and nephews. "Yeah. In one of the house fires."

"And then threatened the other kids." He flipped to the next paper in the stack. "Sick son of a bitch."

"He is that."

"It also means he's getting desperate."

Otto shifted on his feet. "I thought he was just a psycho."

"That too." Dom straightened. "But if you take away the thing people live for, they become much less likely to do whatever you say."

"Like if you kill their kids."

"Exactly. Varda knows that. If he's taking out two-year-olds as part of his strategy, it'll eventually backfire."

"Maybe he didn't know the kid was in there?"

Dom shook his head. "Varda knows everything about his people. Probably knows when they sit down for a shit. He knew. He just didn't care. And that might work to our advantage. Any update on a reaction to Cipriani?"

"Rossi's got one, I think."

"Good. Send him up."

Otto inclined his head and slipped out, leaving Dom alone with the map and his thoughts. What a blood bath this war could end up being if Varda was willing to use children as cannon fodder.

"You wanted to see me?"

Dom looked up at Rossi framed in the doorway and had to fight the quick flash of jealousy that had taken root since he took Rossi and his other capos to the restaurant. He wanted to get another look at that pretty waitress, not give Rossi an opening to put his fucking hands all over her.

He'd known Franco all his life. It was rare that their taste in women overlapped. But apparently it did with Emilia. And each time Rossi touched her the night before, Dom wanted to snap his fucking hands off. It was a miracle he'd managed to keep his cool.

"Otto said you had an update on the Cipriani fallout."

Rossi grinned. "Hot off the presses, as it turns out. I just spoke with my cousin, who's managed to wriggle a little further into the org. Turns out you were right.

"About which part?"

"About how vital Cipriani was to keeping some people loyal. The men he was courting and convincing are starting to whisper that maybe it was Varda who killed Cipriani."

Dom's eyebrows winged up. "Why would they think that?"

"Because Varda has been getting increasingly paranoid. That's one of the main reasons so many capos and soldiers are falling back or outright defecting. He lost a whole family to Gallo this week."

"Gallo pays better. With all those government connections."

Rossi snorted. "I'm sure the weapons dealing helps too."

"So he's falling apart."

"Seems to be on his way, at least."

Dom picked up one of his markers and spun it around in his fingers. "So why isn't he making a move?

"Because he doesn't have the men in place?"

"Even with all the defections, he's got more than enough soldiers to take a run at us." He set the piece back on the edge of the map with a thud. "He's waiting for something. But what is it?"

Rossi frowned, moving closer to study the map. He pointed to some new locations Dom had marked earlier. "Are these more private properties?"

"Yeah. That brings the total up to sixteen."

"That's a lot of fucking houses." Rossi ran a hand through his hair. "What the hell is he up to?"

"I don't know. But I've got Otto passing along the message to some of our deeper spies to check them out. Find out exactly what kind of supplies they've got hiding in there."

"Smart. Lunch is up. I'm going to grab something to eat before my afternoon training."

"I'll come with you." Dom followed him out and down the stairs.

"You see the granddaughter of the cook your sister hired? She's got a nice tight ass."

"You cannot fuck the help, Rossi."

"I'm just saying," Rossi mumbled as they reached the main level.

"You cannot fuck Emilia either."

"The waitress? Why no—" Rossi looked up from his phone, and his eyebrows shot up. "Oh. Interesting."

"It's not interesting," Dom assured him.

"Uh huh. I don't think you've ever called me off a piece of ass before."

"Well, today I am."

"Fine, fine. She looks like an exceptional fuck, though. So you'll have to let me know how it goes."

"Shut up before I have to cut out your tongue."

Undeterred, Rossi grinned and kept pace with him toward the large formal dining room that was nearly big enough to seat everyone at once, even though they rarely all sat down to eat together. It was generally used more as a buffet line. People came in and out to eat when it fit their schedule.

Dom was adding ravioli to his plate when someone called his name.

"Got a minute?"

He glanced up at one of the youngest soldiers in the house. "What did you need?"

"We were taking a report from one of our Varda spies. Something told me he wasn't being truthful, so we brought him back to the house. He's in the cellar. Thought you might be able to get him talking. Unless you want me to see if Alexei is free."

Dom set his half-full plate on the table and motioned toward the door. "No. We'll try my powers of persuasion first. If that doesn't work, then we'll call Alexei."

They took the fastest way to the cellar, out the patio door, and past the pool house, rounding the side of the house and taking the deep, narrow steps cut into the earth. This was probably part of whatever original structure this house was built on.

The house itself was too modern for a cellar as rough as the one they discovered on their second day. It's not like the former owner was going to store wine down here, although that's probably what it was used for once. There was an expensive temperature-controlled room on the other side of the house for that.

They'd quickly decided to turn it into an interrogation room. The dirt floor made cleanup a breeze. Shovel out the blood and gore, dump it over the cliffs, and then bring in fresh dirt to replace it.

Dom recognized the man bound to the chair in the middle of the small room, one of his men standing on either side of him. This guy had approached him three weeks ago, saying he was married to a Varda cousin. He swore he had information on Varda's dealings and a hungry family to feed after losing his job.

Dom didn't much trust defectors. If you were willing to turn once, you were willing to turn again. But so far, he'd been able to verify all the intelligence this guy had given them. That was over now, though. Assuming his man's gut was right and he was jerking them around.

But when the guy tied to the chair saw him, his eyes went wide, and Dom knew his man was spot on. Otherwise, why be afraid to see him?

"Gildo." Dom crouched in front of the man so their faces were level. "I hear you have some new information for me."

"I-I do. But I don't understand what I'm doing here. What is this place?"

"I hardly think that has anything to do with what I pay you for. Do you have anything? Or have you outlived your usefulness?"

"No, no," Gildo said. "I have something. I swear."

"Well?" Dom twirled his hand in the air. "I'm waiting."

"Right." Gildo tried a half-hearted smile. "I heard something about these houses Varda keeps buying."

Dom glanced up at Rossi, who'd followed him down.

Their information about Varda properties came from reliable sources he would trust with his life. If Gildo was going to lie to them, it would be easy to spot.

"What about them?" Dom decided to test the waters. "Is he abandoning some of them?"

Gildo nodded his head violently. "Yes, yes. Good. You've already heard. I was worried I was too late to warn you."

Dom pushed to his feet and shared another look with his men. "Warn me about what?"

"About how he's getting rid of properties in the east because he's in talks with Antonetti."

"Is he?" Dom slowly turned, eyebrows raised, and pinned Gildo with a hard stare. "Last I heard, Antonetti was refusing to get involved. Switzerland and all that."

"W-Well, that was the case b-before. But not now," Gildo stammered.

"That's very helpful, Gildo. It's made the decision on what to do next very easy."

"Really?" Gildo sounded relieved. "What are you going to do?"

Dom clenched and unclenched his hand into a fist. "I'm going to kill you."

"What? No! Please!" Gildo begged, thrashing against his bindings as Dom moved behind him and gripped his head in both hands. "I told you the truth." Gildo sobbed. "I swear it."

"You shouldn't swear on lies. It's bad for the soul."

With a quick twist of his hands, Dom rotated the man's head at a sharp angle, snapping his neck. When he released him, Gildo slumped forward.

"You could have at least let us rough him up first," one of his men complained.

Dom rolled his shoulders. "Don't worry. You'll get to take out plenty of Varda trash before this war is over. Do we have to worry about Gildo's wife in all of this?"

"Maybe. It's hard to say whether he was keeping her in the loop about any of his activities."

"Watch her. If she starts acting suspicious or looks like she's going to run to Varda, take her out. But make it quick, and it's best if it looks like an accident. Anything else?" They all shook their heads. "Good. I'm going to go finish my lunch."

He jogged up the steps and through the grass. If Varda was trying to plant his own spies, he'd have to try a lot harder than that.

# Chapter Nine

She sat across the street from the Varda mansion, sipping her now cold coffee. She'd gotten up early, hoping to slip out of the house before everyone else was up. But Bella hadn't grown out of being an early riser and was already awake doing yoga in the living room.

It seemed unnatural for a teenager to be awake so early. Emilia couldn't fathom why anyone would want to be up before the sun. She'd sleep until three in the afternoon every day if she didn't have to get up and go to work.

Luckily, her distraction tactic of offering to take Bella and Antonio for lunch and to the beach had worked like a charm. It would be nice to spend some alone time with her siblings. Usually, between work and school, the only time they had to spend together was over dinner, their mother lurking over their shoulder, muttering under her breath no matter the topic of conversation.

Dom's generous tip from the night before meant she could buy them a nice lunch and not feel guilty about it. So long as her mother didn't find out. If Maria discovered they were treating themselves while Emilia monitored her mother's finances like a warden, Emilia would never hear the end of it.

Maria could never stop at just one thing. If she went out to even one lunch with the girls during the week, she'd want to do it again and again. She'd thought her mother's spending habits were an addiction at first. But it didn't take her long to realize it wasn't that Maria couldn't stop—it was that she didn't want to.

That's what had gotten them all into this mess in the first damn place. It's why she wasn't in Rome right now, windows thrown open to hear the birds and the bells and the people walking by on the street while she snuggled into the pillows and drifted back to sleep. It's why she was sitting in front of this stupid, ugly mansion at this god-awful hour.

The gate she'd driven through earlier in the week suddenly swung open, drawing her gaze, and the man who'd collected her from the house walked down the short drive. His hands were tucked into his pockets, and he looked to all the world like he was about to go on a leisurely Saturday morning stroll. She knew better.

Pausing at her rolled-up window, he rapped it with his knuckles, then leaned down when she opened it. "You're early."

He held his face so close to hers she could smell the mint on his breath. Better than the alternative, at least. "I like to be punctual. Can he see me now so we can get this over with?"

The man cocked a brow at the sass in her tone but didn't comment on it. Giving a quick nod, he stepped away from the car and waited for her to roll the window back up and step out. She followed the same path as yesterday. Up the short drive, across the courtyard—empty this time—into the house, and down the hall to the dead end.

Varda was seated on the couch instead of behind the desk, but he looked much the same. Too tan against his white hair, with a gaudy gold chain hanging in the open neck of his navy blue button-down shirt. The rings on his fingers made a faint clicking sound when he waved her into the room.

"So?" he asked impatiently once she'd taken a seat.

Emilia rubbed her sweaty palms on the thighs of her jeans. What was the most diplomatic way to say you didn't have shit? "I'm working on it still."

He frowned, white brows slashing down over dark eyes. "What does that mean? Working on it?"

"It means I don't have anything. Yet."

He sucked his teeth, propping his ankle on his knee. "And why is that?"

"I've been to that bar you told me about every night this week. He hasn't come in once. At this point, the bartender is tired of me ordering soda water and waiting around for several hours."

She'd decided last night, shortly after they'd left the restaurant, not to tell Varda about Dom and Franco and the others showing up to eat there. Something in her gut told her to keep that information close. Apparently she was dumb enough to listen to that insistent little voice.

"I don't have months to wait, girl."

Like she wanted to still be in this position months from now. "I know. I'm sorry. I don't know what else to do. Unless you know somewhere else I might be able to run into him."

"I have no idea where else Bianchi and his vermin might like to hang out."

She straightened at the name. "Bianchi? I thought I was supposed to get close to Franco Rossi."

Varda waved a dismissive hand. "Domenico Bianchi. He was his father's top general, and now he's his brother's. A thorn in my fucking side."

So Dom wasn't just Franco's boss; he was *the* boss. Commanding an entire army. An army waging war against the man who held her family's life in his hands. Jesus fucking Christ. What had she gotten herself into?

Varda rose and turned toward his desk. "I'll give you one more week to bring me something I can use."

"And if I can't?"

"I suggest that you do," he snapped.

Her irritation got the better of her, and she darted to her feet. "I can't control when and how he decides to go for a goddamn drink."

Varda closed the distance between them with surprising speed, gripping her ponytail and yanking it so hard her back bowed. "You think I called you in here for your attitude, little girl?"

"No." She swallowed down the whimper that wanted to escape.

"You have a job to do and a family to save. That's why you came down to Sicily, isn't it? To get your precious mama off her knees and save your pretty little sister?"

"Leave my sister out of this," Emilia demanded, struggling against the hold he still had on her hair. "She has nothing to do with what's between you and my mother and me."

"But she could. That's the thing people like you always forget. I can change the deal and the terms any time I fucking feel like it." He released her hair and shoved her toward the door. "Get out of my sight. And don't come back empty-handed a second time."

She weaved out of the office, down the hall, back across the courtyard, and down the driveway to her car on shaky legs. It took her three tries to get the key in the ignition because her fingers wouldn't stop trembling. Squealing away from the curb, she drove until she couldn't see the road through the tears in her eyes.

Pulling onto the shoulder, she leaned her forehead against

the steering wheel and wept. It wasn't fair; none of this was right. Emilia was already paying for her mother's mistakes. She didn't want Bella to have to pay for hers as well.

The girl deserved to grow up and get the hell away from here. Antonio too. She had to figure out a way to make sure that happened, even if she had to make deals with the devil to do it.

Maneuvering back into traffic, she swiped at her tears and took a deep breath. At this point, running into Rossi was the least of her problems. Before she had a snowball's chance in hell of getting close to him, she'd have to get past Dom and the possessive, neanderthal claim he thought he had on her.

*I saw you first.* That's what he'd said. Right before he'd taken the only chance she had at keeping her little brother and sister safe from this madness and dropped it in a glass of water. She'd have to figure something else out. There was no other choice.

When she pulled up to her mother's house, she texted her sister to come out instead of going inside. There was no way she could face her mother right now and answer a million questions about where she'd gone so early and what she was planning to do all day and why she didn't tell her she had plans. It wasn't worth the inquisition.

Despite her rough morning, Emilia smiled when Bella came bouncing out of the house, a big bag slung over her shoulder and her dark red hair, so much like Emilia's, flowing behind her.

"Where's Antonio?" she wondered as Bella climbed into the car.

"Still sleeping. Girl's day! I figured you didn't want to come in and run into Mama, so I grabbed your swimsu—What's wrong?"

"What?" Emilia glanced up at her face in the mirror,

noting her damp lashes and the redness in her eyes. "Nothing."

Bella twisted in her seat. "Something made you cry. Or someone." She gasped. "Did a man hurt you?"

Emilia pulled away from the curb with a chuckle. "Sort of, but not really."

"That's a terrible answer. What happened? Really."

"It doesn't matter. I'll handle it, and it'll all work out in the end. Which beach did you want to go to today? The one out by your school doesn't attract as many tourists."

"Can we go to the beach near your restaurant?"

Emilia made a face. "That one's always full of Americans."

"Yeah, but there's a cute guy who works the gelato stand."

"Oh, is there?" Emilia teased, waggling her eyebrows.

Bella groaned. "Don't make me regret telling you. And don't tell Mama."

"Isabella Sagona." Emilia pressed a hand to her heart in mock offense. "I can't believe you would even say such a thing to me."

Her sister rolled her eyes and slumped down in her seat. "If he hurt you, find somebody who won't."

"If who hurt me?"

Bella's voice was soft when she said, "The guy who made you cry."

"It's not that simple," Emilia replied.

"Of course it is," Bella insisted, kicking off her flip-flops and propping her bare feet on the dash. "Find someone who can give you exactly what you want. And then rub the other guy's face in it."

But who could give her exactly what she wanted? She wasn't nursing a broken heart here. This was life and death, and she was caught between two dangerous men. One who owned part of her soul and one who wanted to.

And if she couldn't get Varda the information he wanted, he could and would do whatever pleased him to punish her. Ever since she'd waded into this mess, she'd been at his mercy, forced to play by his rules. And he wasn't the kind of man who liked to play fair.

It probably didn't matter what information she brought to him. He'd always find a way to move the goalpost, to up the price for freedom. The only way to get out from under Aroldo Varda's thumb was in death. Hers or his, it didn't make much difference. And hers was far more likely.

Unless she could manage to strike a deal with a different devil. One with dark eyes and a rough, deep voice that sent electricity racing over her skin. They had the same end goal, after all. They both wanted Varda dead. And if anyone could give that to her, if anyone could assure her escape from this nightmare, it would be Domenico Bianchi.

She would just have to be very careful not to let him drag her into his darkness.

# Chapter Ten

"Another soda water?"

The bartender stopped in front of her and ran a rag over the glossy surface. The man looked as annoyed by her constantly taking up space at this end of the bar as she felt by standing here with nothing to show for it. Dom hadn't been back to the restaurant in days. And she hadn't seen him in the bar either.

It was hardly her fault if Varda's intel was bad, but he'd blame her for it anyway. She had to meet with him again soon, and again she was going to have nothing to show for it.

Anger licked at her sternum. If Dom hadn't dissolved Franco's number like a spoiled child who didn't want to share his favorite toy, she might actually be somewhere right now. Somewhere other than constantly worried about what Varda might do to her sister if she came back empty-handed.

"Actually," she said when the bartender began to move away. "Could I get a glass of Prosecco?"

The man flashed her a smile for the first time in days, and she returned it. She needed something stronger than soda water to deal with her disappointment. If she couldn't make this deal with Dom, if he rejected her, she was screwed. She couldn't unring this bell, couldn't pull the words back once they were free. Once she played her hand, that was it. And if he said no…

The bartender set her glass on a small napkin, and she watched the bubbles fizzle and pop. It was getting late. If they hadn't come in by now, they probably weren't going to, and her feet were starting to hurt. She'd been standing all day and then balancing on heels for hours, hoping he showed. It was stupid, and she felt stupid for doing it. Even if she didn't have any other choice.

Taking a sip, she closed her eyes as the bubbles exploded over her tongue and the Prosecco slid down her throat, warming her from the inside out. She never indulged in more than a glass of wine at meals most days.

There was a time when she'd have gone for a quick drink almost every night after work, talking and laughing with friends and coworkers about the day before splitting off. Those who were married would head home, and the singles would hop from the bar to a restaurant for a meal. She missed the days when all she had to worry about was if she'd packed all her SD cards for the next day's shoot.

Sighing, she turned to lean back against the bar and took another sip. Then, as if she'd summoned him, he was walking through the door of the bar, stopping short when he saw her. Franco ran into the back of him, his complaint silenced when he saw her over Dom's shoulder. He grinned and walked around Dom to her side.

"I thought I'd never see you again." Franco pressed a hand to his heart. "How could you not call?"

Her gaze flicked from Franco to Dom and back again. "I lost your number."

Franco chuckled, tucking a loose strand of hair behind her

ear and brushing his thumb over her cheek. "I imagine you did."

"Rossi," Dom growled, appearing at her elbow.

"I know, I know. Pity," Rossi murmured before moving away.

Dom moved into the empty space in front of her, eyes dropping to her mouth when she took another sip of Prosecco. "Did you warn him off me?"

His lips twitched at the corners, and he leaned his elbow on the bar. "I might have."

"That seems very rude. Considering you didn't give me any way to contact either one of you."

He ordered a glass of grappa when the bartender came to check on them and then fixed those dark eyes on her again. "If I wanted you to contact him, I'd have left his number in your palm."

"But you didn't want me to contact you either."

"I never said that. I went back to the restaurant the next night."

"My day off." She frowned. "You could have given your number to someone else. They'd have passed it on to me."

He stepped closer, twirling a strand of her hair around his finger. "I didn't want to give it to anyone else. Besides, we're both here now."

"We are."

Her gaze snagged on his lips, and she couldn't stop herself from wondering what he tasted like. Could she have just a little taste before putting her head on the chopping block and praying he didn't lop it off? One kiss could hardly hurt anything.

The problem was, she didn't think she'd be able to stop at just one. And it would be almost impossible to get him to trust her if she had sex with him. Then it would seem like she was working some kind of angle. The man wanted her, but he didn't owe her anything. And he could take her life as easily as Varda could if he wanted.

That thought sent a little shiver through her. And she hated that it enticed her as much as scared her. These last six months had really warped her fucking brain.

"Maybe we could go somewhere quieter. And talk."

His eyes flashed with lust as the bartender set his drink on a napkin and moved away. Dom downed the entire thing in one swallow and grabbed her hand, dragging her to the door and down the narrow walk. He took a hard left and marched them toward a dense cluster of trees. Heart racing, she vaguely registered the thought that being alone with him in a secluded area was probably not the best idea.

But then he was pushing her up against the rough stone, and his hands and his lips were on her, and she couldn't think of anything else. How could an idea this bad feel so good?

His hands were rough and urgent as they skimmed down her hips and around to her ass, cupping and squeezing as he trailed kisses and nibbles across her bare collarbone. Thank god for this dress. It really had been worth every penny.

Dom dragged his teeth over the spot where her neck joined her shoulder, and she let out a soft moan, his hands tightening on her ass at the sound. His kisses burned a trail up the column of her throat and across her jaw until his mouth finally claimed hers. Hot. Hungry. Demanding.

He tasted faintly of sweet and spice and the sharp tang of alcohol, and she wanted more of him. More of his hands on her skin, his lips, his teeth. His cock. The more he touched her, the more desperate she was to be touched by him, to lose herself in the steady pounding of her heart and the feel of his body against hers.

Sliding her hands up into his hair, Emilia gripped it tight in her fingers, claiming every one of his bruising kisses as her own. His hand skimmed down the back of her thigh and fisted the hem of her dress. She barely registered the sensation of cool air over her heated skin until his fingertips brushed the bare globe of her ass and he groaned.

"Wait, wait," she said, panting against his cheek. She felt his hold tighten on her dress, but he didn't move. "Are you really Domenico Bianchi?"

He went rigid in her arms and jerked back, his eyes narrowing on her face. "Why would you ask me that?"

She took a deep breath, her hands braced on his chest. He hadn't moved away. He still held her dress in his hand, and the other was wrapped around her waist, but his eyes were full of suspicion now.

"Because if you are, I have a proposal for you."

He sighed, his breath feathering across her cheek, and stepped away. She shoved down the disappointment and the emptiness she felt now that he was no longer touching her. She needed to get a fucking grip.

"I don't pay for sex."

Anger punched to the surface. "Excuse me?"

"Your proposal." He waved a hand at her. "I don't want it."

He started to walk away, and she grabbed his arm, pulling him back against her. "I am not a prostitute. But I do have something you want."

Grinding the length of his cock against her hip, he grinned when she bit her lip and moaned softly. "Obviously you do. But I'm not interested in games."

He stepped away again, and she knew she had to say something or lose this moment forever. "Aroldo Varda wants me to spy on you."

Dom froze but didn't turn around, so she shifted to stand in front of him again. He looked angry now, and she nearly lost her nerve. But it was too late to take it back. The only thing she could do was push forward.

"My mom owes him a lot of money. I moved down here to help her pay it back."

"And how did you get from being in his debt to being a spy?" His voice was cold, and he wouldn't meet her eyes.

"One of his enforcers picked me up one day before work and said Varda wanted to meet with me. Varda said if I could bring him valuable information about your war, he would wipe out my mother's debt. And we'd be free."

Dom snorted. "And you believed him?"

"You think he gave me much of a choice?" He looked at her then, finally, but she couldn't tell if he believed her or not.

"So he told you to cozy up to me, and what? Get me to spill all my secrets?"

She shook her head. "Not you. Franco."

"Rossi?" His eyebrows shot up.

"He said I was just his type."

Dom gave her that appraising look that never failed to heat her blood. "He wasn't wrong. But you thought you'd go for a bigger fish."

Crossing her arms over her chest, she arched a brow. "If you'll recall, I tried to flirt with Rossi, and someone got jealous."

He moved forward slowly until he was crowding her against the wall, the length of her body pressed back against it while he pressed against her. Could he feel the rapid beat of her pulse behind her sternum? It felt like her heart would explode from her chest if he touched another part of her.

His lips grazed the shell of her ear when he whispered, "Why are you telling me this, Emilia?"

"Because," she whispered back, "we want the same thing."

Increasing the pressure on her body, he traced her earlobe with the tip of his tongue, and she sighed. "I don't think we do."

"We both want Varda dead."

He paused, slowly pulling back to look down at her, and braced his hands on either side of her head. "You want Varda dead." It wasn't a question, but he sounded skeptical.

"It's the only way to be free from him."

Stepping back again, he shoved his hands into his pockets and studied her. "I doubt he keeps you in his confidence. What use are you to me?"

"I might not be able to tell you anything. But I can slip him whatever information you want him to know. As long as you don't double-cross me and have me give him something that gets me or my family killed."

Dom chuckled, but it was a cold, harsh sound. "I think if anyone has to worry about being double-crossed here, it's me."

"But you're interested?" His silence gave her hope. He wasn't outright refusing her. It had to be a good sign.

"When do you meet with him again?"

She gripped her wrist, feeling the pulse fluttering under her fingers as she took a step toward him. "Saturday. After I get off work. I didn't have anything for him last time. And he..."

"He what?"

"He threatened my sister." She couldn't stop the tears that welled in her eyes, but she blinked against them. Her voice was thick with them when she spoke. "I don't know what he might do to her if I show up empty-handed again. So I'm here." A tear slipped past her defenses and rolled down her cheek. "Putting my life, my sister's life, in your hands instead."

Dom reached up to swipe away the tear with the pad of this thumb. "What's your name? Your real one."

"Emilia Serena Altieri Sagona."

"You have two last names." He frowned. "Are you married?"

"No. My stepfather insisted on adopting me. A million years ago when he married my mother."

"And your real father?"

She barked out a humorless laugh. "If you can find him, let me know."

He watched her for a moment longer, lips pursed, and she could hear nothing but the deafening rush of her heartbeat pounding her ears. His lips moved, but she couldn't make out the words, forced to shake her head so the world rushed back to her.

"What did you say?"

"I said meet me here tomorrow at seven. We'll talk more then."

"Wait." She laid a hand on his arm when he moved to brush past her. "So we have a deal?"

"We'll see. I'm still not convinced you aren't a very bad idea. Tomorrow at seven."

She watched him disappear inside the bar and slumped against the edge of the building, bracing her hands on her knees and forcing herself to take slow, deep breaths. This had to work. He had to say yes. If he didn't, she was out of options.

She really hoped she had made the right choice in coming to him. Because if she hadn't, she'd just signed her family's death warrant.

# Chapter Eleven

"Are you sure this is a good idea?"

Dom glanced up at Rossi and then back at the paper he was studying. "No. But I'm going with my gut on this."

Rossi was silent for a beat. "Your gut or your dick?"

He pinned Rossi with a warning glare until Rossi held his hands up, palms out in surrender. "I had to ask the question. We don't know if we can trust this chick."

"We don't know if we can trust any of the spies we recruit from behind enemy lines. And besides, if she is spying for Varda, telling me so would be a pretty stupid thing to do when it was clear she could have gotten close to me without it."

"How much money does she want?"

"She doesn't. Or so she says."

"There's no fucking way. Why would she stick her neck out like that and potentially get herself killed for nothing?"

Dom flipped the page and scanned the one underneath it. "Not nothing. She wants me to kill Varda."

Rossi whistled through his teeth and leaned his hip

against the edge of the table where Dom was working. "Maybe you're right. Maybe she is legit. Or crazy. Just watch your back. In case she goes all psycho on you."

"I always do. Now go away. I have to meet with her in an hour, and I want to make sure I have these details memorized first."

"You got it, boss." Rossi gripped the handle of the pool house door and paused. "Oh, I heard from Alexei this afternoon."

"Did he finally give us a date for his knife training?" Dom asked without looking up.

"Yeah. Said he'll be here on Wednesday."

"Good. Out."

When the door finally clicked closed, he took a deep breath. Rossi could hang around all fucking night and talk about nothing if he let him. Flipping to the third page of Luca's very extensive background check, he read the details of her life carefully.

Tonight he wanted to test his gut feeling about her. He didn't know why, maybe his expert skills at reading people from a lifetime of standing off to the side and watching as the second son, but he believed her.

Bribing a woman who couldn't say no to his proposal to do the near impossible just by spreading her legs seemed exactly the kind of thing Varda would do. He picked a woman who had plenty to lose and gave her hope.

Dom knew Varda wouldn't keep his word. The man needed the cash too much, and even if he didn't need it, he delighted in fucking with people. He likely had no intention of forgiving Emilia's debt. And she was smart enough to figure that out. Because she was right. The only way out of one of Varda's deals was death.

And since Dom didn't plan on leaving Varda or any of his distant heirs alive when this was all said and done, he could pretty much guarantee they'd both get what they wanted at the end of the day.

He was halfway to trusting her, but as much as he hated to admit it, Rossi was right. He had to be sure he wasn't thinking with his dick. Tonight he needed to look her in the eye, see if she would corroborate these details from her background check or lie to him. He wanted to get a feel for her, to push her a bit and catch her off guard.

He'd let himself get a little too lost in her last night, fully prepared to take her up against the side of that bar for anybody walking by to see. Tonight was about business. He had a job to do, a family to protect, a territory to claim, a war to win.

After scanning the details of her background check one last time, he shoved away from the table and made his way to the bar to meet her. He wanted to know more about the woman who'd called to him from the first moment he saw her. And if she passed his initial round of questioning, he was going to send her to Varda with a little test. See if she really was willing to follow orders.

She was already waiting for him when he arrived, standing at the same spot in the bar she'd been last night, and when he walked in, her eyes found his instantly. She fidgeted, her fingers playing with the hem of her shirt. She was nervous.

No dress tonight. Instead she wore jeans that hugged every curve and rode low on her hips. Her shirt was loosely fitted, and he found himself wishing he could see the shape of her. Christ knew she was nice to look at.

He gestured to one of the tables with his chin, and she met him there, dropping into the seat and folding her hands in her lap. The waitress came and took their drink order, leaving them in uncomfortable silence.

"I wasn't sure you were actually going to come," she said.

"I'm the one who asked for the meeting."

"I know, but…" He waited for her to continue. "You didn't seem all that interested in hearing what I have to say."

He was more interested than she knew. "How long have you been in Sicily?"

"That's what you want to talk about?" Emilia asked as the waitress set their drinks on the table and left again.

Taking a sip of his wine, he raised a brow. "Yes."

"Okay, then. I've been in Sicily a little more than six months. Going on seven now, I guess."

"And where did you live before?"

"In Rome." She gave a wistful sigh. "I was a photographer there."

"For a newspaper." He watched her carefully to see how she'd react to the lie, but she only shook her head.

"No. A fashion magazine. It paid well, but I didn't like it much." She laughed softly, her eyes far away as she remembered. "I love photography. A total fanatic from the time my grandfather bought me my first camera. When I found out I could get paid to take pictures I…" She rubbed her fingers over her lips, like she'd said too much, and looked at him. "Sorry, what was your question?"

"Were you seeing anyone? Before you came here?"

Cocking her head, Emilia studied him. "How many connections do you have if you were able to dig up my relationship status?"

Dom bit the inside of his cheek to keep from grinning. She was sharper than he gave her credit for. And he found it sexier than he ought to.

"Not that many. Which is why I'm asking."

"I was single. I dated a guy who cheated on me, and I was shy about taking a chance after that. I hadn't been attracted to anyone in a long time. Not until y—"

Color rose to her cheeks, turning them an enchanting

shade of pink, and she quickly averted her eyes. It took every bit of willpower he had not to drag her across the table and take her on top of it. He took a lazy sip of his wine, setting it gently on the table before asking his next question.

"You have a little sister, you said?"

"And a brother. They're twins. Bella and Antonio. From my mother's second marriage. Half siblings, I guess."

"What made you decide to stay in Rome instead of moving down here with your family?"

"My stepfather was an asshole."

His eyebrows winged up at the venom in her tone. He'd expected her to say university, since her background check said she'd gone to school there to get her bachelor's in photography. He wondered what her stepfather had done to earn such vehement dislike.

An idea occurred to him. One that made him want to resurrect the fucker and kill him again.

"Did he abuse you?"

Her eyes widened over the rim of her wineglass. "No. Nothing like that. At least, not physically. He adopted me legally for appearance's sake. So people wouldn't ask too many questions. But I was never his. He had Bella and Antonio. He didn't want me. I got out of there as fast as I could."

Curling his hand into a fist in his lap to resist the urge to comfort her, he searched his memory for another question, but she hadn't lied to him so far.

"Have I passed your test? Or should we talk about my secret foot fetish now?" she quipped.

Unable to help himself, he laughed. "I think we can skip that one."

"You don't have any reason to trust me, Dom," Emilia said, sobering. "But my brother and sister are the most important people in the world to me. I would never do anything to jeopardize them. Ever."

"I believe you." And he did. Every word out of her mouth rang true to him.

The tension drained from her shoulders, and she blinked rapidly, looking quickly away at a point over his shoulder.

"I don't know exactly how I got here," she whispered so low he could barely hear her. "But I think you're the only person who might be able to help me get back out again."

He shifted in his seat, drawing her gaze. Those gray eyes glistened with unshed tears. "And what about payment?"

"You want me to pay you?" Her brow creased, and she rubbed at it with her fingers. "I don't make enough money to pay you and Varda. I'd have to get another job. And I—"

"I meant how much money did you want me to pay you? For spying."

She whipped her head up to look at him, and her distress melted into confusion. "I don't want your money. I told you what I wanted out of this last night. And it would look suspicious to my mother anyway."

"She wouldn't be happy about some extra cash?"

Twirling her glass on the table, Emilia heaved a deep sigh. "She's a complicated person, my mother. Things are better the way they are. I can't deal with her and you and this nightmare with Varda all at the same time. I can't add one more thing to my plate and hold it all together. So keep your money."

He leaned forward, bracing his elbows on the table. "The only thing you want is Varda dead?"

She captured her bottom lip between her teeth and eyed him thoughtfully. "What happens to my debt if he dies? Does it become yours or something? And I owe you or your brother or however this works?"

"Your debt disappears with his death. As if it never existed."

"Then yes," she replied with a decisive nod. "The only

thing I want is him dead. Just tell me what I have to do to get it. I'll do anything."

"Careful, Emilia," he warned. "Don't make promises people can take advantage of."

She studied him for a long moment, and he noticed how blue her gray eyes looked in this light, like the sea on a cloudy day. "Are you planning on taking advantage of me?" Her voice was teasing, but her eyes were serious.

"When do you meet with Varda next? Saturday, you said?"

The crease reappeared in her brow, and she nodded. "Yes. After work."

"Good." He dug into the pocket of his jeans for the scrap piece of paper he'd stuffed there. "I want you to give Varda these three names and tell him you found them on a list of spies. There were more names, but these were the only ones you were able to write down without getting caught."

Her lips moved as she recited the directions to herself silently, staring at the names on the paper. Eventually she nodded, shoving the names into her pocket and looking back at him.

"How am I supposed to contact you to let you know it's done? Or to meet again?"

He drained the rest of his wine and stood. "I'll find you."

She nodded but didn't speak, and before he could stop himself, he reached down and pulled her to her feet, tilting her head up by her chin to claim her lips. There was no resistance from her; if anything, she leaned into him, one arm circling his waist, the other braced against his chest.

He wanted to drag her out to his SUV, strip her naked, and drive his cock inside her until they were both sweaty and panting. But not tonight. Soon. He already knew he wouldn't deny himself much longer. Nibbling her bottom lip, he released her and left the way he came.

The possibilities were endless when it came to the intel he could feed Varda through Emilia. Varda would think he was getting the upper hand while Dom shepherded him right where he wanted the son of a bitch.

He believed her story, and he knew she'd be one of their best assets in this war. But she could be dangerous for him. He couldn't let his focus stray from his goal.

# Chapter Twelve

Emilia lifted the lid on the pot of sauce simmering on the stove and gave it a stir, the scent of it making her mouth water. She'd needed something to do with her hands after her meeting earlier with Varda. And making her grandmother's spaghetti and meatballs from scratch seemed like the best way to do that.

There was something endlessly soothing about making the pasta, scooping and kneading with her bare hands until it was soft and pliable. Rolling it out until it was just right and feeding it through the machine like her grandmother taught her. The meatballs were a labor of love, mixing the ingredients—a little ricotta to keep them nice and tender—and rolling the tiny balls by hand.

She'd considered making bread, but it wasn't her strength, and Bella had promised to pick up a loaf on her way back from the beach where she'd been hanging out with friends. She was due back any minute, and her mother was upstairs taking a nap. Antonio was in the other room playing video games. Every so often, she heard a shouted curse when someone died or something blew up.

She finished frying up the last of the meatballs and added them to the sauce, giving everything a stir to bring it all together. She'd drop the fresh pasta in the water as soon as Bella got home, and by the time the bread was sliced, they'd be ready to eat.

The small shining spot of normal was a welcome relief from the unexpected turn her life had taken in just a few weeks. Rome seemed a distant fairytale now that she was wrapped up in Mafia wars and dangerous men who didn't trust her but still wanted to use her for their own ends. But that was fine. She was using them too.

Now that she'd given him information he deemed valuable, Varda and his man seemed in much better spirits when she dropped off her most recent payment. And Dom was getting whatever he was getting out of this arrangement by handing those names over to his enemy.

Presumably, they were people he wanted killed at Varda's hand, but she thought it best not to ask too many questions. Just because blood was being spilled didn't mean she wanted to know whose or how much. The thought struck her, and she shook her head.

Six months ago, a thought like that would never have crossed her mind. If it had, she'd have been appalled at how casually she could turn her head away from death and let it be someone else's problem. The need to survive put a lot of things in perspective. But the oddest part was, she wasn't sure if she was becoming unglued or a truer version of herself.

The sound of the front door drew her attention, and Bella's voice in greeting a scant second later made her smile. Antonio even paused his game to follow his twin into the kitchen, leaning casually against the door frame with his arms crossed over his chest while Bella set the bread on the table and hung her bag on a hook in the closet.

"Did you make pasta from scratch?" Antonio asked, eyeing the noodles drying on a rack in the corner of the counter.

"I did. And meatballs and sauce."

"I wish I'd known," Bella said, washing her hands in the sink. "I'd have bought fancier bread."

Emilia laughed. "I'm sure whatever you brought is fine. Antonio, can you go tell Mama dinner will be ready in about ten minutes?"

He grimaced and shared a look with Bella only they could decipher. They'd always been like that. From the moment they could communicate, they did so only with each other in ways Emilia or their mother or the twins' father could never understand. Emilia was the only one who found it endearing instead of annoying.

"Did you ever deal with your man problem?" Bella asked as the sound of Antonio's feet trudging up the stairs echoed in the front hall.

"I don't have a man problem," Emilia replied, dropping the fresh pasta into boiling water and stirring it so it didn't stick. "But yes, I did."

"See, you keep giving me mixed signals like that. Do you...want to talk about it?"

"It's grown-up stuff, Bells."

Bella scoffed. "I'm almost an adult, you know. I'm sixteen."

"Almost," Emilia agreed, tugging her sister's ponytail. "But not yet. Is there something you want to talk about?"

"Like what?" Her sister tried to keep her voice casual, but her cheeks pinked, and Emilia grinned.

"Like that boy from the beach. Gelato boy."

Bella groaned and set her phone down on the counter. "Oh my God, you cannot call him that! His name is Theo."

"Theo." Emilia wrinkled her nose and fished a piece of pasta out of the water to test it. "What kind of name is that?"

"I don't know. His dad is English. Who cares? He's hot."

Emilia chuckled, biting off half the noodle and handing her sister the rest. "Do I need to worry about him?"

"No. I know how to be careful. About everything," she added, shooting Emilia a warning look when Antonio and their mother came down the stairs.

There was nothing that could make her break the sister code. Emilia had known Bella was having sex when she asked her to take her for birth control two Easters ago. Emilia figured if kids were going to have sex, they should be as safe as possible. And the best way to know if Bella was or wasn't being safe was to be open and honest and not judge. So far, it had been working well.

Antonio, not so much. If he was having sex, he didn't want to talk about it, not with his big sister, and Emilia felt a fresh wave of sadness that he was a boy without a father to guide him. Her stepfather might not have been a good dad to her, but he loved the twins. That was something she'd never doubted for a second.

"What's all this?" Maria asked as Emilia carried the bowl of pasta and bread to the table.

"I made dinner. Antonio, can you bring the sauce, please?"

He grabbed the bowl she'd filled and set it in the middle of the table before claiming his seat across from Bella. Emilia took her usual chair and held her hand out for Bella's plate, adding pasta and sauce to it.

"Are those meatballs?"

"Yeah." Emilia tried for a smile, not sure what to make of her mother's tone. "Nonna's recipe."

Maria smiled, accepting her full plate from Antonio, and for the first time in a long time, she actually looked happy. "I remember the first time she taught you to make this. Standing on that ugly orange step stool in the kitchen."

"And still, I could barely see over the counter."

"You always were a natural with pasta. I could never get it right."

Emilia tensed, waiting for the insult that usually came after a sentence like that, where Maria would make a dig to make herself feel better about coming up lacking next to her own child. But her mother only twirled the pasta around her fork and took a bite.

"It's just like I remember it." Maria looked at Emilia across the table, nothing but happy memories swirling in her eyes. "You have a knack."

"Thanks," Emilia replied after a minute of stunned silence.

It was like her mother had taken a nap and become a different fucking person. The fact that her mother's kindness made her suspicious somehow hurt worse than the criticism she was expecting.

"Antonio, how did your science test go?"

Maria glanced at her son, who was also clearly surprised by this turn of events. Emilia couldn't remember the last time Maria had asked a question like that. She was usually the one dragging conversation along behind her so they didn't eat in silence every night.

"Uh, it was good. Aced it."

"Of course you did," Bella replied with a roll of her eyes. "You ace everything, and it's so annoying."

"The tests are easy." Antonio shrugged, dipping a piece of bread into the sauce on his plate.

"You don't even study!"

"Did you try that doodle thing I told you about?"

Bella nodded at her sister. "It worked for history, but not for math." She sighed. "Nothing works for math."

"What doodle thing?" Maria wondered.

"I used to draw in the margins of my notes next to things my teacher said were important for a test. I don't know how it worked, but if I doodled a cat next to everything I was supposed to know about Mussolini, it helped me remember."

Maria frowned. "I used to yell at you for fooling around and drawing when you should have been studying."

"Yes," Emilia said. "You did."

"Well, why didn't you tell me it was helping you?"

Emilia shrugged and shook her head. "It was a long time ago, Mama. Hardly something to worry about anymore."

Not to mention the fact she had tried to tell her mother, and it had only ever made her yell louder. Emilia couldn't remember a single moment from her childhood when her mother let her get a word in edgewise. If Emilia wasn't nodding along in agreement or apologizing for something she didn't do, her mother had little interest in what she had to say.

"Still," Maria said, her voice going sulky. "You could have said."

"Does it really matter?" Antonio asked. "It was, like, a million years ago."

"Thank you, Antonio," Emilia said dryly, and he grinned.

"I don't appreciate the attitude, young man."

"There's no attitude, Mama," he insisted around a bite of spaghetti. "It's just not a big deal. How was your day?"

"My day was fine," Maria sniffed, her fork clinking aggressively against the plate as she resumed eating. "I had to work, and then I came home and took a well-deserved nap. But I guess that doesn't matter either, since I didn't slave away in the kitchen making dinner."

Bella sighed softly, and Antonio rolled his eyes.

"I made dinner because I wanted to," Emilia said. "Not because it's a competition or something."

"You're always telling me how I failed you. It's a wonder I come home at all."

"Then don't," Antonio said, voice low and snapping with anger.

"Tonio!" Bella hissed, but he ignored his twin.

"What did you say to me?" Maria demanded, slamming her fork against the plate and shoving back from the table.

"If you hate being here so much, then don't fucking come back." Maria gasped and clutched her chest. "You ruined a perfectly good dinner doing what you always do."

"And what is that?"

"Making everything about you."

"Well, I apologize for trying to contribute. I promise to never do it again."

Maria stood so quickly her chair fell over backward and banged into the wall. Her footsteps stomped up the stairs until her door slammed, and Emilia heard what sounded like a picture crashing to the floor. She shook her head and looked at Antonio.

"If you're going to yell at me for that, can you wait until I'm finished eating?"

"I'm not going to yell at you," Emilia said, spooning more pasta and sauce onto her plate and digging in.

"You're not?"

"Did you lie?" Antonio shook his head. "Did you yell?" Another shake. "Were you unnecessarily rude or hurtful?"

"I didn't think so," Bella said.

Nodding, Emilia turned back to her brother. "Me either. So, no. I'm not going to yell at you. I'm not going to make you apologize either. You can decide if you feel bad about what you said and apologize if you want to, though."

Slowly chewing a bite of bread, he considered her words for a moment. "I don't feel bad about what I said. She's always been like this. It's just gotten worse since Papa died. And since you moved in."

Emilia's heart sank. "I didn't mean to make things worse for you."

"You didn't," Bella insisted. "Mama did by acting this way. You're trying to help, and she's too proud to let you."

"Even though she really fucking needs it." Antonio finished his plate and carried it to the sink. "Dinner was really good, by the way."

"I'm glad you liked it."

Emilia watched her brother disappear into the living room, the sound of his video game resuming, and blinked back tears. She didn't want to cry. She was tired of crying. Why the hell hadn't she run out of tears yet?

"Don't let her get to you." Bella stood and cleared the rest of the dishes. "It isn't worth it."

Emilia helped put the food away and wash up, leaving Bella making cookies and humming to herself. Climbing the stairs, she paused long enough outside her mother's door to retrieve the photo that had fallen. A picture of Bella, Antonio, and their parents. One that had always made her sad.

The twins were young, maybe five or six, standing in front of their parents with their arms raised and big smiles on their faces in front of the Eiffel Tower in Paris. Emilia would have been about fifteen when this picture was taken. And she wasn't in it because she was behind the camera.

It wasn't that she didn't want to be in it or that she'd begged to use the new camera her grandfather had given her for her birthday. It was because once she'd discovered her love of photography at twelve, her stepfather had used it as an excuse to exclude her from every family photo. And her mother had let him.

The one time Emilia brought it up, Maria assured her she was being ridiculous, melodramatic. So Emilia had taught herself to use the timer function and saved up money to buy a little remote. Still, she was always conveniently relegated to family photographer. Slowly and deliberately chipped out of their lives until she finally extracted herself on her own terms.

She hated knowing she was the reason for bringing so much animosity to the house when she'd moved down here. But what were a few shouting matches when the alternative was death?

Hanging the photo on the protruding nail, she closed herself in her room and flopped on the bed, staring at the ceiling. Eventually this would all be over. One way or another. Maybe when she went back to Rome, she could take the twins with her. Get them away from their mother's toxicity and give them a fresh start. Maybe.

Assuming she didn't get herself killed with this insane plot to set them all free.

# Chapter Thirteen

He circled his opponent slowly, the knife threading through his fingers at his side. This guy was impatient. He'd try to wait, but he could never wait long. It's why his forearm was dotted with shallow cuts, angry and red.

Dom preferred a gun or his fists to a blade, but there was a certain kind of invisible power that came with the weapon. It thrummed up his arm and sang through his chest. He wondered if that's why Alexei preferred them.

You had to get close to your kill with a knife. Like your fists, it was personal, but you could inflict a death blow with the flick of your wrist. He twirled the knife a final time and let it settle loosely against his palm.

The man wouldn't wait much longer. Dom watched his body for tells. They were easy to spot when you were impatient. There, in the dart of the man's eyes, searching for a good target for his blade. Another tell in the tightening of his fingers on the handle. A third one in the bunch of his muscles and lean of his body.

Dom anticipated his strike, spinning out of the way and

coming up behind the man. He wrapped an arm around the man's shoulders and yanked him back against his chest, knife point pressing against the pulse in his throat.

Slow, sarcastic clapping rang out behind him, and Dom released the man to see Alexei striding into his view. "Dom. You've been holding out on me. So good with a knife, yet you still insist on killing with a gun."

Flipping the blade of his knife closed while his man recovered, Dom shrugged. "Guns are faster. And I like the feel of a well-aimed fist, bone crunching under your knuckles." He grinned. "It relaxes me."

"That's how your sister feels about blood on her hands," Alexei said, chuckling. "Next pair."

Dom claimed a spot at the edge of the crowd and watched the next two men spar with each other, Alexei circling them both and offering tips and pointers. Half the men were out on recon, picking up supplies, meeting with spies, and gathering reports. The other half were here for this training.

He'd have to make sure Alexei came back next week to work with the rest. It was good practice. Varda liked to fight dirty, and when it came to it, they would need every tool in their arsenal. Plus, he was still waiting to see if Varda took the bait. He couldn't make his next move without it.

Otto appeared at the edge of the patio where it met the grass and signaled him. Leaving Alexei to his training, Dom jogged over to meet him and took the folder from his hands.

"Tell me," he said, leading Otto away from the grunt of blades landing and Alexei barking commands to change grips or fix a stance.

"Our deep cover is still working on the private properties angle. No news yet. But he said he lost touch with one of his contacts."

Dom frowned. "Which one?"

"Dispenza."

One of the names he'd given Emilia for Varda. Interesting. "Is that it?"

"There's some small shit in the report. Nothing I can't imagine you couldn't have worked out for yourself."

"Still. Nice to have confirmation."

"My thoughts. Need anything else?"

Dom shook his head, and Otto disappeared inside. Dom knew some of their spies were in contact with each other, but only he and his capos knew who was on their payroll in the Varda organization. As far as any of his own deep covers knew, they were talking to loyal Varda men.

He wanted to leak Dispenza's name to Varda as a rat because the guy had gotten greedy in recent weeks, demanding more money and skirting around the edges of blackmail. He'd be impressed that the guy had balls if it didn't piss him off so much.

Hopefully his deep had lost contact because Dispenza was dead. If Dispenza had worked out the real identity of his man, then it was doubly good that he could be swimming at the bottom of the Mediterranean right now. And it meant Emilia had delivered his message exactly.

His phone rang, and he fished it out of his pocket. Matteo. They weren't due for a face-to-face for another couple of days. Connecting the call, he pressed the phone to his ear.

"Domenico," Matteo growled. "Why the fuck am I looking at three dead bodies outside my casino?"

"How the hell am I supposed to know about your dead bodies in Palermo when I'm all the way down here?" Dom rolled his eyes and tucked the folder under his arm.

"Because the note pinned to their very mutilated bodies says, 'Returning your spies a little worse for wear.' Signed A.V.," Matteo added through gritted teeth.

"Excellent," Dom breathed.

Varda had taken the bait, which meant Emilia had

dangled it perfectly. It also meant she was ready for her next assignment. If she kept to her regular schedule of weekend meets, he had plenty of time to intercept her and give her the next message. Which meant a quick trip into the village.

He swore he could still taste her on his lips even though it had been days. The woman haunted his fucking dreams. He kept trying to wash her out with cold showers. They weren't working.

"I don't consider dead men in my parking lot excellent."

Dom pinched the bridge of his nose. He didn't understand his brother. All that savagely leashed control had to be exhausting to maintain. "Cheer up, brother. This is progress."

"Not when you're the one who has to clean it up. What are you going to do next?"

"I'm going to get under his skin."

Disconnecting the call, Dom brought up Rossi's number and sent him a quick text to let him know he was going out and Rossi was in charge while he was gone. The drive into the little village was a short one on narrow streets, and he parked in a public lot, walking the couple blocks to Emilia's restaurant. If she wasn't working today, he might just go in search of her.

A woman he recognized but whose name he didn't know lit up when she saw him, a big smile stretching across her full, bright pink mouth. He might have been inclined to give her a good ride in the alley if not for a certain redhead invading all his thoughts.

"You've finally come to see me," she purred, leaning on the edge of the bar so her breasts pressed together between her arms.

He didn't even spare her a glance. "I'm looking for Emilia. Is she working today?"

The woman pouted. "She got off about an hour ago. Said

she was going down to the beach across the street before she went home."

Dom dashed between the cars and down the little hill until his shoes toed sand. He scanned the beach, his heart nearly stopping when he saw her stretched out on a towel as blue as the sky and dressed in a deep purple bikini that made him think of mermaids and peeling it off her.

He started for her and then stopped. Someone else was watching her. A man dressed all in black and looking very out of place among the other sunbathers there. Was Varda having her followed?

The idea constricted his chest, and he struggled with the overwhelming urge to protect her. Except what could he do? Short of assigning her a 24/7 bodyguard, something she was sure to reject. She'd put herself at risk making this offer to him. They'd both have to live with it. For now.

Weaving through the other people sprawled out on towels and chairs, he stopped beside her and lowered himself to the sand. "You should really be more aware of your surroundings," he said when she didn't move.

"I knew it was you before you sat down."

He shifted to face her. "Did you now?"

She rolled onto her side on the towel, propping her head in her hand and giving him a good view of her cleavage and the outline of her nipples. He wanted to roll her onto her back and taste every inch of her.

"Mmm," she murmured. "I did."

"And how did you know it was me?"

"You smell like the earth after it rains, woodsy and fresh." He lifted a brow, and she laughed. "It's a compliment, I promise. What are you doing here? Was your test a success?"

He watched her sit up, sand sparkling where it stuck to the flat plane of her stomach and the smooth arch of her legs. She looked even more delicious up close.

"It was. But someone is watching you."

"What?"

Her body jerked, and before she could scan the beach looking for the man he'd spotted, he yanked her into his lap, barely biting back a groan when her ass ground against his cock.

"Don't look, for fuck's sake." She shifted, and he grit his teeth. "Why is someone following you?"

"How should I know why you people do what you do?"

Something foreign flared in his chest when she lumped him and Varda into the same category, but he brushed it away. "Is Varda suspicious of you?"

"I get the distinct impression he's suspicious of everyone."

She moved until she was straddling his lap and could scan the beach around them less conspicuously. He settled his hands on her thighs, barely resisting the urge to stroke her skin with his fingertips.

"Oh," she said when she finally pegged him. "That's his enforcer. Or at least the one assigned to me."

Dom frowned. Odd for Varda to assign an enforcer to watch her. It didn't sit right with him.

"Varda thinks you slept with me to get the information you gave him, right?"

She captured her lip between her teeth and slowly released it. "Not exactly."

He gripped her thighs, and she jumped. "What did you tell him?"

"He assumed I cozied up to my original target."

"Rossi." She nodded. "And you didn't correct him?"

Her eyes were a storm cloud when she met his gaze. "No, I didn't. I wasn't sure what he would do with that information, and I didn't want to…didn't want to give him ammunition against you."

His lips were on hers before she finished her sentence, and

she immediately leaned in and gave him more. More of her kiss in the sweep of her tongue against his, more of her body pressed against him, hips rocking against his thighs.

Her hands combed through his hair, and he skimmed his fingers around to the backs of her thighs, bringing her body down flush against his. She broke from his kiss on a throaty moan when he ground the already hard length of his cock against her core. He couldn't remember the last woman who made him hard as fucking steel in a finger snap.

"We should go on a date." The words were out of his mouth before his brain fully engaged, and the shock on her face mirrored his own.

"A date? Why would you want to do that?"

"Because," he said, fishing for the excuse in the impulse, "if Varda thinks you're hooking up with me—"

"Not you, Rossi."

"Well, you're not going on a fucking date with Rossi," Dom growled. "He'd have your panties around your ankles in five minutes."

"Not if I don't wear panties."

He ground into her again, and she groaned softly. "That mouth of yours will get you into trouble one day."

"My mother is always saying that," she replied, a little breathless. "Why do you want to take me out? Really."

"Because now that we've been seen together, Varda is going to know it's me you're getting information from, not Rossi. You need to keep up the facade." And because he couldn't let the idea go now that he had it. "If Varda is having you followed and all he sees is the two of us meeting for a quick five minutes and going our separate ways, he's going to know something's up."

Fear replaced the arousal in her eyes, and he regretted putting it there. "How long would we have to do that for?"

"Tired of my company already, Emilia?"

Her lips twitched, but she didn't smile. "More worried about what might happen if I spend more time with you. And what'll happen to my panties."

He pressed a kiss to her chest between her breasts and growled against her skin. "When is your next day off?"

"Sunday. But I work in the morning tomorrow. Should be free after about four."

"I can pick you up at your house."

"No. God, no. Meet me at the restaurant. I don't want my family to know about this. The less they know, the better. Besides, how would I explain I'm dating a Mafia general when one is currently trying to ruin our lives?"

When she slid off his lap, he frowned. Maybe she really did see him the same as Varda. The idea of it sliced deeper than he wanted it to. Pushing to his feet, he brushed the sand from his pants and looked out over the water.

"I'll see you tomorrow at four. Wear panties."

# Chapter Fourteen

Standing in the single-stalled bathroom of the restaurant, Emilia stared at herself in the mirror and held her hair up at the back of her head. She'd been obsessed about whether to wear it up or down for roughly ten minutes. Maybe longer. In the end, she decided to wear it up to keep her from playing with it all night.

Dom inviting her on a date, whether it was to keep up the charade or not, had made her nervous. She'd dropped two plates today, and her stupid manager promised to take it out of her next check. No doubt he would hit on her in the near future and use that as leverage. Like the creep he was.

Giving herself one last look and taking a deep breath, she left the bathroom and headed for the door. She didn't make it ten paces before her manager slid in front of her, blocking her path.

"Where are you going all dressed up?"

Emilia glanced down at the lavender dress she'd brought from home. It was similar to the one she'd worn to the bar. The one she'd nearly let Dom fuck her in. A part of her hoped this one had similar effects. She couldn't look at him without remembering the feel of his lips on hers, and she wanted to feel a lot more. No matter how terrible an idea that might be.

"Going out."

"With friends?"

She swallowed a sigh and forced a smile onto her face. "I guess you could say we're friends. Excuse me. I don't want to be late."

When she tried to move around him, he grabbed her arm and held her in place. "When are we going to go out?"

The second of never. "I don't think it's appropriate to date coworkers." She tried to shake his grip, but he tightened his fingers. "Please let go of my arm."

"You walk around here teasing me all the time like you don't know what you're doing."

"I walk around doing my job. Nothing more."

"You want me to stare. You want to lead me on."

"I—"

"Emilia." Dom's voice was a threat, and her manager instantly dropped her arm, stepping to the side. "What's going on here?"

"Just talking with my employee, sir. If you have a seat, one of our waitresses will be right out to serve you."

Dom held out his hand, and Emilia went to him, biting back a smile at the way her manager's eyes widened. "If that's how you treat your employees, maybe you shouldn't run a fucking business." He turned from the man to her, his tone softening. "Ready?"

"Ready."

"Have fun with the stuck-up bitch," her manager muttered. "No one else gets to."

Dom reacted so fast she didn't have time to stop him, his forearm against her manager's windpipe while he flailed against the wall in seconds. "What did you fucking say?"

"N-nothing!"

"What I thought I heard was you calling my woman a bitch." Dom increased the pressure, and her manager sputtered.

Something hot and bright flared in her chest when Dom used the words *my woman*, and she smoothed a hand over her belly to quiet the butterflies. Nothing about this should be sexy. And yet…

"Your face looks familiar." Dom cocked his head. "What's your game? Blackjack? No." His grin was cold. "Roulette, right?"

Her manager nodded. "I haven't gambled in weeks."

"Not since you paid off the last debt and tried to cheat the house." He flashed the lone tattoo on his forearm, and her manager's face went white. "I decided to let you live after that. If I find out you talked to her like that again, I won't be so benevolent a second time. Do you understand?"

Her manager nodded as much as Dom's arm against his throat would allow and doubled over coughing when Dom released him. Then Dom calmly took her hand, lacing their fingers together, and led her from the restaurant.

"That was…" Bad. Exhilarating. Sexy as fuck. "Something. But I'm not sure if you just made the problem worse or better."

"If he touches you again," he growled, "I better be your first fucking call."

"I can't."

His eyes darkened, and he yanked her against his side as they walked. "You'd fucking better."

"I *can't*," she said again, stopping short and pulling him back to stand in front of her. "I don't have your number."

He considered that fact for a moment then held his hand out palm up. "Phone."

She dug it out of her purse and unlocked it before

handing it to him. His fingers moved quickly over the screen, and then he gave it back to her. "Now you do."

Taking her hand again, he led her down the sidewalk toward the noise of a street festival. She'd heard the other waitresses talking about some local saint day this morning. Rome celebrated feast days, but this was something else. There was a quaintness to it.

The street was lined with food and craft stalls, the smells wafting through the air and voices overlapping as children darted around in the street, shrieking and calling to each other. People milled about, quickly licking gelato before it melted and haggling with the vendors over their wares.

"I was thinking a restaurant, but..." He looked at her for confirmation.

"This is good," she assured him. Less pressure than the awkward conversation of a quiet dinner.

He squeezed her fingers, and she saw Varda's man before Dom pointed him out. She had absolutely no idea how long he'd been following her. She'd barely been able to sleep the night before for worrying about it. He could have been tailing her for weeks, and she might never have known if Dom hadn't said something.

They wandered up one side of the street without speaking, and she found herself content just to be near him. He had a strangely calming presence, despite how lethal he obviously was. That look in his eyes when he'd held her manager up against the wall by his neck. Dom had killed before and he'd kill again, and the idea of it didn't bother her nearly as much as it should.

He paused at a stand to look over some sugared fruit and bought a tray of orange slices, the clear candy shell glinting in the sunlight, and offered her one. When she reached up to take it from his hand, he pulled it away and brought it to her lips.

"What's the matter? Don't like oranges?"

She licked her bottom lip, and his gaze dropped to her mouth. "I can feed myself."

"I know."

Opening her mouth, she closed it around the fruit, grazing the pad of his thumb with her teeth and swallowing a moan when he dragged it over her bottom lip.

"Tell me about your work," he said when they resumed walking again.

"At the restaurant?"

"No." He chuckled. "When you were a photographer."

"Oh." The dull ache that usually accompanied those memories pulsed in her chest. "It was a good job, paid very well. But designers are pains in the ass."

"Funny. I would have thought it would be the models."

"Some of them can be. But Rome is cutthroat. I think most of them are happy to just be working. The designers, though." She rolled her eyes, and he laughed. "Have you ever seen a man dissolve into a screaming fit because a blazer didn't lay just so?"

"I can't say that I have."

"Count your lucky stars. What about your work?" she asked after a beat.

"You don't want to hear about my work."

She traced her fingertips idly over the tattoo on his forearm. The one her manager had been so afraid of. "But I do. That's why I asked."

He stopped to look at her and shook his head. "Next question."

"Tell me about your family."

"Nope."

"Oh, come on!" she protested. "You know about my daddy issues." She thought she saw a small smile, and she decided to push her luck. "Please?"

He sighed. "I have an older brother and a younger one and a little sister."

"Parents?"

Something swept across his face. Grief? Relief? But it was gone so fast she couldn't name it. "Both dead. My mother from cancer. My father by his own hand."

She squeezed his arm. "I'm sorry. Were you close with them?"

"Not really. My father favored Matteo, and my mother favored Carina. So I made my own way in the world."

"As your father's top general." He slanted her a look. "That's what Varda called you."

"It's an accurate description."

"How did you know my manager liked to gamble on roulette?"

"My family owns a bunch of casinos."

He didn't offer up any more than that, and she decided to let it go. There was only so much she needed to know about just how deadly he really was. They wandered for a little longer, until the smells and the sounds started to give her a headache.

She craved the quiet. She didn't get nearly enough of it anymore, living in a house with three other people.

As if sensing her discomfort, Dom led her away from the street and down to the water. It was rockier on this end of the beach, the waves buffeted by cliffs as they climbed down a set of steep stone stairs. She liked this part, the way the waves echoed off the rock.

"Better?" he asked, wrapping his arm around her shoulder and pulling her back against his chest.

"Yes," she sighed, drawing the sea air deep into her lungs. "I didn't realize how pretty it was here. Or how you could drive for an hour and see a city, a farm, and a mansion."

He chuckled in her ear, raising goosebumps over her cheek. "Sicily is an interesting place. Full of contradictions."

"It's an illusion. Nothing is as it seems."

"Nothing?"

"Nothing." She turned to face him. "Except maybe…"

Without thinking about it too much, she pushed onto her tiptoes and pressed her lips to his. His arms were around her in an instant, hauling her body closer while he angled his head and deepened the kiss. His tongue swept against hers, and she slid her arms around his neck, giving him as much as he would take.

When he tilted his head to skim his lips along her jaw to her earlobe, flicking it with his tongue, she sighed. She should stop this. Giving in to Domenico Bianchi was a recipe for disaster. But if he was fire, she wanted to be consumed by him.

"I have to tell you something," she said, giving him access to her neck while her fingers tangled in his hair. "I didn't follow directions."

"Which directions?" he asked against her throat.

"I didn't wear any panties."

He froze against her, his fingertips tightening on her hips. "You're bare for me under this dress?"

"Yes."

He released her so fast she stumbled back a step, her heart sinking that she'd said the wrong thing as his eyes swept the beach. Landing on something, he grabbed her hand and pulled her over to a cropping of rock and around the far side of it.

Spinning her until her back was pressed against the hard surface, he ran his hands down her arms and moved them above her head, pressing them against the stone. "Keep your arms there and don't move them until I give you permission."

Her whole body shivered at the command, and she didn't

even consider not obeying. His hands dropped to the hem of her dress, his fingers digging into her skin as he dragged the material up her thighs and over her hips.

She was already wet for him, and now she was desperate to be touched by him, her whole body quivering in delicious anticipation. His fingernails scratched lightly across her thigh, the sensation making her knees go weak. When he grazed her pussy with the tip of his finger, she groaned, her arms coming away from the wall in an instinctual need to touch him.

"Ah, ah," he scolded, pulling his hand away until she pressed her arms above her head again.

As soon as they made contact, he was cupping her, his finger slipping between her lips and grazing her clit, steadily increasing the pressure until she gasped and bucked her hips. He ran it down to her entrance, using his other hand to spread her legs wider and slipping it inside her.

A groan rumbled through her as he entered her pussy. She was so wet, hot, needy. On fire for more than his finger inside her. It wasn't enough, but it felt good as he moved it in and out of her, faster and faster, until her breath came in shallow pants and her hips rocked with the steady rhythm of his hand.

He slipped in a second finger, curling them up to rub against her g-spot, and she shuddered, her fingers scrambling to find purchase on the rough surface of the rock face. He drove her relentlessly, his thumb rubbing pressure against her clit as he pumped his fingers in and out.

"Fuck," she groaned, straining with the effort of keeping her arms over her head when all she wanted to do was touch him.

But the pain of the effort translated to pleasure as he shifted, changing the angle of his fingers and hitting her g-spot each time he filled her. "Let me hear you," he demanded, rubbing her clit in fast, rough circles until she couldn't hold back any longer and he wrenched the orgasm from her body with a searing cry.

Her arms fell limply to her side as she sagged against the wall, and she watched him bring his fingers to his lips, tongue darting out to clean her wetness from them.

"I'm going to enjoy getting my tongue between your thighs," he said, his hands going to his belt. "But right now I want to feel you come on my cock."

He freed his thick length, and she reached out to stroke it from root to tip, rubbing her thumb over the head and making him hiss. It was as perfect as the rest of him, and she stroked him again, squeezing gently until he muttered a curse.

"Turn around. Hands on the wall."

She obeyed, and he ran his hands up the backs of her thighs. She jolted at the contact, then melted back against him as he squeezed the curve of her ass and continued his exploration over her back, gripping her shoulder.

His cock brushed her slit when he leaned down to whisper against her ear, and she whimpered. "You have about five seconds to change your mind before I fuck you."

Saying nothing, she rocked back against him, his hard length dragging against her, the friction making her shiver. A distant laugh registered in her brain, but she didn't care who saw them now. The only thing she cared about was the feel of his cock as he bottomed out inside her.

She dropped her head between her shoulders and groaned.

"You like taking my cock with so many people close by?" he demanded, one hand gripping her hip, the other tight on her shoulder so he could set a fast, hard pace.

"Yes," she breathed, using the wall to push back against every thrust.

"You would have let me take you against the side of that

bar, where anyone could have wandered past and seen you bent over for my cock." His hand snaked up to squeeze her breast, roughly twisting her nipple. "Wouldn't you?"

Her pussy contracted around him, and she whimpered. "Yes."

"That's a good little slut." His hand dropped to her clit, rubbing it roughly as he leaned over her back, his thrusts brutal. "My little slut," he whispered against her ear.

She wanted to agree with him but couldn't make her mouth work as her orgasm ripped through her, racing along her skin until she was electric with it. His thrusts didn't slow, his hips slapping against her ass with each one.

"You have another one for me," he said, his fingers returning to graze against her swollen, sensitive clit.

"I can't," she sobbed, jerking against him to try and get away from his insistent fingers.

"You can," he insisted. "Come again for me. Do it, Emilia."

He gave her no choice, savagely wringing another orgasm from her until she was sure she would fall over if he wasn't still inside her, his hands tight on her waist. Then he slammed deep, his chest pressed against her back, and emptied himself inside her.

"You're perfect." He pressed a kiss to the nape of her neck.

"A perfect what?" she panted.

She felt his lips curve into a smile against her skin. "My perfect little slut."

She shivered, grateful when his strong arms pulled her up and held her in place so she didn't collapse. "That's not exactly what I was anticipating when I decided not to wear panties."

"What were you anticipating?"

"That you might try to finger me under the table at a

restaurant or something." He chuckled against her cheek. "This was better."

"Much better. I hope you know we're doing that again."

"Very, very soon," she agreed, sighing when he stepped away and tucked himself into his pants.

"Somewhere more private."

She shimmied her dress back into place, fixing her hair as she felt him slide down her thighs. She could use a pair of panties right now. "I thought we just established I liked it like this?"

He reached for her hand and brought her knuckles to his lips. "I want to take my time with you. See what else you like."

"Well," she breathed. "I won't say no to that."

# Chapter Fifteen

Pulling up the long, tree-lined drive, Dom made a face at the sight of that ugly stone fountain his father had installed several years ago. Maybe Matteo would let him take a sledgehammer to the god-awful thing now that he owned the villa.

He let himself in through the courtyard gate, crossing the expanse of grass with the sun shimmering through the shade trees. The house was quiet as he made his way down to his brother's study. Stopping short in the doorway, he frowned. Empty. Where the hell were they?

Checking his watch, he turned away from the room and went to check the family room. Also empty. He dug his phone out of his pocket, prepared to send a text, when he heard the unmistakable sound of his sister's trilling laughter.

Turning toward it, he skirted the smaller dining room and glimpsed his family by the pool, umbrella guarding against the worst of the sun and lunch spread out on a large table. When he let himself out through the patio door, everyone looked up.

"Welcome home," Carina said as he claimed an empty chair and filled a plate.

"Yeah. Apparently I'm late for today's society luncheon."

"You know, Dom," Carina said, taking a sip of wine. "Of all my brothers, you're the grouchiest."

Dom laid a hand over his heart and pinned his sister with a serious look. "Thank you."

Carina's mouth ticked up at the corner, and she shook her head.

"Now that you're here," Matteo began, "we can get started. What's the status of our campaign against Varda?"

"It's progressing. I tested a new spy, and they did well. Varda took the bait I gave him."

"The dead bodies I found at my casino."

Dom inclined his head. "Yes. The dead bodies. They were spies I needed disposed of. I figured letting Varda take them out while also feeling a sense of accomplishment that he was purging his own ranks would help give him that false sense of security I'm after."

"And did it?" Luca wondered.

"His activity has increased at these houses we've been watching for weeks. I'm not sure if they're safe houses or not, but something is definitely going on with them."

Carina shifted in her chair, flicking a glance at Alexei, who reached for her hand. Dom had nearly forgotten his sister had been kidnapped and almost burned alive doing her own safe house investigation a few months ago.

"What's his deal with them?" Alexei wondered. "What's he using them for?"

"I'm not sure yet. Some of them are more well-known among his ranks, some of them are more top secret. But he has a lot. And I'm still gathering more intel on why."

"If he's setting them up as some kind of stronghold," Matteo began.

"Then we want to take them out before we make our big move," Luca finished.

Dom nodded. "Right. Exactly. I have a deep cover who could get closer to them to get a better idea of what we're dealing with. But I need Varda distracted when he tries. I can't afford to have Sforza's cover blown right now."

"And how do you intend to do that?"

"My newest spy has direct access to Varda. I'm feeding him information that way."

Matteo's brows shot up. "He's in Varda's inner circle, and you trust him?"

"I do." Dom decided not to correct his brother's assumption that his spy was a man.

He didn't know why he felt the need to protect Emilia's identity from his own family. Rossi was still the only one who knew about her, and for now, Dom intended to keep it that way. Whether it was to protect her or protect whatever this thing that was building between them, he wasn't sure.

"So what's the next move?" Matteo asked.

"We're going to leak that we're planning a raid on one of his properties. Sources say he keeps cash and some weapons there."

"You want him to ambush you?" Carina asked, brows raised.

"We'll be prepared for it, but yeah. The circle of people he trusts gets smaller and smaller every day. If we keep him busy on one end of the territory, my guys can check out those houses on the other end with fewer distractions. I'm betting he'll pull his best guys off them for a chance to try and kill me and some other Bianchi soldiers."

"And if he does kill Bianchi soldiers?"

Dom turned to Luca. "War requires sacrifice. But I'm going to do my best to make sure that doesn't happen. We have to play along like we don't know the ambush is coming so I can protect my person on the inside, but I'm going to do my best to bring all our people home. I always do."

Matteo rested his elbows on the table, steepling his fingers. "And after this fake ambush?"

"We could coordinate an attack on multiple houses."

"Weaken his position," Alexei said.

Dom nodded. "That's right. Varda hasn't taken any direct shots at us because he's not exactly sure where to strike, and he doesn't have the manpower to match us. But that won't last forever. I want to siphon off as many of his resources as I can before he gets desperate enough to make a move."

"I imagine it won't be long."

"No. He thinks he has the upper hand with this spy. That he's slipped a mole into our ranks."

"But he hasn't," Carina said.

"No. And it'll make him overly confident for a little while."

"Which gives you the opportunity to use that hubris against him," Matteo said.

"And he won't realize you have until it's too late," Alexei added.

"That's the idea."

Matteo slapped Dom on the back and grinned. "Good work, brother. No wonder Father encouraged you to use your fists so often."

Dom's smile was thin. He'd been forced to use his fists, not encouraged. Every decision his father had ever let him make had to be earned in blood, proven in sacrifice.

Their father honed Dom's basic instincts to razor sharpness. The same way he had with Alexei, finding him on the streets of Naples and molding him into a killer. But Lorenzo Bianchi had a way of chewing people up and spitting them out, his sons included.

"What happens when this is all over?"

Matteo looked at Carina, a frown creasing his brow. "What?"

"Well, when we were battling against the Romanos, you wanted to control their businesses. Varda doesn't have businesses, aside from those shitty pizzerias he maintains as fronts. His money is in loans and threats. Is that what we plan to do once he's gone?"

"I don't care about petty extortion. I'm not interested in threatening civilians for cash," Matteo said. "Varda's problem, the reason his position is so weak, is that he refuses to modernize. The old ways don't work the way they used to."

Luca nodded. "You can't get every cop and politician in Sicily to turn their head. There's always going to be someone trying to make a name for themselves by bringing down a Mafia Don."

"Exactly," Matteo agreed. "The trick is to camouflage yourself better. Rub elbows with the elites instead of paying them off."

"Is that what you've been doing these last seven years? Rubbing elbows with the elites?" Dom wondered, an edge to his voice.

"I've learned a lot about how to run an empire that stands the test of time." Matteo kept his voice even, refusing to rise to the bait.

Dom scoffed. "From who?"

"The Irish. They continue to operate under their government's nose despite being at war with them for decades. They're thriving. In the States too."

Carina scoffed at that with a wave of her hand. "You're dealing with Americans now? What is the world coming to?"

Matteo chuckled. "They have connections all over Europe. It's hard not to hear the Callahan name whispered by someone when you're doing business."

"Aren't those the people who killed DiMarco?"

"Yes. Apparently DiMarco's lust for his Don's daughter finally got him killed." Matteo skimmed Carina with a glance, and she shivered.

"May he rot in hell," Alexei replied, bringing Carina's hand to his lips and pressing a kiss to her palm.

"It still doesn't answer my question," Carina said. "How does taking down Varda contribute to the empire you want to build in Sicily?"

"I don't want his business, but I need his strength and his land. I can't go after Gallo and Antonetti without it."

"And you'll install one of his heirs like you did with Davide? He doesn't have sons, right?"

"He doesn't have any children," Luca confirmed. "Not even bastards running around. His heir will be a nephew."

"I'm not installing any Varda, heir or not, in that territory," Matteo replied.

"Who then?" Dom wondered.

Matteo met Dom with a searching look. "I was thinking I'd install you, actually."

"Me. You want me to run Varda's territory?"

Inclining his head, Matteo drummed his fingers on the tabletop. "And his army once we can make them loyal with an influx of cash. I'll need the threat of both to keep Gallo and Antonetti from doing something stupid. They're already in negotiations to join their families by marriage, but they won't strike against me if I can control what's left of Varda's land and men while I deal with them."

"And you think I'm the person for that particular job?"

"You don't?"

Dom sat back in his chair with a huff. He hadn't considered it. Running a territory had never been in his job description. Until Matteo took off out of the blue, he'd been raised to support the heir. To ensure the health of the family businesses by whatever means necessary and to enforce his brother's word as law.

That's what their father's brother had done until he died. It's what Dom had always intended to do. No matter how much he and Matteo argued, his loyalty was to the family and its legacy, not the man.

"And who sees to things here if I'm permanently set up in the south? Enforcement at the casinos? The men?"

"I do still know how to kill people," Alexei drawled. "And my apprentice is coming along nicely." Carina grinned.

"That is where I need you," Matteo insisted. "But if you're not interested, I can choose someone else."

"I didn't say I wasn't interested," Dom bit off. "But your offer is unexpected."

"Take time to think about it then." Matteo's phone signaled, and he stood from the table. "But I need your answer by the next time we meet. If you don't want it, I have to pick someone else. Now, if you'll excuse me. Luca and I have a meeting with Davide."

"Without me?"

"I thought you hated these financial meetings," Luca said.

"I do."

"So yes," Matteo replied. "We're meeting without you. I'll text you a summary."

"I think you should say yes," Carina said as Matteo and Luca disappeared through the patio doors.

Dom glanced at Carina. "Trying to get rid of me?"

"I am officially moved into the villa in Marsala," she replied with a roll of her eyes. "I'm already rid of you. You know Matteo wouldn't make this offer lightly."

"I know."

Running Varda's territory, maintaining it as a Bianchi stronghold while Matteo continued his campaign to the east.

He could do it, but when the war was over, when Matteo sat on Sicily's throne and every family bent the knee, then what?

He'd watched Matteo dangle the promise of revenge in front of Carina where Romano was concerned and then take it back when it was convenient for him. He had no proof he could trust his brother's word on something like this, not for the long term.

Dom shook his head and looked out over the water. Another problem for another day. Right now he had to focus on the next step in the battle right in front of him. Looking too far ahead was a recipe for disappointment. By the end of the weekend, Emilia would whisper his plans in Varda's ear. And next week, he'd set everything in motion.

# Chapter Sixteen

The room was thick with anticipation, the men ready for tonight's raid. Emilia's confirmation text had come through Saturday night like clockwork, and he'd spent every minute of the last three days drilling the plan into the heads of the men he'd chosen for this mission.

As ready as they were for an ambush, they needed to appear unprepared. If they gave Varda even the slightest hint they knew he'd be lying in wait for them, Emilia could be in danger—and so could their ability to outmaneuver Varda. He didn't want to risk either one.

Sforza had confirmed just a few hours ago that he was good to check out three of the houses that seemed more top secret than some of the others and that Varda would send the men on this ambush Dom had suspected he would. If Dom could bring his men home alive, the mission would be a resounding success.

Once his men were gathered, Dom took them through the plan one final time. They'd arrive at the location in two cars. One group would go around the back to make entry and watch their six, and the other would go in through the front.

Odds are Varda would put his men inside to take them by surprise.

It wasn't a big place, a small, squat building Varda used as one of his collection centers on the far side of Agrigento. The money and weapons were supposed to be in the loft space. They were purposely planning to leave them behind.

They were a distraction so his men could get into those houses without arousing suspicion and nothing more. He needed that intel to set the next piece of his plan in motion and further destabilize Varda and his control.

"Any questions?" Dom looked around the room, nodding at a guy in the back who lifted a finger in the air.

"We taking anyone alive, or do you want them all dead?"

"Dead," Dom replied. "The whole damn thing is supposed to look like a failure. We're not even taking anything out of the house with us. I want Varda to think we had to run with our tails between our legs. Anything else?" When no one spoke, Dom twirled a finger in the air. "All right. Let's roll out."

The men filed to the waiting SUVs, and Rossi pulled Dom aside. "You sure you don't want me to go with you?"

"I'm sure that if something goes sideways, I need you here," Dom said. "You're the one who'll be sending in backup if we need it."

"It was a good idea to station a third car nearby." Rossi hesitated. "I don't like the idea of you going into this without me watching your back."

"You just want to shoot someone."

Rossi grinned. "That too."

"I'll need you on the next one." Dom squeezed Rossi's shoulder and climbed behind the wheel of the first SUV.

They rode in silence, the third car breaking off to circle around to the location from a different direction once they crossed the border into Varda territory. The streets were quiet when they drove by the first time. Dom slowed in front of the building but kept driving.

Adrenaline sent pulses through his nerve endings, every sense hyper alert as he pulled parallel with the curb a few buildings up and cut the engine. He waited until the second car pulled into the alley before getting out and meandering down the sidewalk.

They'd look less out of place if the street wasn't so dead and the buildings weren't so rundown. A text came through, a signal that his men were in place at the rear, and even though he'd rather blow the door off its fucking hinges, Dom had to play his part.

"Open it," he said to the man beside him, watching him crouch down and work tools into the lock to pick it.

It only took a few seconds before the lock clicked and the door swung in silently. It was dark inside, darker than he anticipated it would be, shades closed so the street lamps couldn't penetrate. There should be security lights on along the back wall, but they were out. Varda must have cut the power to keep them in the dark.

Weapon drawn, he stepped over the threshold, straining his ears for the sound of movement. But it would be impossible to tell if that was Varda's men or his own coming in from the back. Aside from the loft, this building had two larger rooms, one bathroom, and three smaller rooms that could be storage areas or counting rooms.

The loft is where the goods were. If Dom had to bet money on it, Varda and his men would probably be hiding in the large room beside the stairs to the loft. It would be the perfect place for an ambush. Trap his men up there and shoot them like fish in a barrel.

Heartbeat thudding thick in his ears, he took his men down the far hallway, away from the loft. The other group would move in that direction and hopefully engage Varda's men before going up to avoid being cornered.

It wasn't long before they heard the unmistakable sound of exploding bullets. Dom spun toward the noise, racing back the way they'd come, his eyes finally adjusting to the darkness. The narrow hall spilled back into the room where they'd entered, and he jogged across it, darting through the door in the corner and down another short hallway.

Varda's men looked up at the sound of pounding footsteps, surprise clear on their faces even in this light. They weren't expecting two groups of Bianchi soldiers. Varda's mistake and poor planning were going to make this ambush look better than he thought.

Taking aim at the man closest to him, Dom dropped him with a single bullet. The man behind him turned too late, and he fell on top of his friend. The next guy was more prepared, squeezing off a series of shots and forcing Dom to duck into one of the smaller rooms.

One of his men from the second group joined him a scant second later. "How many?" Dom demanded.

"Eight when we came in, I think. Saw two dead bodies on my way to you, and we've dropped two ourselves. Makes four left if there aren't more. Otto's hit, though. Might be in the shoulder. Hard to tell since it's so fucking dark in here."

Dom cursed under his breath. "We got guys in the loft?"

"Yeah, at least one. No idea if the stuff is actually up there."

"Okay. Take two men from my group and sweep the rest of the building to make sure there aren't any surprises. And figure out how to turn the fucking lights on."

The man nodded and left, the hail of bullets ebbing as people reloaded, and Dom reemerged. He counted three bodies on the floor now, but two of them were face down, so it was impossible to tell which man belonged to which crew.

He saw the flash of a muzzle before he felt the bullet whiz past his head, and he ducked to run across the hall to the room where the last man in his group was taking cover.

"You good?"

"Nicked in the thigh, but I'll live. You?"

"Fine. I'm going to try and get closer. Cover me."

His man nodded, moving to the door and opening fire down the hallway. Dom seized the opportunity to run into the next room, the second large space, and meet up with the second group. A Varda soldier charged him, and Dom dropped him with shots in rapid succession.

"How many left?" he demanded of the man closest to him.

"Two at least, maybe three."

"I've got a team doing a sweep and looking for the fucking lights. Then we can—"

The building lit up, and Dom nearly groaned with relief. The three Varda men were very exposed, comfortable in the dark but not taking any precautions in the light. Two more were dead before they could even take aim, the third caught in the back as he tried to run out the door.

Dom swept into the last room to clear it, noting a single Varda soldier huddled in the corner. At the sight of Dom, he tossed his gun to the ground and threw his hands up.

"Looks like we got ourselves a lone survivor," someone said from behind him.

"A relation. That's Varda's nephew. His least favorite one after tonight. I want him," Dom said, changing his mind about not taking anyone alive. "Take him to the car and make sure he doesn't know where he's going."

Two men stepped forward, producing a ski mask from a pants pocket and shoving it over the man's head backward while someone else zip-tied his hands behind his back. Dom pulled out his phone and called the third car to meet them.

Heading back out into the main room, he stopped at the base of the narrow stairs leading up to the loft.

"Find anything?" he called up.

"You're definitely going to want to take a look at this."

There was something in his man's tone that didn't sound right, and he frowned. Keeping his gun ready at his side, he slowly climbed the stairs. It was darker up here, the whole space illuminated by a single bare bulb, and it took his eyes a second to register one man unmoving on the floor and the other with a gun to his head.

"Domenico Bianchi. Big fish for such a small raid. Varda will be interested to hear about that."

"Too bad you won't make it out of here alive to tell him," Dom said.

"Maybe," the guy said with a malicious grin. "But I'll still kill you in the process, and that seems like a win to me. Taking out the Bianchi general. Your brother's a fool to risk the backbone of the Bianchi army for a few thousand dollars and some guns."

"What's life without a little risk?" Dom said, making eye contact with his man and waiting for his nod of understanding. "I'll be sure to tell my brother what you think of his leadership skills. I'm sure he'll be crushed. Now," he barked.

His man shoved away from Varda's lackey and dove for the floor. Dom seized on the surprise by firing into the guy's chest once, twice, a third time, satisfied when he jerked violently and collapsed back against the boxes piled around him, smearing the cardboard with blood.

"Nice shot," his man said. "He's not ours," he added, hooking a thumb at the other guy when Dom got up to check for a pulse.

Dom rolled the guy onto his back, and sure enough, he was a Varda man. Good. The bastards. Holstering his weapon, he climbed down.

"Did we lose anyone?"

"No. Otto took one in the arm, but he'll be fine."

Dom nodded. "The nephew?"

"In the truck. What do you want to do about the bodies?"

Dom surveyed the seven men on this level, blood oozing out in widening pools and soaking into the floor. "Nothing. There's two more dead up there. This way it looks like we got spooked and ran. And I want to spread the word that we lost a couple men. Let Varda think he actually got off a few good shots."

"Instead of being a complete and utter failure?"

"Exactly," Dom said with a grin. "You take the nephew back. Put him in the cellar and call Alexei to work his magic. If we can't get anything out of him, I want it to look like a suicide. The rest of you split between the last two cars and head back to the house. I have something I have to do."

They nodded and filed out. Dom sped off after them, taking a right when he should have gone left to get back to the house. Pulling into the public lot, he parked and dug his phone out to text the only person he wanted to see right now. The only person he wanted to work off this adrenaline high with.

The only person who could give him exactly what he needed.

# Chapter Seventeen

*What are you doing right now?*

Emilia smiled at the text from Dom, untying her apron and slinging it over the hook in the small room where she stored her purse. Looping her bag over her shoulder, she fired off a quick response.

*Just leaving work. You?*

Flipping off the lights in the break room that was little more than a closet with two chairs against the wall and some cubbies for personal belongings, Emilia let herself out the side door into the alley and checked it was locked behind her.

*Waiting patiently.*

She tilted her head and read the message a second time, a small smile playing on her lips. So cryptic. She knew he was running his raid sometime in the next few days. He hadn't given her specifics for her own safety, and that was just as well because she didn't want to know details.

What happened between him and Varda was his own business as long as Varda was dead and buried when this was all said and done. She doubted he was in anything other than work mode if he was waiting to do whatever it was he was about to do.

*Waiting for what?*

She looked up to cross the last street to the parking lot and stopped short. Dom's SUV was parked next to her car, and he was leaning back against it, the phone in his hand illuminating his face. Even from this distance, he made her mouth water.

She hadn't physically laid eyes on him since they'd had sex on the beach. No. Since he'd fucked her on the beach. With every inch of his cock. Biting her lip at the memory, she crossed the street and the lot, stopping next to her car.

He looked up, smiling, and her phone dinged in her hand. *You.*

"Well, here I am." She dropped her phone into her purse and tilted her head with a smile. "Did you—"

Her words were silenced when Dom gripped her by the shirt, hauled her up against his chest, and claimed her mouth. He tasted sweet, like he'd been eating candy while he waited, and the flavor of him was such a stark contrast to the rough way his hands roamed over her body, gripping her ass and lifting her just enough to grind his cock against her core.

She wriggled against him impatiently, her body already on fire for him. He could press her back against her car and take her in full view of the parking lot for all she cared. The desperation to feel him inside her was like fire snapping under her skin. She'd never wanted a man the way she wanted him.

He dipped his head to flick his tongue over her collarbone, scraping it with his teeth and making her sigh. She rocked in his grip until he groaned against her skin, sinking his teeth into the flesh of her shoulder until she cried out.

"Dom," she whimpered.

"Yes, kitten?" He tortured her with another slow roll of his hips.

"Your car or mine?"

He set her on the ground and reached behind him to open his car door, helping her into the backseat and climbing in behind her. As soon as the door closed behind him, the car plunged into darkness, and he hauled her onto his lap.

Straddling him, her hands immediately went for the hem of his shirt, tugging it up and off. She leaned in to press a kiss to his nipple, dragging her tongue across it and smiling when he shivered, his hand sliding into her hair and tightening against her scalp.

He let her tease him a second time, then brought her mouth to his, his tongue tracing along her bottom lip before sliding against hers while he cupped her breast, squeezing her nipple hard through the fabric of her shirt and bra.

"Off," he commanded, breaking the kiss and skimming his lips along her jaw to her earlobe.

She quickly undid the buttons on her shirt with shaking fingers and then the front catch on her bra. She groaned when he roughly palmed her breast, pinching her nipple between his thumb and forefinger. Arching against the pain, she couldn't relieve it with his grip on her hair, but she didn't want him to stop. She wanted more.

He teased his teeth down the side of her neck, nipping and sucking the skin while she trailed her fingernails down over the defined muscles of his abs, tracing each one. She made quick work of his belt and zipper, reaching her hand in to cup him and squeezing gently when he groaned.

"For the record, this wasn't the place I had in mind when I said I wanted to take my time with you."

She laughed softly, freeing his cock and wrapping her fingers around it. "It's more private, though. There are walls. And tinted windows even."

"But you're very loud, kitten."

"I'm not that loud." She pouted, stroking her hand down and back up. "I was being quiet on the beach."

He growled, thrusting up into her grip. "If that was you being quiet, then I definitely need to get you somewhere soundproof. Emilia?"

"Hmm?" she murmured, dragging her thumb roughly over the tip of his cock.

"Why are you still wearing shorts?"

Grinning, she shifted to his side and worked down her zipper, wriggling out of her shorts in the confined space and then tossing her shirt and bra on top. There was something very sexy about being fully naked while he still had his jeans on, his thick cock hard and waiting for her.

She repositioned herself on his lap, breath catching in the back of her throat when he slid against her, coating himself in her wetness. Having him inside her again was all she'd been able to think about for days.

Dom leaned in to capture her nipple in his mouth, wrapping his tongue around it as he slid his hand down to her clit, circling it with his finger. He teased her with light strokes while his tongue and his teeth increased the pressure on her nipple.

Reaching for his cock again, she grumbled in protest when he grabbed her hand and trapped it against her thigh, holding her wrist firmly and slipping first one, then two fingers inside her.

"Fuck," she sighed, grinding against his hand while his teeth closed around her nipple, pulling it away from her body until she shuddered.

Dom released it, blowing cool breath against the wet bud. "Come on my fingers like a good slut, and then you can have my cock."

He added a third finger and pushed them deep while his

thumb circled her clit. Switching to her other nipple, he slowly drove his fingers in and out, picking up the pace as she met his lazy thrusts with her own needy ones, her hips gyrating each time he buried his fingers inside her to increase the pressure on her clit.

"That's it," he taunted when her thighs started to shake, his fingers moving faster until they were slamming in and out of her, his thumb applying deliciously painful pressure to her clit. "Come for me. Now, Emilia."

He rammed his fingers deep, and she exploded around him, fingernails digging into the skin of his forearm until she drew blood. He flipped her onto her back as the last of the orgasm faded and traced her lips with his wet fingers, pushing them into her mouth.

"You come so well for me," he said, teasing her slit with his length while she cleaned her wetness from his fingers. "Should I taste you, or do you want my cock?"

He gripped the base of his shaft and tapped the head against her clit, grinning when she arched under him and rocked her hips.

"Your cock," she panted, reaching for his shoulders to try and pull him closer. "Please, Dom. I need you to fuck me."

"Okay, kitten. Since you came for me so beautifully." He slid deep, grinding against her. "But I will get my mouth on you eventually."

"Yes," she breathed, wrapping her legs around his waist.

Pulling out, he sank back in slowly, rocking into her hips to put pressure on her clit. He fucked her torturously slowly, his lips and tongue circling her nipple until she writhed under him, needy and panting. His level of control was a mix of pleasure and irritation. She needed to be fucked, to be used, to have him push them both mercilessly toward the peak.

"You're killing me," she gasped when he ground against her clit again, sending tingles up her spine.

"You need more?" He rocked his hips a second time, and she nodded, unable to speak. "Be careful what you wish for, kitten."

He reared his hips back until only his head was inside her and then drove inside her so hard she arched up, her breasts dragging against his chest. His pace didn't slow, hips slapping against hers as he fucked her roughly, breath hot on her skin as he trailed his teeth from her shoulder to her neck to her jaw.

Tugging on her earlobe with his teeth as he fucked her, each deep thrust of his cock had her clenching around him, desperate to come for him, to feel him explode inside her.

"Rub your clit," he whispered roughly, hissing when her pussy gripped him tightly at the command.

Slipping her fingers between them, she drew quick swipes over her painfully sensitive clit. "Dom, I..."

"I know." He grit his teeth, hips moving at a punishing pace, and she could tell he was close too. "You take my cock so good, Emilia. Be my good little slut and come for me, and I'll give you what you need."

"Fuck," she groaned, one hand working her clit, the other wrapped around his neck as he plowed into her.

With one final deep thrust, his teeth on her skin, she arched against him, breath lodged in her throat as the orgasm ripped through her, stars dotting her vision. She cinched her legs tight around his waist, exhaling against his cheek as he spent himself inside her.

"Fuck, fuck, fuck," he muttered into her hair, and somehow she summoned enough energy to chuckle. "I should have let you ride me," he said, shifting back on the seat and pulling her with him, groaning low in his throat when she slid against his softening cock.

"There's always next time. And the time after that and the time after that." He chuckled and pressed a kiss to her shoulder. "Are we going to celebrate like that whenever you have a raid that goes well?"

"How do you know the raid went well?" He leaned back and tucked her hair behind her ears.

"Let's call it a wild guess. I don't mind celebrating with you." She pressed a kiss to his lips, moaning softly when he deepened it, his arms encircling her waist. "What happens now?"

"I need some time to plot it through, gather some intel. I'll—"

"Be in touch. I know." She sighed. "I should probably get home."

When she shifted to move off his lap, she felt his cock grow against her thigh and bit her lip. His arms tightened on her waist when she hesitated, and he pulled her flush with his cock again. Rocking his hips up to slide his length against her slit, he grinned when she dropped her forehead against his with a breathy sigh.

"Round two?" she asked.

He slid inside her so fast her breath caught in the back of her throat. "Since you asked so nicely, kitten."

# Chapter Eighteen

The plan had gone off without a hitch. Once word spread that Dom had lost three men and left without the goods they came for, Varda was pleased with himself. He didn't seem to care that he'd lost ten in the process, only that Dom and the Bianchis also suffered some losses and had nothing to show for it since he still had his money and his guns.

The nephew wasn't as helpful as Dom had hoped he might be. Close enough to Varda to be sent on this mission but too far removed to know much about Varda's next steps or plans. With Alexei's help, they'd made it look like he'd slashed his wrists at home with a note apologizing for being a coward. Varda didn't appear all that broken up about it.

He had multiple nephews spawned from multiple sisters, and several he liked better than useless little Ricardo. He hadn't officially named an heir yet. It kept his nephews on their toes, eager to please him to hopefully inherit the territory one day. Not that they'd live that long.

Now Dom was braced for retaliation. If Varda was going to, now was the time. When he thought they were grieving and burying their own. So far, nothing had happened, and the fact it hadn't made Dom restless.

But this morning, Otto delivered the dropped report from their embedded spy, and it was full of information he could use to inform his next moves. He hadn't given Emilia a tip for her weekly meeting with Varda yet, and he was cutting it close.

There'd only been time for Sforza to get in and out of three houses, but they were the newest ones, often watched by men Varda trusted most. Dom had hoped Varda would leave them vulnerable the night of the raid, but he hadn't, assigning some of his second-tier men to keep an eye on them. Something that apparently comprised sitting in the living room of the house playing on their phones and smoking cigarettes.

Sforza didn't even need to be coy about snagging a spot on the detail. One had been offered to him. The fact made Dom smile. Varda had traitors and loyal Bianchi soldiers in his ranks and had no fucking idea. No wonder his control of his men and his territory was slipping. But he wasn't to be underestimated. Cornered animals bite.

Glancing up at a knock on the door, he waved Rossi in, accepting the glass of wine Rossi handed him before taking a seat on the couch. Rossi took a deep drink and sighed, but said nothing.

Dom attempted to ignore him, making notes as he scanned the shorthand report. The houses were older buildings, probably purchased cheap. It didn't need to be pretty to be useful.

They weren't as secure as he'd expected, considering the number of man-hours Varda was spending to keep them guarded. He could pay half the men if he installed a couple security cameras. But Varda was nothing if not old school, and that oversight would work in their favor.

The constant presence of men was their biggest obstacle. Not an insurmountable hurdle by any means, but a messy one. These houses were in residential neighborhoods, and by the looks of it, not everyone was Mafia. It would do them no good to breach the house guns blazing and have the neighbors call the cops.

Tossing back the rest of his wine, Rossi sighed again.

"Dear God. What?" Dom said, setting his pen down on top of his pad of paper.

"I need pussy."

Dom rolled his eyes. "You're not going to find any of that here, I'm afraid."

"I know that, you prick. I meant, let's go out."

"I don't want any pussy." That wasn't true, but there was only one he wanted, and she was busy.

"How is that possible? You chase more skirt than me."

"Because I need to finish going over this report and figure out what the fuck I'm going to do next." He gestured at the pages spread out in front of him. "This war isn't going to win itself."

Rossi sat forward, arms resting on his thighs. "You've been staring at those reports all day. You need a break."

"I still have two I need to finish. And then I have to figure out what the fuck Varda is doing with these houses. Why does he have so many? And where is he getting the money for them? If I take them out, am I showing my hand and how much intel I have? Does he want me to take them out because they're really a trap?"

"See? That's why you need a break. You're spiraling."

Dom shot Rossi a look. "I'm not spiraling."

"You're sure as hell giving Varda too much credit. At his core, the man is a coward. If he wasn't, he'd have taken his so-called army, the one he's always bragging about and posturing with, and hit back at us already."

"He's up to something," Dom insisted. "And I want to know what."

"You'll think clearer once you get laid."

"Rossi, please. I'm begging you. Go out and stick your dick in something. I need the peace and quiet."

Rossi grunted. "I need a wingman."

"Take Otto. He's an excellent wingman. And he's got battle scars now."

"Why are you dodging this so hard?"

Dom gestured at the papers laid out in front of him. "I told you. Work. War. Things to find out, people to kill, territories to conquer."

Cocking his head, Rossi narrowed his eyes. "No. That's not it. We've been in tighter spots. You never said no to a good hard fuck to clear your head before. Unless…"

"Rossi—"

"Unless you're already getting laid. By a certain little waitress." Rossi pointed his finger when Dom rubbed his fingers over his eyes and pinched the bridge of his nose. "I knew it! You said you were going to tell me how good she was in the sack."

"We haven't made it to the sack yet. And I'm not going to tell you either way. Get out."

"Not going to tell me? Why the hell not?" Rossi demanded. "Since when do you not kiss and tell?"

"Since now. Go away."

Rossi dropped his head into his hands and groaned. "You can't catch feelings, man. I've lost three friends to women in the last year. Don't do it. It's a trap."

"I'm not catching feelings." His stomach twisted sharply, but he ignored it. He wasn't. That was that. "But I am sleeping with her because she has something I need and vice versa. There's nothing more to it."

"Sure," Rossi said, pushing off the couch and retrieving his glass. "Just better hope she doesn't become a distraction."

"Don't be a dick. I know what I'm doing. If you don't trust me to keep my head in the game and get the job done, then run home to my brother."

"That's not what I said."

"Great. Glad that's cleared up. Now get the fuck out."

Rossi stalked out of the pool house, slamming the door behind him, and Dom tossed down his pen again. He wasn't catching any fucking feelings. He was perfectly capable of fucking someone and not getting attached. Even someone as perfectly suited to him as Emilia, with the way she responded to his words and his cock and his fingers and—hopefully very soon—his tongue.

But Emilia and her pretty lips wrapped around his dick in the backseat of his SUV when they'd gone for round three was the last thing he needed to focus on right now. He had to finish reading through these goddamn reports. He couldn't plan his next move until he knew what Varda was hiding in these houses.

Pushing Emilia and Rossi out of his mind, he got back to work. He scanned the page quickly until a word at the bottom jumped out at him. Weapons. The first and second levels of the house had been normal. Sparsely furnished with folding chairs but nothing that seemed out of the ordinary.

Until Sforza stumbled on a door in the floor leading down to a cellar. He hadn't had time to explore it fully, but when he opened the door to peek inside, there'd been weapons. Many of them lined up on tables or leaned against walls. Ammo stacked on metal shelves and crates Sforza suspected held larger caliber guns.

Varda was bleeding money after his nearly one billion euro loan to the Romanos went unpaid after their death. So much so he hadn't been paying his men very well for months.

Where the fuck was he getting the cash to buy that many weapons?

Sforza confirmed that similar caches appeared at the other two houses he was able to get into the night of the raid as well. There was no telling how many weapons caches Varda had been stashing around the territory. But there was no way he was footing the bill for any of them. Someone was helping.

Another knock on the door had him groaning. "I'm not in the mood, Rossi!"

"It's Otto."

Dom looked up and waved Otto in. "Didn't want to go pick up chicks with Rossi either?"

"We're on our way out. I figured you'd want to see this."

"What is it?" Dom accepted the sealed envelope from Otto and ripped into it.

"An emergency drop from Sforza."

Dom's gaze snapped to Otto's as he shuffled the paper out. The message was short, sweet, and to the point.

*Weapons delivery scheduled. Two days. 10 p.m. Enna.*

"Holy shit," Dom mumbled.

"What is it?"

He shoved the paper at Otto and flipped to a fresh page on his pad. "Somebody's helping Varda stockpile weapons. And in two days, we're going to find out who. And then I'm going to fucking kill them."

"Do you need me to stay?"

Dom shook his head. "Go get laid. I'm going to need everyone's head in the game on this. Get it out of your systems now so you can focus."

Dismissed, Otto left, the door clicking softly closed behind him. They'd need another distraction. Pull focus away from the weapons exchange like they had with the raid. This time he didn't need it to look like a failed mission. He'd make sure their involvement in the weapons exchange was recon only.

Watch the exchange, follow the inventory to its location, attempt to gauge the number of weapons, report the intel back. With a time and location, he didn't need to rely on internal spies. He could send his own men. Between that and the raid on two, maybe three other houses, he'd get Matteo to send down some backup. He already had names in mind.

Someone was backing up Varda, getting more involved than they should be. Enna was in Romano territory, though Dom couldn't imagine anyone in Romano ranks had the money to bankroll something like this. Giuseppe and then Elio Romano had been deeper in the hole than Varda was now.

It was more likely this was an attempt to meet on neutral ground. But Romano territory wasn't neutral. It was under Bianchi control. And whether it was Gallo or Antonetti wading into the fight, their interference wouldn't go unanswered. Dom would make sure of it.

# Chapter Nineteen

Exhausted, Emilia dragged herself up the front walk and sank onto one of the small chairs her mother kept on a flat patch of grass behind the bushes. She'd managed to get up and out of the house even before Bella was awake in an effort to avoid suspicion. But hiding what she was doing was getting harder and harder.

She had so many secrets now. Pretending to spy for Varda, actually working for the Bianchis, sleeping with Dom. It weighed on her, all these half-truths and outright lies, and she wasn't sure how much longer she could hold herself upright under them.

The front door opened with a squeak, and she jumped, watching with wide eyes as her sister joined her in the cool morning air. Bella silently handed her a cup of coffee and took the second chair, tucking her feet underneath her.

"Another early Saturday for you."

"Yeah. I went for a walk." Emilia wrinkled her nose at her own lame excuse. "Might go in and take a nap before I have to head to work this afternoon."

"A walk."

Emilia took a sip of her coffee, glancing at Bella out of the corner of her eye. "Uh huh."

"You hate walking."

"I don't hate walking, Bella. I have to walk everywhere. It's how you get around when you have legs."

"You know what I mean," Bella replied, a crease forming between her brows. "You don't like to just go out for leisurely strolls, and definitely not this early in the morning. Sleep is your favorite activity."

"You're making me sound lazy. That's just hurtful."

Bella rolled her eyes. "Where have you been going every Saturday morning? And why do you always look so upset when you get back?"

"I…it's not important, Bells. It's just gr—"

"Grown-up stuff. Yeah. Whatever. That's what Mama says when she doesn't want to talk about something."

Emilia winced. It was true, but it still felt like an insult to be compared to their mother. "I don't want to lie to you, Bella. Believe me when I say I don't. But I need you to trust me on this. I can't tell you because I want to keep you safe."

Bella was silent for a long moment, the steam from her coffee mug curling around her face and swirling away from her with each breath. "Does it have something to do with the guy you're seeing?"

Emilia jerked so hard she sloshed coffee over the mug's rim and spilled it all over the thigh of her jeans, hissing as the hot liquid soaked into the fabric and made contact with her skin. She dabbed at it with the hem of her shirt, but that didn't do anything other than make it dirty.

"What makes you think there's a guy?"

"Wow," Bella said, voice monotone. "One, you spilled coffee all over yourself when I asked. Two, I saw you sneaking in late the other night. "As far as I know, the restaurant isn't open until three in the morning."

"I wasn't sneaking," Emilia replied, though she could hear the guilt in her own voice.

"Okay, then. You were coming in very, very, very quietly, trying not to wake anyone up. We can pretend that's not sneaking. Even though if I did it, it would totally be sneaking."

Emilia wasn't ready to tell her sister about Dom. What would she say? I'm dating a powerful Mafia general who's the best sex of my life. Oh, and I'm also kind of a spy so we can finally be free from this fucking debt to live our lives? Yeah, that sounded normal.

But the lie that there was no guy tasted bitter on her tongue. She was tired of holding everything in, and what's more, she hated that look in her sister's eyes. Like she was disappointing her by not being open. Honesty was a two-way street, after all. But there were lines she wouldn't cross, things she couldn't share. Not just because her sister was sixteen, but because she really did want to keep her safe.

"So, what if there was a guy?"

Bella took a sip of her coffee, eyes warming. "Then I would want you to tell me everything about him. Obviously."

Emilia grinned. "We met at the restaurant. A few weeks ago. He came in and I saw him, and there was just…"

"Chemistry," Bella breathed.

"Yeah." Emilia chuckled. "Chemistry. Electricity. He touched my wrist, and I thought I was going to combust."

"Did he ask you out?"

"Um. Actually. I asked him out." It wasn't totally a lie. She had made Dom the offer that started this whole thing in motion.

"That's very modern of you. Maybe I'll ask out Theo since he's taking his own sweet time about it."

"You should. Don't you have that dance coming up? The fall music thing?"

"It's more like a concert with a reception after, but yeah." Bella considered, tilting her head in a way that reminded Emilia so much of their mother. "I could ask him to that. That's a good idea. But don't change the subject. We're talking about your love life, not mine. This guy. What's he like?"

Emilia smiled into her coffee, crossing her legs and leaning back in the chair. "He's different. So different from anyone I've dated before. Protective, smart, interesting, mysterious. He makes me see everything in a new light. He's constantly looking at everything from five separate angles and three steps ahead."

"And the sex?"

Choking on a sip of coffee, Emilia coughed and sputtered, shoving Bella's hand away when she patted her back and giggled. "I'm really not sure that's appropriate, Bells."

"Oh, come on! We're both having it!"

"You're currently having sex?" Emilia raised a brow.

"Well, not with anyone right this moment. But I'm not a virgin."

"I know that. It's just...I don't want to make it weird."

"Sex isn't weird," Bella assured her. "This conversation is making it weird. Is he doing freaky stuff to you or something?"

Emilia tried to hide her blush behind her coffee mug, but Bella gasped. "Oh my God, he likes to spank you!"

"Jesus Christ, Bella. The whole neighborhood doesn't need to hear that. There's no spanking," Emilia insisted. "But he is the best I've ever had. For sure no other guy compares." That was the truth. And it left out all the details she was never ever going to tell her kid sister.

"Good for you," Bella said, dropping the subject and lapsing into silence. "Does he make you happy?"

"Does he make me happy?"

"Yeah."

Emilia chewed on her bottom lip. "We've only known each other a few weeks. Only been out a handful of times."

"But does it really take all that long to know if someone makes you happy or not?" Bella turned to study her sister.

"No. I guess it doesn't."

Did Dom make her happy? She was so miserable before it wouldn't have taken much to make her feel something above despair. But happiness seemed a realm all its own. Happiness was something that had felt out of reach for such a long time.

He made her smile. Was that happiness? When she got a text from him, her heart beat a little faster in her chest. When they had sex, she'd never wanted or needed anyone more than she needed him in those moments. Never craved what only he had been able to give her. But was that happiness? Or lust?

"I don't know if he makes me happy," she said honestly. "But I know he makes me feel good. He makes me smile. He gives me something to look forward to."

"That sounds pretty good to me. Will you promise me something?" Bella asked after a beat.

"Of course. Anything."

Bella's eyes followed a bird that landed on the bush in front of them. The bird hopped in a circle, tweeting for its mate. When it saw the two of them sitting there, it cocked its head and studied them with wary eyes. Then it gave a final warbling call and took off for the trees.

Once it was gone, Bella turned toward Emilia, gaze serious. "When this is all over. When the stupid loan is paid off, and me and Antonio and Mama are all safe again. Promise me you'll figure out how to be happy."

Tears sprang to Emilia's eyes, a lump forming in her throat. "Sure, Bells. I can do that."

"I mean it," Bella said. "If anyone deserves to be happy, it's you. Promise me."

Emilia reached for Bella's outstretched hand and gave it a squeeze. "I promise. You're too wise for your own good," Emilia said, sniffling into her now cold coffee.

"Remember that next time I forget to finish my homework or wash the dishes."

Laughing, Emilia drained her mug and stood. "I'll keep it in mind. Thank you." She leaned down and pressed a kiss to the top of Bella's head. "I love you, and I'm glad you're my sister."

"I love you too. Now go take a shower and a nap. You look like shit."

With a laugh, Emilia ruffled Bella's hair and let herself into the house. Setting her mug in the sink, she climbed the stairs to her room and collected her towel and robe before shutting herself in the only bathroom. The shower groaned to life when she twisted the knob as hot as it would go.

Stripping off her jeans and t-shirt, she tossed them into the laundry basket, followed by her bra and panties. She'd put her happiness on hold over half a year ago and hadn't thought about it since. Every day was simply a routine of waking up, going to work, getting her check, and giving that check away to the man her family owed money to. Wash, rinse, repeat.

That was it. There wasn't time or energy or space for happiness. She hadn't even taken a photo since leaving Rome. The only way she'd been able to survive was to focus on the here and now and not think too far ahead. Thinking too far ahead only left you disappointed when nothing worked out the way you thought it would.

Before she quit her job, she'd been angling for a senior photographer promotion. More freedom to design her own shoots, choose her own models, and increase her chances of being specifically requested by a designer or editor. And it came with a nice pay bump too.

She'd spent so much time thinking about what her life would be like if she got that promotion, and for what? Now she was stuck in this house, trapped by a debt that wasn't hers, and her career was in the toilet. There was no way she'd work in fashion photography ever again. Not with the way she'd walked out on her boss and left the magazine in the lurch days before the start of a new campaign.

Stepping under the spray, she tilted her head back and let the water run over her hair and face. Dom might make her happy now, but weren't they just using each other for their own ends? How could any of this survive once they both had what they wanted and Varda was dead?

It was too much to think about, a future that was too far-flung. She still had to operate in the here and now. The only things that mattered were Varda's death and her family's freedom. Anything beyond that was a distraction.

No matter how good Dom made her feel, how much he made her smile, how many times she thought about him or wondered what he was doing when they weren't together. She had to get through this first. Then she could entertain the idea of happiness and what it might mean and who she might find it with.

Even if it seemed impossible.

# Chapter Twenty

It was quiet on the outskirts of Enna. The city sat perched on a hill, lit up against the dark, with rows of homes and churches and an old crumbling castle that attracted tourists during the busy season. Then the land turned rough, craggy, dipping with hills and valleys and sheer rock faces.

Everything was swallowed up by the darkness, shrouded by the dense growth of bushes and trees. It was wild here, and Dom's eyes flicked to the clock on the dash. 9:56.

The raids on the two unassuming houses deep in Varda territory were well underway, bolstered by the extra men Matteo had sent down the day before. Dom wouldn't hear the outcome of those until after. Rossi was supposed to make contact as soon as the situation was under control.

If the statement with the first raid was one of being caught by surprise and having to haul ass, then this one was intended to look more like retaliation. He wanted Varda to know who hit him and how. Whatever Varda was hiding in those houses would belong to the Bianchis before the night was over.

9:58. He scanned for headlights, but the road remained dark. If they were meeting in Enna, as Sforza said, this was the only way in and out coming from either the Gallo or Antonetti territories. He couldn't imagine they'd want to loop around to the far side of the city and risk being in Bianchi-controlled Romano territory any longer than necessary.

Emilia said Varda bought the story that Dom was retaliating for his lost men by hitting some random Varda properties. He'd nearly shared more than he should have when they went to the movies. She was far too easy to talk to. But keeping her safe was a priority. And leaving her in the dark was the best way to do that.

The sweep of headlights caught his eye, and he straightened in his seat, the men with him shifting to get a better look through the windshield. An SUV followed by a large panel van turned left on a dirt road ahead of them, and Dom instructed his man to keep the lights off but creep up behind them.

He didn't want to be seen here. The point was to remain invisible. Watch and gather information. All he wanted to know was who was bankrolling Varda's impressive gun collection.

The road was narrow and pocked with holes, and he had to admire their commitment to staying out of sight. Taillights flashed up ahead and stopped, and they pulled onto the shoulder, angling the dark SUV into the shadows of the trees to keep it hidden from view.

He rolled the window down, but the incessant chirping of bugs drowned out whatever conversation was being had as the double doors opened on the back of the truck. The flame from a lighter flared and went dark again, leaving only the glowing embers from a cigarette. He had to get closer and see.

"Stay here," he said, reaching for the door. "Remember, we're only watching."

"If they make you?"

"Then meet me back at the road."

"You want us to leave you with them and haul ass?"

Dom thought of Emilia and what might happen to her if she got made, if Varda suspected her of double-crossing him. He could take these guys if he had to. She could not stand against Varda. Her safety trumped his.

"Yes. I want you to leave me and meet me back at the fucking road."

Slipping silently out of the car, he picked his way carefully through the brush, avoiding downed branches and the leaves that had begun to fall. He skirted the area in a wide circle until he was close enough to hear the murmur of voices.

He crept forward, avoiding the beams of light from their headlights, and leaned his shoulder against a tree. At this distance, he could make out six men, but he'd seen two more get into the back of the van to check out the inventory. Eight total. At least. But how many were for Varda, and who the fuck did the rest belong to?

"This is your last shipment until there's some progress on your end. We're not going to keep shoving guns into your hands for you to use against us later."

"We have a deal. You can trust Varda will hold up his end of it as long as you hold up yours."

"This is the sixth shipment of guns we've provided to you, and you haven't made so much as a single strike against Bianchi. He's already taken down the Romanos, and now he's after you. We don't want him coming for the far side of the island too."

"The Romanos were weak. They needed money."

"A position you currently find yourself in."

There was some grumbling, and the voices fell silent, replaced by grunts and the shuffle and scrape of wooden crates being removed from the van and shoved into the back of the SUV. Dom didn't recognize either voice, and the crates weren't marked with a logo or name as far as he could see. He couldn't leave here without one.

While they continued to load, he chanced moving closer, ducking behind a tree right on the edge of the dirt path and crouching behind it. The rough click of a lighter and another flare of light illuminated the face of Varda's favorite nephew, Georgio.

The last of the crates were loaded into the SUV, the doors slamming shut, and Georgio reached out and gripped the forearm of the man standing in front of him.

"My uncle thanks you for your help."

"Tell your uncle we want to see progress, or you'll get nothing more from us."

"We've already taken out three Bianchi men after they attempted to raid us and failed. There's another raid going down tonight. I'm sure we'll have more dead bodies before the night is over."

"Yeah, well, do us all a favor and try to show a little initiative for once in your existence."

Georgio dropped his cigarette on the ground and toed it out with his boot. "Gallo will have his progress very soon. Have patience."

Dom's jaw clenched. Nero fucking Gallo. He should have known. That bastard would align with the devil himself if it meant saving his own skin. That was all he cared about in the end. He could and did switch sides as quickly as he changed mistresses. Matteo was going to love that development. Dom knew he had big plans for dealing with Nero Gallo.

A tree branch snapped behind him, and he froze in his retreat to the car. He heard no other rustling or footfalls through the brush, just the low hum of voices and slamming of car doors as they prepared to leave. Probably someone taking a piss before they got back on the road.

He'd wait until they both pulled out before making his way back to the SUV and checking in with Rossi. Leaves rustled behind him seconds before he felt the hard press of a gun against the back of his head.

"A spy. How interesting. Arms up and turn around."

Dom pivoted, hands held out at his sides. He didn't recognize the man aiming a gun at his face, but the man recognized him.

"Not just a spy. A big Bianchi fish. This is our lucky night."

"Only if you make it out alive."

Dom leapt forward, grabbing the barrel of the gun and spinning to plow his elbow into the man's face. The guy's head snapped back, and he snarled, jerking his weapon free and taking aim at Dom's chest. But Dom was faster, shoving the man's hand up until the gun fired at the sky.

Fuck. The scramble of noise from behind him was immediate. Car doors slamming, men shouting, feet crunching over dried leaves. He rammed his body into the asshole who tried to kill him, shoving him back against a tree and slamming his wrist against it until the gun fell from his grasp and got lost in the brush.

Drawing his own weapon, he fired until the guy stopped moving. Backing away from the body, Dom didn't bother to be quiet now, sprinting back toward the main road. If his men had listened to him—and they damned well better—that's where they'd be.

Feet pounded the forest floor behind him, and the breath sawed in and out of his lungs as he crashed through the trees, branches clawing at his arms. He could move to the dirt track, eat up the distance to the main stretch a little faster, but he didn't want to give anyone a clear shot at him.

He thought he saw it, a break in the trees, and then suddenly headlights winked on, forcing him to squint against the sudden brightness. Shots rang out behind him, his pursuers making use of the new light source, and two of his men jumped from the SUV to lay down cover fire while he closed the distance between him and the truck.

When his feet finally hit pavement, the car sped forward and swerved to the side. His man leaned across the steering wheel and opened the passenger side door.

"In!" Dom shouted, catapulting himself into the car and slamming the door shut behind him. "Go, go, go!" he demanded once everyone was securely in their seats.

Bullets uselessly pinged the car as they sped away, but the men chasing them were on foot. By the time they made it back to their own vehicles, Dom and his men would be long gone. But he watched for headlights to follow them out anyway.

"Fuck!" he screamed, pounding his fist into the dashboard.

In and out unseen. That was the most imperative part of this mission, and he'd fucked it up. Now Emilia might be in danger. His heart squeezed at the thought.

"What's the update from Rossi?" he demanded.

"I don't know. He hasn't—"

Dom's phone rang, and he swiped his thumb across the screen, putting it on speaker. "Tell me."

"They were more prepared this time," Rossi said. "More men than what you said were at the last one. At least two dozen. It's good you had your brother send backup."

"Weapons?"

"A fuck ton of them in what probably used to be a root cellar." Rossi paused. "Dom, take me off speaker."

Dom didn't like the shift in Rossi's tone, but he did as he asked. "What else?"

"We lost two guys."

Dom scrubbed a hand over his face. "Who?"

"Abela's second son, Fiero, and Carmine Barone."

"He's eighteen."

"Yeah," Rossi said softly. "He was. How'd it go with you?"

"Not as planned. We're taking the long way back through Romano territory. Send as many men as you can spare back to the house and take the bodies home. I'll meet you in Palermo."

Dom disconnected the call and gripped his phone tight in his fist until the urge to throw it through the windshield ebbed. Casualties were an inevitability of war, but that didn't mean he liked looking mothers in the face and telling them their sons would never come home again.

"We lost two. Fiero Abela and Carmine Barone. Rossi is going to meet us in Palermo."

No one spoke. No one moved. Dom dialed his brother and read him in on the situation. The raid was a success, all things considered, even though the loss sat heavy on his shoulders. They'd confiscated money and weapons this time and killed over a dozen Varda men. But he'd fallen short on his recon mission.

They knew it was Gallo bankrolling Varda's defenses now. And Matteo had snarled at that. Dom hoped Gallo's involvement was the thing they needed to push Matteo to act. Because soon Varda was going to learn someone had been spying on his handoff.

Varda might not know it was Dom who'd seen them, but he'd be able to put it together that it was likely someone from the Bianchi camp. And that could make Emilia a target for Varda's wrath if they didn't play it right.

Disconnecting with Matteo, he pulled up Emilia's number and started a new message.

*When are you working this weekend?* Their code for her meetings with Varda.

*Sunday morning.*

Good. He had a few days to handle business in Palermo before then. He wanted to see her before she spoke to Varda, make sure they were on the same page, make sure she knew exactly what to say to keep suspicion off her.

*I want to see you. Dinner Saturday night?* he said.

*I'd love to. Everything okay?*

He ran a hand through his hair and stared at the screen. *Yeah,* he lied. *Just tired. See you Saturday.*

Tonight could have gone better, could have gone worse. But as they drove toward Palermo in silence, Dom knew he was done with recon. He was ready to hit Varda hard and end this. Time to move on to the next phase of his plan.

# Chapter Twenty-One

Standing in front of her closet with her hands on her hips, Emilia surveyed her options for dinner tonight. She hadn't done more than text with Dom since he'd surprised her after work and taken her to a movie. The emergency note for Varda had made her uneasy, though.

She hadn't gone to him outside of their usual weekend meetings before. But he seemed to buy the missive Dom had made her memorize, and she got to spend an evening with Dom. Everything felt one step closer to being finished for good.

Plus, being with Dom made her feel calm, centered. Even if it was just to keep up appearances. Watching some action movie with bad dialogue but great explosions, holding hands, and sharing popcorn had felt so normal, more normal than she'd felt in a long time. And she gave herself permission to have it for a little while.

Eventually it would end, and then she'd have to figure out what to do next. But what was the harm in soaking it all in while she had the opportunity? If a sexy, rich, protective bad boy wanted to take her out and slip his hand under her skirt in a dark theater, she wasn't going to say no to that.

What was the alternative? Sitting at home on a Saturday night watching her mother read? No thanks. Besides, she missed him. The sound of his voice and his laugh, the brush of his fingers on her skin, the way he called her kitten—that had seriously caught her off guard in the best way.

She answered his questions, and he answered hers. Sometimes. The more she thought about him, the more she wondered at her sister's words. Maybe he did make her happy. And if he did, then what? Emilia shook her head. That was too big a question to ponder with everything else going on right now.

Instead she'd focus on the next right thing, and that was picking something to wear tonight. A dress or maybe a skirt. Easy access was always a good idea when she was with Dom. He couldn't seem to keep his hands to himself. Not that she was complaining.

She pulled out a blue dress that played up her eyes and held it under her chin. This one never failed her; it hugged her curves in all the best ways. It was a tight fit, but Dom seemed to like that anyway.

When she went to put it back, the dress next to it fell off the hanger. As she stooped to pick it up, her eyes snagged on the box hiding her camera. That was another thing she couldn't stop thinking about. Taking his picture.

There was a moment when they left the theater after the movie, when the setting sun hit his face just right, throwing one side in shadow and the other in bronze relief. The fading light made his black tattoos stand out against his skin, and the gold chain he wore around his neck glinted. With the colorful buildings at his back, it would have been a stunning shot.

Dropping to her knees, she pulled the box forward and

opened it gently. Her camera bag sat nestled in a pile of scarves, and she ran her finger over the seams with a smile.

Before she took the job at the magazine, she thought she loved photographing people. Any person or situation would do. But that wasn't it. She'd quickly discovered it was candids she loved, not people. Capturing someone in a human moment and immortalizing it.

She'd kept beautiful shots of her mother in a box as a child. Her mother reading in a nook they had in their old house outside of Rome. Another of her making risotto, little Bella at her elbow watching with wide eyes. A third of her mother teaching Antonio how to ride a bike. She'd loved those pictures.

Until she came home from school one day and they were strewn across the kitchen table, her mother demanding to know why Emilia had insisted on taking such ugly photos of her. Despite Emilia's tearful protests, the photos had been thrown in the trash.

If not for her grandfather, Emilia might have given up on photography altogether after that. But he'd encouraged her to keep going, keep translating what she saw in her head into the camera. And she had. But somewhere along the way, she'd gotten away from that. She wondered if she could get it back once this was all said and done.

Reaching in to undo the clasp on the camera bag, she jolted when someone banged on the front door so hard she heard the glass rattle from all the way in her room. Shoving the box back in the corner, she glanced at the clock and made her way downstairs.

Bella and Antonio were out with friends, and her mother was at some coworker's wedding today. Who the hell was banging on the door? Another insistent pounding and her heart with it. Dread curled in her belly as she closed her hand around the knob and pulled the door open.

"Varda." He stood on the front step, seething, with three men at his back. "I thought we weren't meeting until to—"

His hand shot out to grip her throat, squeezing roughly as he shoved her back into the house and up against the wall. A picture fell to the floor, and she heard the glass shatter. His men stepped calmly inside and closed the door like they'd been invited over for coffee.

"Who the fuck do you think you're dealing with here, bitch?"

"What?" she rasped. "I don't understand."

"Your information was a little lacking at our last meeting, don't you think?" His fingers tightened on her throat, and she clawed at the back of his hand, desperate for air.

"I-I…don't…"

Varda brought his face inches from hers, his breath hot and sticky against her cheek. "You told me Bianchi was going to attack two of my properties on the east side."

"Yes. That's what I found on his phone."

"And you expect me to believe," Varda growled, "you just happened to miss the fact he was planning on intercepting my delivery?"

"Your what?" Dom's insistence on never giving her any details about what the information she was passing along meant finally came in handy because she had no idea what Varda was talking about.

Varda wasn't convinced, though. He pulled her away from the wall and slammed her head back against it, causing black spots to explode across her vision.

"Don't play coy with me, you stupid cunt. I was generous when I forgave you for cozying up to Bianchi instead of Rossi and not telling me. I am not inclined to be generous again if I find out you're lying to me."

"I swear," she coughed, terror thrumming in every nerve ending. "I have no idea what you're talking about. I only saw the"—his grip tightened, and his scowl deepened—"the texts about the raids. Please."

A tear slipped down her cheek, and something like amusement lit his eyes. Whether he believed she'd lied to him or not, he was enjoying this. Enjoying holding her life in his hands and watching her squirm. Her lungs burned, and her vision dimmed as he squeezed again.

Fuck. He was going to kill her. And then what would happen to Bella and Antonio and her mother? Would they come home to find her dead body? Would they be next?

Without warning, he released her, and she collapsed to her knees, inhaling deep lungfuls of air with gasping breaths. Her throat was raw and it hurt to swallow, but she wasn't dead. At least not yet.

Varda stalked away and then back again, reaching down and gripping her by the hair to yank her to her feet. "If I find out you know more than you're saying, that you've been stabbing me in the back and lying to my face, I will make you pay a thousand times over."

"I swear," she said, unable to keep the rough tremble from her voice. "I'm not lying to you."

"Let's fucking hope not. Because if you are, I will gut your mother, your sister, and your brother right in front of you. You can listen to their begging, pleading screams as they die so they play in your head over and over again while my men pass you around as their plaything."

He released her and took a step back. "I can make your life miserable in unimaginable ways, Emilia. Don't fucking test me. Do you have any information for me?"

"No, I—"

The backhand to the face caught her off guard, and she stumbled into the small table in the front hall, knocking her mother's hand-painted vase onto the floor, where it shattered.

"Fucking useless. I'll be back in three days to collect your payment and more information. Better hope you have something for me by then."

Pain radiated across her cheek and down her neck as Varda left the way he came, slamming the door behind him. On a choked sob, Emilia slid to the floor, drawing her knees up to her chest and resting her forehead against them.

He was going to kill her. That was the only way this ended for her if Varda won. He was never going to let her family out of this debt, never going to let them go free and live their lives. He'd always intended for it to end in her blood. And the idea that he might get his way terrified her.

Dom was the only thing standing between her and certain death. And she so desperately wanted to hear his voice in her ear. Needed him to tell her he was going to fix this, make it all go away.

Pushing to her feet, she picked up the pieces of her mother's vase and carried them into the kitchen. She'd have to figure out how to explain that, but later. Grabbing her phone off the counter, she dialed Dom's number.

It rang twice before she realized her mistake. Dom would be livid. He'd threatened her boss for far less. This would make him murderous. And she couldn't afford for him to lose sight of the goal now.

Disconnecting the call before he could pick up and tossing her phone on the counter, she pressed at the tender spot on her cheek where Varda's hand had made contact and winced. She'd have a bruise there soon if she didn't already. It was probably best if she canceled tonight with Dom. Make up some excuse about a stomach bug or something.

Her phone rang, and she jumped, her heart catapulting into her throat. Dom. If she talked to him now, she'd burst into tears. He'd want to know what was wrong, and then she'd be right back in the same spot she was before. She sent the call to voicemail and picked up the ruined vase.

It was an ugly cheap little thing, but her mother loved it. Maria would be upset it was broken. And Emilia doubted she could come up with a story good enough to explain it away. It would all be her fault in the end. Her mother might never know everything Emilia was putting on the line to free them. Worse than that, she likely wouldn't care if she did.

She wondered sometimes if coming down here was a mistake. Maybe there was more she could have done from Rome instead of pushing in on her mother's life and her mother's business.

Maybe she could have gotten Bella and Antonio out instead. Safely removed them from a situation they never should have been involved with in the first fucking place. Let her mother deal with the consequences of her own actions for once instead of someone swooping in to save her.

A second and then a third call from Dom came through, followed by a string of messages. She should call him back. She could fake her way through a single phone call. Just tell him she wasn't feeling well and needed to cancel.

In the end, she chickened out, sending him a quick text that she wasn't feeling up to it tonight and could she take a rain check. Wandering into the living room, she called her boss next and let him know she was sick and couldn't make it into work. He wasn't happy about it, but the raspiness from her bruised throat helped sell the lie.

Dropping her phone on the coffee table, she curled into a ball on the sofa, buried her face in a pillow, and let the sobs overtake her.

# Chapter Twenty-Two

Dom circled the block in front of Emilia's house three times, satisfied she wasn't being watched, before pulling even with the curb and stalking up the front walk. Her hang-up call had piqued his interest, ignoring his calls had made him suspicious, and canceling their date had made him worry. Worry he couldn't ignore, abandoning his meeting with Rossi and Otto to come down here and make sure for himself she was okay.

He knocked, listening for sounds on the other side of the door. Nothing. She had to be home. She wasn't supposed to be at work for another hour or so, and her meeting with Varda wasn't until tomorrow.

He heard a faint shuffling sound and knocked again. This time he heard a soft yelp, and his worry intensified, twisting his stomach into knots.

"Emilia! It's me! Open the door!" If she didn't, he was going to break the fucking thing down to get to her.

He heard the snick of the lock, and the door swung in on her tear-stained, wide-eyed face. She reached out to grip his shirt and yanked him inside.

"What are you doing here?" she hissed, eyes darting across the front yard. "You know they watch me."

Seemingly satisfied, she stepped back and closed the door. He saw it clearly then, the edges of a blooming bruise on her cheek. He took a step closer, and she flinched. Was that a fucking handprint on her neck?

He barely checked the fury he felt at someone putting their hands on her when he demanded, "Who the fuck touched you?"

"It doesn't matter." She swallowed, and her bruised throat bobbed.

"The hell it doesn't. Tell me, Emilia. Now."

"Dom, it's not...it doesn't..." Her voice quivered and her eyes misted, darting everywhere but his face. She shook her head. "It was..."

She dissolved into tears, and he caught her when she stumbled, drawing her against his chest and holding her close. He ran a hand down her hair, pressing a kiss to the top of her head.

"Tell me, kitten. Please," he pleaded. He needed to know who'd done that to her. Because he was going to murder them.

She shook her head against his shoulder. "You're only going to kill them," she said, as if reading his thoughts.

"Fucking right I am. Carve the flesh from their goddamn bones." He jerked her back to look down into her eyes when an idea occurred to him. "Was it your boss? Did he do that to you because you wouldn't sleep with him?"

"No." Her voice was hoarse, and the sound of it only served to further fill him with rage.

"Who, Emilia? I need you to tell me."

"Varda. It was Varda."

The image flashed into his mind. Varda with his hands around Emilia's throat, threatening her for something that wasn't her fault. Exactly what he'd been afraid of made manifest because he hadn't been careful.

"I'm sorry, kitten. I'm so sorry." He pulled her close again, squeezing her until she protested with a squeak. "Where's your family?"

"My brother and sister are out with friends. My mother's at a wedding." She jolted in his arms. "Why? Do you think they're in danger too?"

If they were, it would be too late to do anything about it now. But he couldn't say that to her. No need to make her worry. "No. They're probably fine. But you're coming with me, so you need to go pack a bag."

"What? I can't go with you."

"You can, and you are," he replied, voice stern.

Dom dug his phone out of his pocket. He'd have a man sit on the house, make sure her family was okay. But he wasn't going to let her out of his sight for a while. Not until he had a better bead on Varda and a solid plan on how to make the fucker pay for touching her.

"Go pack. Right now."

She crossed her arms over her chest and cocked a hip. There was that fire he loved so much snapping in her eyes. "I can't just leave my family here and go off wherever with you."

He held up his phone. "I'm having someone come watch the house. You technically live in Bianchi territory anyway. And whether it was you or someone else, we'd defend an attack on our side of the border. He won't strike here. At least not tonight."

Gripping her shoulders, he turned her toward the stairs and gave her ass a gentle pat. "Go. Or I'll move into your bedroom, and you can introduce me to your whole family."

Emilia whirled to face him. "You wouldn't."

Dom cocked a single brow and watched her debate with

herself. He absolutely fucking would, and she knew it. Which is why she turned on her heel and jogged up the stairs. He listened to her rummage around in drawers while he coordinated a detail on her house.

He still had some extra men hanging around from the most recent raid bunking on the couches in the great room. They could work twelve-hour shifts, starting immediately. Because he wasn't letting Emilia out of his sight, but he knew she wouldn't go without knowing her family was safe.

At the sound of her feet on the stairs, he glanced up to see her coming down with a bag slung over one shoulder and what looked like a camera bag in her hand. He knew she was a photographer, but he'd never seen her take a single photo. Not even with her phone.

She caught him eyeing the bag and blushed. "It's probably stupid to bring it with me. I'll put it back."

Grabbing her hand before she could turn around and run back up the stairs, he pulled her close for a kiss. "It's not stupid. Ready?"

"Yeah." She chewed her bottom lip, looking past him to the door. "What if he comes back?"

Dom laced their fingers together and drew her to the front window, pointing as a dark sedan pulled up and parked across the street. As soon as the lights went out, his phone signaled an incoming text. He turned it around to show her.

*In position.*

"That is my man. He's protecting a vulnerable house from attack on Bianchi land. In twelve hours, someone will relieve him."

"But for how long?"

"Until I tell them to stop." His eyes dropped to her throat, and he had to shove down the rage simmering just under the surface. "I'm not leaving here without you."

She nodded, and he reached for the door, waiting while

she locked it behind them. His man waved once they were in the car, and she twisted around in her seat, watching her house until it disappeared from view. He let her have the silence as they drove in the fading light back to the compound, but she didn't release his hand, her fingers squeezing tighter on his the longer they drove.

Her house wasn't far from the villa, closer than the restaurant where she worked, and the sun was slipping beneath the horizon, automatic lights blinking to life when he pulled up to the gate. Punching in his unique code, he pulled through and up the long driveway.

He wanted to avoid the rest of the men in the house for now, so he took her through the back gate, leading her around the edge of the yard and past the pool. The door was unlocked; he hadn't secured it in his haste to get to her. He flicked on the lights once they were inside, drawing the blinds over the floor-to-ceiling windows.

"You live in a pool house?" She stood in the center of the room, and in this lighting, he could see her bruises more clearly. Varda was going to wish he'd never put his fucking hands on her.

"Until Varda is dead, yes."

Emilia flinched at the name, and he moved across the room, slipping her bag from her shoulder and carrying it into the bedroom. She followed him in, leaning against the doorway, her camera bag cradled in her arms.

"You any good with that thing?" He gestured to the bag with a tilt of his head.

"Are you saying you ran a comprehensive background check but never googled my work?"

Chuckling, he crossed the room and guided her to the couch, sinking onto the leather and pulling her down with him. She instantly curled into his side and tucked her feet up.

"That's exactly what I'm saying."

She set the bag on the table and tucked her hands between her thighs. "I haven't touched it since moving to Sicily. I don't know why I even brought it with me other than it was sitting out in my closet because I was looking at it before..." Her voice faltered, and he wrapped an arm around her waist, drawing her against his side. "Before Varda showed up."

Pressing a kiss to her temple, Dom ran his fingers through her hair. "Can you tell me what happened?"

"He thought I lied to him. About the raids. He said something about a delivery being intercepted."

His fingers tightened on her hip. "You didn't know about the delivery, though."

"I know, and that's what I told him." Her fingertips lightly traced the column of her throat, and he clenched his jaw. "It took him a minute to believe me."

"But he did eventually believe you."

"I guess. If threatening to gut my family right in front of me and turn me into his sex slave is him believing me."

That motherfucking asshole. Dom pulled Emilia into his lap, wrapping his arms around her waist. "He will never touch you again. Do you understand?"

"What if you can't stop him?" Her breath hitched, and tears gathered in her eyes. "What if he wins?"

"Look at me, kitten," he said softly, waiting until she turned her head to meet his gaze. "Do you trust me?"

"I..." She paused, considering his question, and he felt every heartbeat pound against his ribcage until she finally answered. "Yes. I trust you."

"He will not win this." He pressed a kiss to her lips, cupping the back of her head and pulling her closer. She eased back on a sigh and pressed her forehead against his. "He was never going to win this. And now I'm going to make sure he pays for ever laying a finger on you."

"Do you promise?"

"I swear on my life, Emilia."

Curling into his lap, she rested her head on his shoulder, her breath fluttering against his neck while he ran his fingers through her hair. When he felt her body go limp and her breathing was deep and even, he stood, cradling her in his arms, and carried her into his bedroom.

Laying her gently down on the bed, he tucked her in, brushing her hair back from her face. He didn't care what it took, what he had to sacrifice, who he had to kill to make it happen, but he was going to end this. Varda was going to die by his hand—violently, painfully, and very soon.

Then once her debt was dissolved and her family was safe and he was running Varda's territory, she would be his. And no one would ever fucking touch her again.

# Chapter Twenty-Three

Dom woke early, the gray light filtering through the thin curtains. When he shifted to check the time, Emilia murmured in her sleep and pressed closer, her ass making contact with his cock. He buried his face in the hair at her nape and bit back a groan.

He'd convinced her to stay for two days, and he liked waking up next to her, falling asleep with her tucked against his side at night. It surprised him how much. He didn't keep women. He fucked them until he was bored with them and sent them on their way.

But there was something different about Emilia. There always had been. She was his from the first moment he laid eyes on her at that restaurant, even if he hadn't realized it then. Now that he had, there wasn't a force on this earth that could keep her from him.

He hadn't brought it up yet. Plenty of time to talk about it later. Dealing with Varda was the more immediate need. When he wasn't in bed making Emilia come over and over on his fingers and tongue and cock, he'd been focused on hitting back at Varda, scrapping as many plans as he drew up.

They needed to make some big moves, and soon. Sforza hadn't dropped a report in days, and the long silence was unusual. Dom wondered if he'd been made or was just laying low while Varda scoured his ranks for a traitor.

Truthfully, he didn't need Sforza embedded anymore. Now that they knew the locations of the weapons caches and who was supplying them, all that was left really was to exterminate those loyal to Varda and Varda himself. It was maybe two dozen men, tops.

But Matteo, ever the pragmatist, had pressed pause on forward motion. He was worried a quick and bloody campaign would pull too much attention from the authorities. He wasn't entirely wrong.

They'd heard rumblings from the cops and politicians on their own payroll that Varda's antics in recent months with his extortion schemes and petty arson were drawing a lot of attention. If Dom was a patient man, he might be content to stand back and let the authorities get rid of Aroldo Varda.

But that was before the prick put his hands on Emilia and left bruises on her skin. Now the son of a bitch was going to pay. Every time he saw them, Dom devised new and painful ways for him to die. He was becoming quite inventive.

Emilia rolled onto her stomach, and he traced his fingertips down the length of her spine to the top of her ass, raising goosebumps. The woman slept like the dead. But he liked to watch her sleep, hair tousled, skin rosy and soft. Christ, he had it bad.

A soft knock on the door drifted in from the living room, and he slid out of bed, tugging on a pair of sweats. Rossi waited for him on the other side with a cup of coffee, and Dom stepped out, easing the door closed so he didn't wake Emilia.

"Anything from Matteo yet?" Rossi wondered.

"Not yet. He's not going to get what he wants at this rate. He's just delaying the inevitable."

Rossi nodded. "There's no way to do this part quietly. The minute we take a direct hit, Varda is going to do the same."

"And then it'll be a race to see who kills who faster."

"You know it'll be their heads on sticks."

Dom pursed his lips. "Assuming my brother lets us off the leash. The only thing buying us time is Varda keeping himself busy looking for his mole."

Rossi paused with his mug halfway to his lips. "Have you heard from Sforza?"

"No." Dom frowned. "Not since his tip about the weapons drop."

"If he's made…"

"We'll be burying him next. I know."

Varda obviously knew he had someone on the inside divulging information, and since he hadn't been back to Emilia's in the last couple days, odds are he was looking through his own men trying to find the culprit.

"Are you going up to meet with him soon?"

"Matteo's coming here. This weekend," Dom replied.

Rossi slanted him a look. "What are you going to do with Emilia?"

Sipping his coffee, Dom avoided his friend's gaze. "She's got to meet with Varda tomorrow, and as much as I want to keep her here where I know she's safe, she's eager to go home. I'm going to drive her back today."

"What are you planning to feed Varda next?"

Inhaling deep, he said, "The location of our base."

Rossi sputtered around a mouthful of coffee. "You're going to fucking what? We'll be sitting ducks."

Gesturing at a camera perched on the nearby wall, Dom arched a brow. "We're hardly unprotected. And you're not a sitting duck if you anticipate the attack. I need Varda to make a move to force Matteo's hand."

"And give you an excuse to retaliate." Dom nodded. "Your brother isn't going to like that you're intentionally drawing Varda out."

"I don't plan on telling him. But if he does find out about it, he'll get over it." Eventually. "It's time to end this. We've played Matteo's political games long enough. I gathered his intel. I plotted his strategy. I kept his war under the radar as much as I could. But a confrontation with Varda is the inevitable conclusion."

"And you're going to help it along."

"If that's what it takes."

Rocking back on his heels, Rossi nodded slowly. "And this has nothing to do with the pretty waitress currently asleep in your bed?"

The sun crested the stone wall at the side of the compound and bathed the yard in golden light, burning off the last of the mist that clung to the grass and glinting off the drops of dew. This war was always going to end with Varda dead; it was the only way to secure victory.

Dom knew it, Matteo knew it, everyone knew it. It was them or Varda, and Dom sure as shit wasn't going to let it be them. But he couldn't deny that his insatiable desire to finish this as quickly as possible, even against his brother's wishes and express orders, didn't have something to do with Emilia. But it wasn't like he was changing the game; he was simply bending the rules.

"She's part of it. But there was never any other way this was going to go."

Draining the last of his coffee, Rossi turned for the house. "I'll follow you into every battle, Dom. You know that. But I hope you know what the fuck you're doing."

Sighing, Dom let himself back into the pool house and set

his cold coffee on the table. Pausing in the bedroom doorway to watch Emilia sleep, he smiled. She was worth every lecture he'd get from his brother over this. Matteo had until they met. If Dom didn't get approval by the weekend, then he was going to make a move anyway. He'd ask for forgiveness later.

"It's unnatural for a person to get up as early as you do," she mumbled into the pillow as he slipped out of his sweats and crawled back into bed.

"Maybe it's unnatural for you to sleep until noon."

"I make up for it by being very good late at night."

She rolled onto her back, arching off the bed as she stretched, and he couldn't stop himself from leaning down and sucking her nipple into his mouth. Her hands fisted in his hair while she purred, and he smiled against her skin.

"I like fucking you to sleep," he said, kissing his way to her other nipple and wrapping his lips around it.

"I like waking up to your tongue on my pussy."

Pulling back from her nipple with a pop, he nibbled his way down her stomach, dipping his tongue into her belly button just to hear her soft sigh. He settled between her thighs, looking up at her as he dragged his tongue up the length of her slit and flicked it against her clit.

She pushed onto her elbows to watch him, her thighs spread in offering, and caught her lip between her teeth. Shifting on the bed, he traced his fingers up and down her pussy lips, parting them to reveal her clit and wrapping his lips around it. Her hips jerked, and he increased the pressure, flicking it with the tip of his tongue a second time and forcing a groan from her lips.

She was already so wet for him, and he easily slid two fingers deep inside her, curling them up and tapping until the muscles of her thighs trembled and her hips rocked against his hand. He loved the way she tasted, the sounds she made, his name on her lips when she came for him. He would never get enough of her.

Grazing her clit with his teeth, he added a third finger, forcing them in and out of her tight, wet heat as he teased her sensitive bud with his mouth. Her head dropped back between her shoulders, and she groaned low in her throat.

Her pussy clenched around him, and he drove his fingers in and out faster, eager to feel her pulse around him with her orgasm so he could slide inside her.

"That's it, kitten," he coaxed when her hips rocked in rhythm to the thrust of his fingers and she jerked each time he grazed them against her g-spot. "Are you going to come on my fingers?"

"Yes," she panted.

"Good. I want to taste you before I fuck you."

She groaned, long and low, when he wrapped his lips around her clit again, his fingers working faster, harder, thrusting as deep as he could while he circled her clit with his tongue, testing the pressure with teasing bites until her hips jerked erratically.

Sobbing his name, she shuddered with her release, and he shoved his fingers deep, his mouth still working her clit at a punishing pace until she pulsed around him again, rewarding him with a second orgasm.

With one last soft kiss to her pussy, he pulled his fingers out, swiping them over her sensitive clit and making her shiver. Circling his fingers around her nipples, he leaned down and licked them clean, closing his teeth around them until she cried out.

"Tell me what my slut needs," he murmured against her breast.

"You," she whimpered. "Your cock."

He settled himself between her thighs, rocking his hips so his cock slid up and down the length of her pussy. She writhed at the contact, hooking one leg over his thigh and lifting her hips to grind against him.

"Dom," she groaned in frustration. "That is never what I mean."

He slid against her again, coating his cock in her wetness. "Then you should be more specific."

Dragging her fingernails up his back and across his shoulders, she scored them over his scalp and gripped his hair, bringing his mouth centimeters from hers. "I want you to slide your cock deep inside me and fuck me until I can't form words."

He claimed her mouth, roughly biting her bottom lip as he shifted his hips and drove inside her. "See," he said against her lips, "all you had to do was ask."

"You're so mean to me," she said between gasps as he pounded into her.

"That's half the fun, kitten."

She laughed, her pussy contracting around him when she did, and he groaned, thrusting deep and grinding his pelvis against her clit. She was exquisite, every goddamn bit of her.

He slid out and back in with one rough stroke, fucking her hard and deep. Each thrust dragged her nipples against his chest, making her groan and arch against him, her fingers tightening in his hair.

"Dom. Will you come with me?"

He leaned down to nuzzle the side of her neck, pressing kisses against her skin. "You first, kitten." He slid his hand between them, dragging his fingers over her clit and making her gasp while his cock drove in and out.

When she finally, blissfully, came undone around him, he followed her over the edge and emptied himself inside her. Her breath fluttered against his cheek as he teased her earlobe with his teeth.

"I could wake up to you every day and not get tired of it," he murmured.

"Me too," she whispered.

There was something about the way she said it that had him pulling back to look at her. He turned to press a kiss to her palm when she cupped his cheek, rolling onto his back and pulling her on top of him.

"You're different than I expected," she said, propping her chin on his chest and smiling at him.

"Different how?"

"Before you, the only thing I knew of the Mafia was Varda and the way he treated me and my family. I expected you to be the same, just with the same goal as me."

His chest tightened, and he reached up to tuck her hair behind her ear. "And now?"

"You're not the same at all. At least not in the ways that matter."

"I'm still a dangerous guy, Em. I've killed people before. I'll kill people again."

She pushed to her knees, lip caught between her teeth. "But you would never hurt me."

"No." He traced the outline of her jaw with his thumb. "I would never hurt you. You're mine."

Her mouth rounded into an O, and she blinked in surprise. "Yours?" she whispered.

Sliding one arm around her waist and cupping the back of her head, he pulled her down until their lips were a breath apart. "You belong to me, Emilia. In every way."

Her eyes darkened, and her breath was warm against his lips. "I thought we'd both go back to our lives when this was over."

Pushing against the small of her back until her body was flush with his, his grin was slow and wicked, the hard length of his cock pressed against her stomach. "You think I'm letting you go? You were mine from the first moment I saw you across that patio. You'll be mine long after this is over."

"What if it's not possible?" she wondered, breath hitching when he shifted her onto her stomach on the bed and covered her body with his.

Gripping her ass, he leaned down to whisper in her ear. "There's not a goddamn thing that could stop me from having you. Tell me what you want, kitten."

"You," she murmured, groaning as he slowly sheathed himself inside her.

He fucked her, long and slow and deep, searing a single word on her soul with his touch. *Mine.*

# Chapter Twenty-Four

The street was empty when they made the final turn for home, and Emilia couldn't help but feel torn. She needed to go home. According to Bella, tensions were rising with their mother to a fever pitch, with Maria demanding to know where her oldest daughter was.

Bella figured out Emilia was with her mystery man almost immediately and promised not to say anything, but it was unfair for Emilia to continue to ask her sister to lie for her. She wouldn't be totally honest. She couldn't. Not yet.

But she could go home and reposition herself between her mother and the twins. She'd gotten good at becoming a human shield against their mother's ire.

But she didn't want to be away from Dom, either. Especially not after his confession this morning. That he saw more for them, that he wanted her. Forever, he'd promised, with his cock buried deep inside her. She hadn't thought about anything beyond the next step in such a long time. She was afraid to.

Dom parked at the curb and brought her hand to his lips,

kissing her knuckles. "Are you sure I can't convince you to just grab a change of clothes and come back with me?"

"I think you could get me to do almost anything if you asked nice enough." His eyes darkened, and he leaned over the console to steal a kiss. "But I have to go home, smooth my mother's ruffled feathers."

Frowning, Dom glanced at her house. "What does she know about what's going on?"

"Absolutely nothing." She lifted a shoulder at his raised brow. "My mother is the reason we're in this mess," she said, unable to keep the resentment from her voice. "I honestly can't say I know what stupid thing she might do if she found out."

His eyes narrowed on her face. "You think she would betray you? Betray us?"

Her gaze snapped to his, and she wanted to lie, wanted to tell him of course her mother wouldn't do anything like that. But the truth was far more complicated.

"I don't know."

"Emilia—"

"That's why I'm not going to tell her. She can't do anything if she doesn't know, and it'll all be over soon anyway, right? Once you meet with your brother?"

Dom tapped his fingers on the steering wheel while he studied her. "I don't want to leave you here if she's going to put you in danger..."

"She won't," Emilia insisted. "You'll meet with your brother and figure out what you're going to do next. You'll handle things, and we'll put this behind us." She felt her cheeks heat. "Then we can discuss what happened this morning."

"You need more sex already?" His mouth quirked up at the corner.

"No." She squeezed her thighs together at the challenging

look in his eyes. "Well, maybe. But that's not what I meant. Forever is a really long time."

"Yes," he agreed. "It is."

"Things are more complicated than you make them sound."

"There's nothing complicated about how much I want you," Dom assured her. "Or what I'm willing to do to keep you."

His words sent heat skidding along her skin. "Well, my family doesn't even know you exist. Except Bella. She knows I'm seeing someone, even though I didn't tell her specifics."

"You talked to your sister about me?"

She cocked her head at the surprise in his tone. "I did. Is that okay? She saw me sneaking in late that night you met me after work."

"The night I fucked your pussy and your mouth in my truck, you mean."

Heat washed over her face, and he chuckled. "Yeah. That night. No details because that would be weird." She chewed the inside of her cheek. "I'm not saying no, okay? I'm just saying we should talk about it more."

"Oh, we'll definitely be talking about it more," he replied, and her heart squeezed. "You remember your message for Varda?" he asked as she reached into the backseat for her bag.

"Yes, and I still don't like it. What if he hurts you?"

"I'll be fine." Dom turned in his seat and pulled her closer, sliding his hand around to cup the back of her neck. "I need to end this, for you, for my family. And if that means I have to bait Varda to make a move to do it, then I will."

Running her fingers over the tattoos on his arm, she leaned forward and pressed her mouth to his, nibbling his bottom lip and sighing when he used his hand to tilt her head and take the kiss deeper.

"Domenico Bianchi, if you get yourself killed, I'll never forgive you."

"You won't get rid of me that easy, kitten." He released her, trailing his fingertips over the bruises on her throat. "Now go inside before I haul you into my lap and do unspeakable things to you."

She grinned and hopped out of the SUV, slinging her bag over her shoulder. Dom waited by the curb, watching until she opened the door and stepped inside. As she closed it, flicking the lock into place, she heard the growl of his engine as it sped away. Trailing her fingertips over her lips, she sighed.

She was as eager to be beyond all this as he was, but not at the expense of his life. Still, she trusted him, and he knew his business best. If he said he knew what he was doing and he would take care of it, then he did. And she could make herself be okay with that.

Turning for the stairs, she contemplated whether she'd take a shower or a nap first. It was her usual day off, and she'd declined to switch shifts with someone even though she'd been out the last two days. Still sick, she insisted.

The long weekend had been nice once she'd gotten over the anxiety of not having the money to make her payments to Varda. She had enough to cover this week's, and hopefully after that, she wouldn't need to make another payment ever again.

"Did you have a good weekend?"

Emilia froze with her foot on the bottom step, her heart thumping in her chest. Dropping her bag at the base of the stairs, she backtracked to the living room.

"Mama. How come you're not at work?"

"I needed a sick day. Spending all weekend worried to death over where my daughter might be was incredibly draining."

Emilia forced herself not to roll her eyes and give her mother more ammunition. "I sent you a text saying I was fine. Just staying with friends."

"What friends?" Maria demanded.

"Friends I met at work." It was a half-truth, but it was all her mother would get.

"Oh, lovely. Now you're lying right to my face."

"I'm not—"

"Do you make out in cars with all your friends from work?"

Emilia glanced at the window that faced the front of the house, dragging her tongue over her teeth. Her mother had been watching. Great. The cat was out of that particular bag.

"No," she said slowly. "He's a special case. I'm allowed to date, Mama. I'm almost thirty, for fuck's sake."

"Don't you take that tone with me, young lady."

"I'm not a child, and you lost the right to tell me what to do a long time ago. I'm going to go shower."

"Do you even know who he is?" Emilia paused in her retreat, looking back to her mother. "You stupid girl. He's dangerous."

"What are you talking about?" she demanded, though she already knew.

"He's Mafia. And he's not on Varda's side. Not on our side."

Emilia spun, pinning her mother with a look so sharp Maria's eyes went wide. "Are *you* on Varda's side? Did getting on your knees for his men for so many months warp your fucking brain? That man is going to kill us."

"The only reason he'll kill us is if he finds out you're fucking a Bianchi soldier!"

Emilia stalked forward, her mother stumbling back a step. "And what are you going to do, Mother?" she spat. "Tell him?"

"I-I-I didn't say that."

"If you knew even half the things I've done to keep this family alive, to keep you alive. And you're not grateful for any of it. I should have taken Bella and Antonio away from you and left you on your knees. Let you finally deal with the consequences of your selfishness for once."

Maria stuck her chin out and sniffed. "I was trying to keep a roof over their heads. Like any good mother would."

Emilia barked out a laugh. "You keep fucking telling yourself that. If you want to live through this, then keep your mouth shut."

"Or what?" Maria challenged.

"Or there's nothing I'll be able to do to protect you anymore."

Emilia left her mother standing in the middle of the living room and ran up the stairs, slamming her bedroom door behind her. Would her mother betray her? She honestly had no idea. And that thought settled like a lead weight in her stomach.

It didn't seem like her mother knew which Bianchi soldier Emilia had been kissing. But Varda did. And if Maria went to whisper in his ear about just how close Dom and Emilia looked, he might put two and two together. She was already dancing on the razor's edge where Varda was concerned.

She could only hope Maria's sense of self-preservation won out over taking matters into her own hands. Otherwise, this whole thing was likely to blow up in their faces.

# Chapter Twenty-Five

Swiping a hand through the condensation on the glass, Emilia studied herself in the mirror. The heat from the shower always seemed to make her bruises stand out sharper against her skin. At least she wasn't torturing Dom with the sight of them anymore.

Every time he saw them while they were together, his jaw clenched and his hands tightened into fists. If he'd been ready to kill Varda before, now he was going to revel in it. And something was definitely wrong with her, because she was looking forward to hearing all about it.

After tugging a shirt over her head, she wrapped her hair in a towel and hopped into a pair of jeans. She'd agreed to work a double today just to get out of the house and away from her mother, who had stayed home from work for the third day in a row.

Her mother's icy stares were exhausting, the way she stormed out of every room Emilia entered childish. It was too much. She'd rather be at work, surrounded by people who would at least hold a conversation with her.

Unwinding the towel from her head, she smoothed some

product through her hair and braided it off her face. She didn't have the patience for much right now. There was too much anxiety boiling under her skin. Ever since giving Varda Dom's message yesterday, she'd had a bad feeling.

The way Varda had grinned at the news that Dom had a sort of safe house or home base and the knowledge of where it was turned her stomach. Dom knew what he was doing—she trusted that—but that didn't mean she liked intentionally putting him or his men in harm's way.

But he'd insisted that drawing Varda out was the only way to force his brother's hand, force him to say yes to finally killing Varda and ending this war. And she wanted that more than anything. She was tired of simply surviving.

She didn't know if something good could come after this was done, didn't know if she deserved it. But Dom had whispered words against her skin the last time they were together that made her want. And the wanting was terrifying.

When she first arrived, she'd assumed she'd eventually end up back in Rome. Quickly pay off her mother's debt and get the fuck out of here, maybe take Bella and Antonio with her. This was their last year of school, and then they'd be looking at universities. Rome had some great ones, and if not there, somewhere far away from Sicily and their mother's bad decisions.

But from the moment she'd handed her first wad of cash to Varda's enforcer, her life had not been her own. Eventually, thoughts of returning to Rome vanished, and all she had left were weekly trips to Agrigento, the occasional argument with her mother, and brief moments of happiness with Bella and Antonio when they would laugh like they had when they were younger.

Until Dom. But that couldn't really last. Good things never did for her. They were fleeting, temporary, stolen in a breath. He was Mafia, dangerous, forbidden. How could he possibly keep her? How could they even begin to make this work?

He was caught up in the moment. That was all. When this was all over, he'd go back to his life in Palermo, and she would go back to hers. If not in Rome, then here in Sicily, until Bella and Antonio finished school, at least. Once she wasn't paying Varda anymore, she'd have enough money to move out and get her own place.

Shutting off the light, she crossed barefoot to her room and stopped short at the sight of Bella and Antonio sitting on her bed, heads bent in whispered conversation.

"I thought you two left for school already."

Antonio looked at his twin, waiting for Bella's nod before speaking. "We want to know what the hell is going on."

"What do you mean?" Emilia shifted on her feet and wrapped her arms around her middle. "You're going to be late if you don't get moving."

"We're not stupid," Bella insisted. "Something's happened. You were gone for two days, and now Mama won't speak to you. And then you've got these." Bella brushed her fingers over her neck, eyeing Emilia's bruises.

Emilia's hand flew to her own throat. She'd left her makeup bag in her room and hadn't had a chance to cover them yet. "I didn't realize you'd seen them."

"Like she said," Antonio replied. "We're not stupid."

Easing into the room, Emilia closed the door with a sigh. Some part of her had been preparing for this conversation since Bella had asked her about Dom.

"Look, I don't think you're stupid. I just...I have to be careful with how much I tell you."

"What the fuck does that even mean?" Bella said, throwing her hands up with an exasperated huff and crossing her arms over her chest. "We're not little kids. We deserve to know what's going on."

Grabbing a wooden chair from the corner of her room, Emilia dragged it over in front of the bed. Settling on the worn cushion, she debated how much to tell them. She obviously couldn't tell them everything. The fewer details they had, the safer they were. But she needed to give them something. This affected them as much as anyone.

"Remember what happened right before I moved down here? Mama kept disappearing after dinner and coming home with bruises, and then men showed up at the house?"

"The enforcers," Bella whispered, and Antonio slid an arm around his twin's shoulders.

Emilia nodded. She'd known so little about the situation before that day. Only her mother's lies. The first visit was from three of Varda's thugs, dragging them all out of bed in the wee hours of the morning and telling Maria they were no longer in need of her services and they wanted their money back. And they had one week to make their first payment.

She'd only heard about the story after the fact, but the sound of Bella's terrified sobs in her ear was a memory that would never leave her.

"What did I say when you called?"

"That you would do whatever it took to take care of this and keep us safe."

"That's what I'm doing." Emilia swallowed around the lump in her throat. "I wish I could tell you everything, but I can't. For your safety. Just…it should all be over soon."

"Does this have anything to do with the guy you've been seeing?" Bella wondered.

Pursing her lips, Emilia nodded. "Yes. It does. He's helping me. Helping us."

"Is he giving you money?"

Emilia turned to Antonio and scrubbed sweaty palms on the thighs of her jeans. "I…"

She blew out a breath. There was too much to tell, too

many details that could hurt them. Emilia didn't want to think about what Varda might do to them to get information if he thought they had any. He was capable of so much more than the bruises on her throat. The idea that he could unleash that violence on Bella or Antonio terrified her.

"Believe me when I say the less you know, the better. I'm sorry I can't tell you more. But I'd rather you hate me than put you in danger."

"We don't hate you." Bella reached for Emilia's hand and gave it a squeeze. "But what about you? Are you in danger?"

"No more than I was before," she lied. "I promise when this is all over, I'll tell you everything. Okay? I'll answer every question you have."

Bella looked at Antonio, and they both nodded in unison.

"What about Mama?" Antonio wanted to know.

Emilia straightened. "What about her?"

"If you're fixing it and everything will be fine soon, why is she so pissed off?"

Emilia's hand jerked in Bella's, and she pulled it free, gripping her fingers in her lap. "I don't think she approves of how I'm handling it," she said.

Not that she'd given her mother any details. At this point, Maria knew less than the twins. For once in her life, Maria's silent treatment to make Emilia feel guilty hadn't had the desired effect. Emilia didn't trust her mother. Not with this. Not with the way Maria had seemed so worried about Varda and what he might think. Almost as if his opinion mattered to her and not because she was afraid.

It was hard to reconcile the possibility that her mother might actually *like* the man who'd been tormenting and extorting her family for months. Emilia could hardly fathom it.

"It's not like she was doing a great job handling it before

you got here." Bella snorted, pulling Emilia back to the present. "She's been such a bitch."

"Bella," Emilia scolded, but her heart wasn't in it. With the way their mother had been acting, Emilia couldn't disagree.

They were silent for a long moment, Bella picking at a loose thread on the bedspread. "What happens when we don't owe him money anymore?"

"I don't know yet," she answered honestly. "If I went back to Rome, would you want to come with me?"

Bella's head snapped up, and her eyes were wide. "Would Mama be okay with that?"

"Do we care if she is?" Antonio asked.

Bella shared a long look with her twin. "Maybe not. But I wouldn't want to leave Theo."

Emilia gave Bella's knee a quick squeeze. "I understand that. We don't have to think about it right now. But I don't know how much longer I can stay here."

"I'm sorry we ruined your life, Emmy," Bella said, tears in her eyes.

"Hey." Emilia drew Bella into her lap and gave her a big squeeze. "You didn't ruin my life. I chose this. I chose you. Okay? If I didn't want to be here, I wouldn't. I love you guys."

"I love you too."

"Yeah," Antonio agreed. "Me too."

Bella slid off her lap, and Antonio stood with her. Emilia watched them cross to the door, her heart thundering in her chest. They were her entire world. If anything happened to them because of what she'd done, trying to play the hero with Dom, she'd never forgive herself.

"Wait. I need you guys to do something for me." They stopped and turned in perfect unison, and her mouth ticked up at the corner. "Until I tell you this is over and everything is fine, I need you guys to make sure you're never alone. And I don't just mean with each other."

Bella's nose wrinkled. "I don't get it."

The idea formed rapidly in her brain, and she pushed out of the chair, following them to the door and pulling it open. "No more walking to and from school. I'm going to drop you off and pick you up. If I'm working and can't come get you, then I want you to either stay at school or go to a friend's house, and I'll come pick you up after my shift."

"What if Mama's home?"

Emilia glanced at her mother's closed bedroom door before motioning them to go ahead of her down the stairs and jogging down behind them. "No. Only me."

They shared another look, but ultimately nodded.

"Okay," Antonio said.

"Good," Emilia said with a nod, relief flooding her chest. It wasn't much, but it felt like something. Some small measure she could take to make sure she knew where they were at all times, and that they were as safe as she could make them.

She grabbed her purse off the hook by the door and dug out her keys. "Hurry up and grab your stuff, or you really will be late."

Bella and Antonio scooped up their bags and raced out the door, leaving it open behind them, and Emilia took a deep, steadying breath. Dom's plan better work. Because losing Bella and Antonio would be like losing a piece of herself.

# Chapter Twenty-Six

"What about Marino?"

"We haven't heard from anyone on that list since Monday."

Dom tossed the papers in his hand onto the table and sat back in his chair with a huff. All of their spies had gone dark since leaking the location of their base. Emilia had called after her meeting with Varda to let him know it was done and again reminded him not to get himself killed. He was going to do his best.

Varda's apparent glee over this information and the resulting silence from his spies made Dom think Varda was busy planning some kind of offensive. He'd doubled patrols as a precaution, but so far, nothing. He wanted Varda to strike. That's what would get him closer to his end goal, but the waiting was getting on his last fucking nerve.

So he'd turned his attention to his spies and figuring out possible methods of extraction. He didn't want them embedded when the attacks began, and he sure as hell didn't want to leave them in for Varda to find.

Last they heard, Varda was still looking for the mole

who'd tipped them off about the weapons exchange. Dom wanted to pull them out before that happened, but without communication, it was impossible to know where they were, and so far, no one had responded to their requests for contact.

"And we don't have any other way to get in touch with them?" Alexei wondered, twirling a knife in his fingers.

"Nothing reliable we haven't already tried," Dom said. "Sforza is the only one in deep enough for me to really worry about. His connections go pretty high up the food chain."

"Do you still need him in?"

"He'd make ending this go a hell of a lot faster," Rossi replied. "Without him, it's guesswork and hunches. Not impossible, but..."

"A bigger pain in the ass, for sure," Dom finished. "And I've got enough of a problem getting Matteo to come around."

Alexei snorted. He'd dealt with Matteo's indecisiveness with Romano. It had nearly gotten Carina killed. Dom was not about to let the same thing happen to Emilia. He was going to end this whether Matteo liked it or not. But since he'd prefer not to fight a war on two fronts, he'd give his brother a few more days to make the right decision.

"Is he still coming down on Saturday?"

Dom nodded at Alexei. "He is. He's bringing Luca, apparently."

"Need me to be here?"

"Can't hurt. Unless you're on Matteo's side in waiting for his imaginary perfect moment to strike. If that's the case, you can stay home."

Alexei snarled. "Don't insult me. I'm not on your brother's side in much of anything."

"Unless Carina asks nicely?"

A slow grin spread over Alexei's face. "Lucky for me, she doesn't ask it of me often. Have y—"

"Boss." One of the men assigned to overnight patrol stopped short in the doorway to the solarium, fighting to catch his breath. "There's something I think you need to see."

Shoving to his feet, Dom heard the scrape of chairs behind him and followed the man across the house and down to the security room at a fast clip. Three more men were inside, staring at the bank of screens showing the view from the cameras ringing the property.

Dom moved toward the nearest monitor split into four, each section showing a different view. These cameras looked out over the back of the property, beyond the wall where the extra plots of land had been purchased and cleared for more privacy.

At this time of night, they were usually nothing more than a sea of grass and trees glowing green under the night vision. Occasionally they might see an animal dart across the frame, but this was different. Dom bent at the waist to get a better look.

Black masses bobbed in the dark, moving closer and closer to the wall at the back of the property until they got close enough to form shapes. Men. Eight of them. Dressed in black and sporting guns, extra ammo strapped to their bodies.

"More here."

Dom spun to the next set of monitors. These faced north, directly opposite the cliffs overlooking the sea. Eight more men. No. Ten. Similarly armed and approaching slowly, hoping not to draw attention to themselves.

"Is anyone trying to scale the cliffs?"

"No," a third man assured him, panning the cameras down the sharp angle to confirm. "No one on this side."

"But we've got an SUV at the gate. They look like they're trying to get through by hacking the code."

Dom stood and eyed Alexei in the doorway with Rossi right behind him. His sister's fiancé looked as eager to drop bodies as Dom felt. He reached for the nearby walkie and spoke into it quickly.

"North team, you have ten men approaching your position. We're sending down backup. West team, you've got eight, almost to the wall. Not a single fucking person makes it out of here alive. Understand?"

A chorus of agreement came over the line, and Dom turned to Rossi. "Wake up the whole fucking house and give them their orders. I want a team to move through the trees on either side of the driveway and come up behind the SUV. If our men aren't outside providing backup in ninety seconds, I'll kill them myself and save Varda's men the trouble."

Dom held his hand out for Rossi's gun, and his friend slapped it into his palm. "Mine is upstairs. You need one?" Dom asked Alexei.

Alexei opened and closed the blade of his knife with a flick of his wrist. "I think I'll go for the personal touch."

Dom grinned while Rossi scrambled up the stairs to wake the rest of the men, and Alexei followed Dom out into the night. It was cool, the bite of early autumn hanging in the air. Dom listened for sounds of engagement as he ran toward the north side of the property, but he didn't hear any. Yet.

Tucking the gun into the waistband of his jeans, he took a running jump at the wall and gripped the edge with his hands, using his feet and arms to pull himself up to the top. It was dark, the full moon hidden by clouds, and it took a minute for his eyes to adjust.

Pale light from the house illuminated the grass in big rectangles, and he caught glimpses of movement out of the corner of his eye. Rearming himself, he jumped down and crept forward in the shadow from the wall, turning when he heard Alexei land on the ground behind him. His men were a few paces ahead of them, and he flagged them down.

"They'll be on us any second. I don't think they can see us

any more than we can see them. They outnumber us by four until backup arrives, but if we catch them by surprise, we can whittle that number down fast.

"The floodlights."

Dom nodded. "Once they're on, we're all exposed, though. So shoot fast and well. Not a single one of those fucks makes it over the wall or back to Varda."

"Got it." The man reached for his walkie, and Dom braced himself. "Otto," he said, keeping his voice low, "light it up."

A second later, the patch of grass with the trees beyond illuminated, and Dom instantly saw the placement of all ten of Varda's men. Sprinting toward the nearest one, he dropped him with a single shot to the forehead, spinning as another one rushed him but only grazing him in the arm.

His men scrambled behind him, dropping some of Varda's men with well-aimed bullets, others moving in close enough to disarm them instead. Varda had sent his men in with a lot of fucking firepower. Compliments of Nero Gallo, no doubt.

A third man burst through the trees, firing shots that went wide, and Dom managed to hit him square in the chest even as he lunged out of the way of his rushed attack. The man barely faltered, and Dom realized he was wearing a fucking bulletproof vest. What the hell was this?

"Go for the head!" he screamed over the grunts and shots. "They've got armor!"

The man closed in on him, and Dom whirled, bringing the butt of his gun down against the guy's temple and forcing him back a few steps. While the man recovered, Dom took aim, but he was too slow, and the man dodged the shot.

Before he could raise the semi-automatic rifle and get off a volley of shots into Dom's body, Dom sprinted forward, shoving the muzzle of the rifle into the air and bringing his own gun up to the man's forehead. The guy slapped it away, trying to wrench the gun free from Dom's grasp.

When a pained scream rang out to their left, the man was distracted long enough for Dom to notch his gun under the man's chin and pull the trigger. He slithered bonelessly to the ground, face frozen in a silent scream.

Pivoting, Dom surveyed the field in time to watch Alexei draw the blade of his knife across a man's throat. As more of his men flooded the area, making quick work of the last of Varda's team on this side of the compound, he met Alexei amid the wreckage of bodies, his face splattered with blood.

"West side clear," one of his men said, jogging up and holding out the walkie to Dom. "But the team at the gate wants to talk to you."

"Did you get the SUV?" Dom said into the walkie.

"Yeah," came Rossi's voice. "They surrendered. Might want to come down here."

Dom shared a look with Alexei, and they took off at a dead run around the wall and through the trees lining the drive until their feet hit pavement. Rossi had moved the men off the road, behind the privacy of the gate, and ordered them to their knees, hands laced behind their heads.

"Shit. They really did surrender," Alexei said from behind him. "These must be the scared little boys Varda keeps recruiting. So hard to find good help these days."

The man kneeling closest to them curled his lip, and Dom crouched in front of him. "Why did you surrender?"

"Didn't want to die. Simple as that."

"And Varda sent you here as a sacrifice, did he?"

"He figured you'd kill us, but he was trying to send a message," a second man said.

"Some message," Alexei snorted. "Sixteen dead men and four more to torture. I could have so much fun with you," he added, drawing the blood-slicked flat of his blade across a cheek, chuckling low when the man recoiled.

"That's what Varda wants, though, isn't it?" Dom pushed

to his feet. "For me to bring you inside and try to get information out of you?"

The two men closest to him shared a look. "I don't know what you're talking about. We're not going to tell you shit, no matter what you do to us."

"Well, then." Dom raised his gun and shot the man in the forehead. "Makes my job easy."

Darting forward, Alexei buried the blade of his knife in the throat of the next man, pulling it free and stepping back to watch the man clutch at his fatal wound and gasp for air.

Shooting the third man, Dom moved to the last one, stopping short when he recognized him. This was the guy who'd been following Emilia around for weeks. "Is this a promotion or a demotion for you?"

"I serve at the pleasure of Aroldo Varda," he sneered. "I go where he tells me to go. My only regret is that I couldn't get Emilia on her knees like her—"

Dom backhanded the man, his head snapping back at a brutal angle. "Keep her name out of your fucking mouth."

The man grinned, his teeth red with blood. "I always thought she must have a nice tight cunt. Varda's thought about giving her a ride a few times. Maybe he will now that I'm not around to stop him anymore."

Slowly, Dom pushed to his feet, pacing back to Alexei and holding his hand out wordlessly for the bloody blade. Alexei laid it in his palm, eyes narrowed with interest.

Dom dropped into a crouch again, aiming the knife at the man's crotch and pressing forward enough to slice through the fabric of his jeans and make him yelp. "Just for that, I should cut your dick off and feed it to you." He applied more pressure.

"I-I never touched her. I swear."

Gripping the man's hair, Dom brought their faces level. "You wouldn't lie to me, would you?"

The man shook his head, eyes wide and glassy with pain. Dragging the knife away, Dom stood, and the man sagged with relief. He opened his mouth to speak but was silenced when Dom yanked his head to the side by his hair and plunged the knife to the hilt through his temple.

When he ripped it back out, blood trickled down the man's face, and his eyes rolled back in his head. Dom stepped back to watch the man twitch uncontrollably on the ground. The fucker deserved every bit of suffering for even thinking about touching a hair on Emilia's head, but he didn't have all night. Drawing his gun, he aimed it at the guy's chest and fired three times until he finally went still.

Turning to face his men, he gestured to the bodies. "Clean these up. Once you're done, see if they need help on the north or west side."

Alexei kept pace at Dom's side as they made their way back to the house. "So," Alexei said, and Dom heard the grin in his voice. "Who's Emilia?"

# Chapter Twenty-Seven

Humming along to the music drifting from the old radio in the corner, Emilia ran the soapy rag over the bowl in her hands and dunked it into the clean water to rinse. She watched Bella through the window over the sink, talking to a boy while they stood at the edge of the sidewalk.

It was clear how enamored Bella was over this boy Theo with his gangly arms and scraggly attempt at a beard. He was pale with blond hair, not at all the type Emilia thought her sister would go for. But Bella gave his arm a teasing shove and tucked a strand of hair behind her ear.

She wondered if Bella had asked him to the concert at her school yet. Things had been so crazy between Dom and Varda and everything else that she hadn't spent much time with Bella or Antonio other than dropping them off at school and picking them up, and she missed them.

Maria was still avoiding her, had been ever since Dom brought her home after their weekend together. She needed to smooth things over, if for no other reason than to keep her mother close enough to make sure she didn't do anything stupid.

But that was going to be a tall order and would definitely involve a lot of groveling Emilia didn't feel like doing. She'd considered leaving Maria to stew in her own bad assumptions, but in the end, Dom and his safety and an end to this nightmare won out. Tonight she was going to try a peace offering.

Which is why she'd made both of her mother's favorite desserts, including frying the shells for the cannoli herself and making the ladyfingers for the tiramisu from scratch. There was dough for pizza rising in the cold oven, and once she made a quick run to the store for extra ingredients she knew her mother and Antonio liked, they'd make their own pizzas and maybe watch a movie.

Emilia didn't really relish spending the evening with her mother, who hadn't stopped huffing her way around the house since their argument, but they were too close to their end goal to risk fucking it up now. Dom had called late last night to check in and let her know progress had been made, something to sway his brother to act. He wouldn't say what, but he sounded hopeful if exhausted.

A week, two at most, and they would be free. She only had to keep her mother from doing anything rash for that long. She was probably overreacting. As selfish as her mother was, Emilia couldn't believe she would be selfish enough to put them all in danger just to prove some point.

Movement out the window caught her attention. Theo leaned down to press a quick kiss to Bella's lips, his hand on her hip and Bella pushing onto her tiptoes. Emilia sighed. She missed Dom. Four days without seeing him was four too many.

Theo climbed onto his bike and rode away, and Bella floated into the house with a dopey grin on her face. Emilia chuckled when her sister breezed into the kitchen and grabbed a bottle of sparkling water from the fridge with a sigh.

"Have you asked him out yet?"

"Not yet. I keep dropping hints hoping he'll ask me first. Right before he kissed me, I mentioned the concert, and he said it sounded like fun."

"He kissed you?" Emilia said, feigning surprise.

"Oh, please. Don't act like you weren't standing there staring at us."

"It sounds creepy when you say it like that." Emilia scooped the last of the silverware from the bottom of the sink and gave it a good scrub, rinsing it under cool water and placing it in the drainer to dry. "Don't wait too long. Sometimes you just have to go after the guys you want."

"You're hardly one to give relationship advice, Emilia." Maria breezed into the kitchen and grabbed a peach out of the bowl on the counter. "You let that boy ask you in his own time, Isabella. I'd hate to know I raised two whores instead of just one."

"Mama!" Bella scolded. "What has gotten into you this week?"

Maria sniffed, pinning Emilia with an ugly glare. "I found out what a disappointment your sister was. It's a difficult thing for a mother to realize."

Emilia's laugh was bitter. "That's right, Mama. Such a disappointment to give up my entire life to clean up another one of your messes."

"No one asked you to do that. Sometimes I think you did it just so you could hold it over my head for the rest of my life."

"I did it because if I hadn't, you'd be dead. And Bella and Antonio with you."

Maria waved a flippant hand in the air. "You're being dramatic, Emilia. As always."

"She isn't," Bella insisted. "Those men came here that morning, and that's exactly what they threatened to do."

Maria turned and looked at her youngest daughter, and Emilia read the fear in her eyes at the memory before she smothered it with another wave of her hand. "They were just trying to scare us."

"Well, it worked."

"Do you honestly think they wouldn't have made good on their threats?" Emilia wondered. "You can't be that stupid. Look at what they were doing to you before I got here!"

"I knew what I was signing up for when I agreed to the arrangement."

Emilia scoffed. "And I'm the whore."

Maria rushed forward and slapped her daughter across the face. Emilia heard Bella gasp over the blood pounding in her ears. She reached up to rub her cheek, feeling the heat and the sting under her fingertips. She met her mother's unapologetic gaze with a hard stare until it softened ever so slightly. But even then, Maria didn't apologize. She probably never would. Not for any of it.

"Bells, I'm going to run to the store and grab a few more things we need for pizza," Emilia said, unable to keep the hard edge from her voice. "Did you want anything?"

"No," Bella replied softly.

"Great. Can you shred the mozzarella in the fridge before I get back?"

She waited for Bella's nod before stepping around her mother and grabbing her purse off the hook by the front door.

"You need to get a grip, Mama," she heard Bella say before the door closed behind her.

So much for a peace offering. Every interaction she had with her mother only seemed to make things worse. And she didn't even know what to really do about it. A part of her thought she should say something to Dom, but she was worried about what he might do. Not that he'd hurt her mother, but he'd made his feelings about her very clear, and she imagined there wasn't much he wouldn't do to keep her safe.

But maybe keeping a closer eye on her mother wasn't such a bad idea. Dom had gotten a man to watch their house when he'd taken her after her encounter with Varda. Maybe there was a way she could ask him to do that again without giving him all the details.

Her phone signaled in her purse as she climbed behind the wheel, and she dug it out, smiling when she saw Dom's name on the screen.

*Busy?*

She typed a quick reply. *Just heading out to the store. Need a few things for dinner.*

*Meet me at the one between the restaurant and your house. 10 mins.*

She pulled away from the curb and sighed. Dom would smooth out her nerves so she could get through the rest of what was sure to be a hellish night with her mother. Assuming Maria even wanted to participate after their showdown in the kitchen.

The lot was nearly empty when she pulled in, but Dom wasn't far behind her. Emilia checked her face in the rearview mirror and hid the last of the redness on her cheek with her hair. Hopefully he would assume it was a trick of the fading light and not another mark put on her by someone else.

His eyes dropped to her neck as soon as she got out of the car, and he trailed his fingertips over her throat when she reached him. "Have they healed, or are you wearing makeup?"

"Makeup," she admitted.

His mouth set into a hard line, but he said nothing else, turning to raise the tailgate on his SUV. He sat on the edge and patted the spot next to him, but she stood in front of him instead, wrapping her arms around his waist and laying her head against his shoulder. He spread his thighs to pull her in closer, and she sighed when his arms circled her waist and gave her a soft squeeze.

"What's the matter, kitten?" he asked, his deep voice rumbling in her ear. He pressed a kiss to the side of her neck.

What was she supposed to say? My mother hates me, and I'm worried she'll do something stupid before we can finish this?

"Emilia," he prompted when she didn't respond.

"I'm just ready for this to be over."

He moved his hands to her hips and eased her back, using his fingertip to tilt her head up to meet his gaze. "What happened?"

"I had another fight with my mother. Tensions are high in the house and I'm worried…"

"Worried about what?"

She chewed her bottom lip. She didn't want to lie to him. "Worried my mother knows more than she should." It wasn't all of the truth, but it was enough of it.

Dom pulled her in for a kiss, his fingers stroking lightly against the small of her back. "She saw me drop you off, didn't she?"

"She doesn't know it was you, but she assumed you were a Bianchi soldier. Maybe I should have corrected her, but I didn't. What if she tells Varda?"

"You're supposed to be cozying up to me. That's his whole game. What's she going to tell him that he doesn't already know?"

"I guess. I don't know." She blew out a breath. "There's

something about it that doesn't sit right with me. And I don't want her to jeopardize this for us. Not when we're so close."

"What would make you feel better, kitten?" He tucked her hair behind her ear and then traced his thumb down the line of her jaw to her lips, dragging his thumb across them.

"For Varda to be dead."

He chuckled. "I'm working on that. Matteo is coming tomorrow, and then I'll have more answers for you. And a timeline, I hope. Okay?"

With a nod, she wrapped her arms around his waist again and buried her face against his neck. "Okay. Did you have a message for me?"

"What?"

"For Varda. I figured that's why you wanted to meet."

"Oh. No. I just wanted to see you."

She melted into his arms, her heart fluttering behind her ribcage. He wanted her. Just her. And he was all she was starting to want too. Yes, she wanted her family to be free so they could move on, and she wanted to be out of her mother's house, but the more she thought about Dom, the easier it was to see beyond the end of this.

She wanted something she hadn't let herself want before. A life with Dom. Whatever that meant, whatever it looked like, she wanted it. She hadn't been able to stop thinking about it all week.

Her mother had ruined so many things in her life already and taken so much more. Emilia wouldn't let her have this thing building between her and Dom too. She was finally being offered something good and strong and steady, and she was going to grab onto it with both hands and never let go.

If she was his, then he was hers too. And she sure as hell wasn't going to let her mother stand in the way of that.

# Chapter Twenty-Eight

"You're making me dizzy."

Dom paused in his pacing to glance at Alexei lounging on a chaise by the pool. Matteo was late. And it was starting to piss him off.

"Fucker should have been here by now. In seven years, I can't ever recall a casino emergency so immediate I was an hour late for a meeting."

"Me either. He's doing what he always does. And you're letting him."

"And what does my brother always do?"

"Fucks with you to remind you who's in charge."

With a grunt, Dom dropped onto the chaise beside Alexei and flopped back to stare up at the sky, puffy white clouds floating over clear blue. His brother had been on some kind of sick power trip since returning to Sicily. And that reason, more than any of the others his brother had tossed his way, was likely why Matteo had so far refused to let them take a direct hit on Varda.

Matteo didn't really care about the cops. They'd killed dozens of Varda soldiers in the last few weeks, and the cops weren't breathing down their necks about that. Varda had nothing they wanted, no businesses to secure, no properties to leverage, nothing.

This whole thing was pride and nothing more. An exercise in making Matteo feel better when all he was doing was making himself look weak. The men were starting to whisper about why they were delaying so long, and Dom had stopped silencing them. There was only so much he could do to encourage loyalty to Matteo.

His men had been fighting this war with Varda long before Matteo graced the island with his presence again. They had a long history of dealing with Varda spies and petty border skirmishes. Five years ago, Varda had used the distraction around Carina's wedding to Giuseppe Romano as an opening to set fire to one of the casinos. Luckily they'd been able to put it out before it did too much damage.

But Matteo knew nothing of this conflict except what Dom told him in his weekly reports. And Dom's patience was thinning. He needed Matteo to take decisive action, and the men needed it too. They'd never be able to finish this without it. And they still had two more families to face before this was all over.

The slamming of car doors drew his gaze to the white stone wall circling the backyard. Pushing off the chaise, he crossed the patio and let himself into the house. Otto was leading Matteo and Luca through the front door when Dom and Alexei met them at the base of the stairs.

"You made it," Dom said, and Matteo arched a brow. "We're all spread out in the solarium."

They climbed the stairs in silence, following the long hallway to the back of the house. Rossi was already waiting for them inside, fiddling with one of the pieces they'd been using to mark properties Varda owned on the map.

"You've been busy, little brother," Matteo said, surveying the map.

Dom caught Alexei rolling his eyes and barely avoided doing the same. "We haven't exactly been sitting on our hands down here."

"Good. I'd hate to think my investment was going to waste." Matteo moved closer, slipping his hands into his pockets. "What's the update?"

"We had two guys make contact and were able to pull them out."

"Sforza?" Matteo wondered.

"No." Dom shook his head. "He's still dark. But our other guys had some new information about safe houses." Dom indicated the green squares with a wave of his hand. "And they confirmed what I had already suspected about Varda and where his head is right now."

"And where is that?"

"He's paranoid. He knows we have someone on the inside, and he's desperate to find them. And because he's desperate, he's making mistakes."

"What mistakes?" Luca asked.

"He found out the location of our base and totally botched his one and only attempt at raiding us."

Rossi raised his brows at Dom's lie but said nothing. Dom didn't intend on telling Matteo he was the reason Varda knew about their southern base. Especially not if leaking the information had the desired effect.

"When the fuck did he try to raid you?"

"Two nights ago."

Matteo narrowed his eyes on Dom's face. "And why am I just hearing about this now?"

"Because we handled it," Alexei said, leaning casually against the wall.

"Because I wanted to tell you in person," Dom amended.

"He's sloppy, Matteo. Distracted. Now is the perfect time to strike at him and take him out."

"I'm not comfortable with the number of eyes focused on this part of the island."

"For Christ's sake. What eyes?" Dom demanded.

"I have my sources." Matteo flicked a glance at the map. "Once I'm confident the cops are busy elsewhere, you can go in and take out Varda and as many of his men as you please. You said you wanted to coordinate an attack on his outer circle first, right? Take out the men protecting him and then go in for the kill?"

"That's right. Something I'm prepared to do right now. Today."

"Not yet," Matteo snapped. "You'll have to trust me on this."

"Trust is earned, brother. Not demanded."

Matteo took a step forward, gaze hard and unflinching, but Dom wouldn't back down. He'd stood up against their father countless times, walking away bloody more often than not. His brother might be the spitting image of Lorenzo Bianchi in his expensive three-piece suits with his neatly trimmed hair and square jaw and impassive expression, but Dom was hardly afraid of him.

"I am the head of this family," Matteo growled. "That should be enough to earn your trust."

"An accident of birth means nothing to me. It means even less after you abandoned this family to fuck off around the world for seven years. Now you want to waltz back in here with big ambitious plans to make yourself a king when you have no idea what's been at play since you left."

"Between you and Luca, I have a good idea of what—"

"Learning it and living it are two different things," Dom replied. "I won't wait around for you forever. If you're too soft to make the decisions that need to be made, I'll make them for you."

"Are you threatening me?" Matteo's voice was low and dangerous.

"It's not a threat," Dom countered. "It's simply information. I'm tired of playing your games, Matteo. Especially when you won't tell me what pieces you're moving. You expect transparency from me, and you aren't offering it in return."

"The big picture at play doesn't concern you."

Dom surged forward, gripping the edge of the table to keep himself from wrapping his hands around Matteo's fucking throat. "The hell it doesn't, you son of a bitch. You want me to control Varda's territory? Hold it for you? You want me to lead your troops and send them into battle at your whim, and you think that doesn't concern me?"

Releasing the table, Dom clenched his hands into fists at his side. "I thought you disappointed me when you left seven years ago. I was wrong. I'm more disappointed by how weak you've become."

Matteo rounded the table in quick strides, stopping short when Rossi and Otto moved in to block him. His lip curled back over his teeth as he scowled at his brother.

"First you insult me, and now you're turning my own men against me?"

"They're loyal to the person who doesn't waste time playing stupid games and leaving them in the dark. I could have taken Varda out a week ago, but I didn't. I waited. I operated by your rules. And because I did, he figured out where we were and attacked us."

Dom pushed Rossi aside and stepped forward. "But because I trained *my* men well, we took down all twenty of Varda's soldiers in less than thirty minutes. You might enjoy sitting in your ivory tower in Palermo's business district, playing at being the Bianchi Don, but you cannot take Sicily without me."

"I'm certainly tempted to try."

"Enough," Luca barked, stalking forward and shoving each of them back a step. "Both of you get a fucking grip. This is the kind of shit everyone on this island expects from us. The Bianchi men always at each other's throats."

"I told you months ago you needed to be a united front if you expect to win this," Alexei said. "You still haven't listened, Matteo."

"If you want this crown, this respect, this power," Luca added, emphasizing the last word, "you cannot do it alone."

Crossing his arms over his chest, Dom waited for Matteo to speak. A muscle ticked in his brother's jaw as he pulled out his phone and typed across the screen. He tapped it against his palm, staring out the windows over Dom's shoulder.

"Nero Gallo is supplying weapons to Aroldo Varda."

"I already know that. I'm the one who told you."

Matteo's gaze focused on Dom's face, and it took everything he had not to punch his brother's smug smirk in. "Do you know how and when Nero transports his stock?"

Dom opened his mouth and snapped it shut. "No. I don't," he replied through gritted teeth.

"Neither do I. But I'm very close to figuring it out. While we still hunt Varda, Nero knows he isn't a target. The last thing I want to do is give him the opportunity to change up his routine before I can figure out what the fuck it is or how to use it against him."

"You want to know how and when he delivers so you can intercept."

"And sabotage. Yes. Because he's too well-connected to take him out without drawing scrutiny. We have to weaken him first."

Fuck. Dom scrubbed a hand over his face. He hated that

Matteo had a good point. But it was hardly a state secret. There was nothing to stop Matteo from sharing that information with him right after the raid weeks ago except his own ego. An ego Dom was getting tired of dancing around.

"You could have told me."

"I could have," Matteo agreed. "I didn't find it necessary."

"United front," Alexei reminded them.

"What would you know about it?" Matteo spat.

Alexei grinned, undeterred. "You seem to forget just how long I've been watching this family from the shadows. I know everything about you, including how much your father taught you to hate each other. And if you're not careful, it'll be your undoing."

"I don't take orders from you."

"Of course not, *Il Signore*," Alexei said with a sneer.

"Dom," Rossi said before Matteo could fire back a retort. "Someone's pulling up to the gate."

"Another raid?" Dom moved to the door.

"I don't think so," Rossi said, following him down. "Looks like it might be just two cars at the end of the driveway."

Dom skidded to a halt in the security room, every man looking up expectantly. "Tell me," he said to the guy closest to him.

"There's no one else." He panned through each camera as Dom, Matteo, and Luca crowded around the screens. "It's just these two SUVs at the end of the driveway idling."

"Wait, is that—"

"Varda," Dom said, jerking up to look at Matteo. "You want to go out?"

"Well, I'm not hiding in the house like a child."

"I didn't mean..." Giving up trying to appease his brother, Dom pivoted to Rossi and Otto. "Rossi with me. Otto, stay here and monitor. If Varda makes a move or advances men toward the compound again, you know what to do."

Otto nodded, stepping into the room to give them space to pass. Dom checked the magazine in his gun out of habit and slid it into the holster at his back. Luca did the same, and Dom's eyebrows went up when he saw the flash of a gun under Matteo's suit jacket. Alexei was flipping the blade of his knife in and out.

"It wouldn't kill you to carry a gun," Dom said, stepping through the front door and waiting for the others to follow.

"It might," Alexei replied, and Luca chuckled.

He set a leisurely pace down the driveway. No need to rush and let Varda think he had them by the balls. Whatever he was playing at by showing up here, Dom intended to learn more about Varda than Varda would learn about him. Nearing the gate and the waiting SUVs, Dom shared a look with Matteo, who nodded for him to take the lead.

Varda stood between his SUV and the driveway, leaning back against it and looking like he was bored to be kept waiting. But Dom could see the tension in his shoulders and face. There was something else there, though. Something harder to read.

"Aroldo. To what do I owe the extreme displeasure?" Dom said, stopping a few feet from the bottom of the driveway.

"Nice place you got here," Varda said. His eyes drifted from Dom to Matteo. "Or is it your place? So hard to remember who's in charge these days."

"I'm bored with this already, Varda," Matteo replied. "Did you have something interesting to say?"

Varda's smile was quick and razor-sharp. "I think I have something that belongs to you."

Dom kept his expression blank, but his pulse pounded. "What's that?"

At the snap of his fingers, one of his men reached into the open backseat of the SUV and yanked out a man, face bloody and covered in cuts and bruises. Sforza. Son of a fucking bitch.

Rossi shifted on his feet and cleared his throat, but his face gave nothing away. Varda pinned each of them with a look, brow wrinkling when none of them reacted. Dom wasn't sure he could talk his way out of this one, but he'd damn well try on the off chance it would save Sforza or they could get off some good shots at Varda in the process.

"Is that it? I'm supposed to be impressed you beat up some nobody?"

"Nobody?" Varda growled. "You're saying this isn't your man? That you didn't slip a spy deep into my ranks?" He turned to Matteo. "That you didn't know about it?"

Matteo shrugged, following Dom's lead. "I don't recall authorizing any deep cover spies. Not after what you did to the last ones."

"I thought leaving them outside the casino was a nice touch," Varda replied with a sinister grin. "If this isn't your man, then whose is he?"

Dom made a show of rolling his eyes, deepening Varda's scowl. "How the fuck should I know? Maybe he belongs to Gallo."

"And why the fuck would Gallo be spying on me?"

"Could be the tens of thousands of dollars worth of weapons he's been lending you," Luca said. "Knowing how you are with money right now, I'd want to make sure my investment was protected too."

"Not that it'll do either of you much good," Matteo assured him. "Since I plan on killing you both."

"You'd like to think that, wouldn't you?" Varda spat, shoving Sforza to his knees. "You'd like to think you've got it all figured out and you'll be able to take me down. You're not the first young Don, high on his new power, who thinks he can best me."

"Maybe not," Matteo conceded. "But I'm the first who's going to succeed."

"We'll see. First let's get rid of our little problem."

"Not our problem," Dom reminded him. "Yours. So hard finding good people to trust these days."

Varda drew his gun and aimed it at the back of Sforza's head, shoving the muzzle against his skull. On instinct, Rossi stumbled forward a step, and Dom shot him a murderous look that stopped him in his tracks. When he looked back, Varda's eyes were alight.

"Ah, so he does mean something to you. Perfect. Say goodbye to your inside man, Bianchi. And good luck winning against me without him."

Dom's eyes dropped to Sforza's, and he saw resignation there. Before he could draw his weapon, a shot rang out, and Sforza pitched forward to the ground, blood seeping out from the wound in his head in a widening pool.

Someone pushed Varda into the backseat of the first SUV as Dom advanced, firing at anything that moved. The rest of the men with him did the same and dropped three of Varda's guards before the SUVs pulled out in a squeal of tires. Alexei pounced on one man who'd only caught a bullet in the leg, stomping his wrist until the gun fell from his fingers, and he screamed before driving his blade into the guy's chest.

Dom turned to find Franco knelt over Sforza's lifeless body, gun discarded on the ground beside him. Franco and Sforza were cousins on Franco's mother's side. Running a hand over his face, Dom looked up at Matteo, whose jaw was clenched tight, fingers worrying the watch on his wrist in an endless circle.

Matteo's eyes were almost black when he met Dom's gaze.

"We should have killed the fucker where he stood. What's your plan?"

"I need more men from Palermo." Dom watched Rossi lay his jacket over Sforza's face and climb to his feet.

"You'll have them. As many as you need," Matteo promised.

"We'll take them out in two phases."

"Loyal men and heirs first," Rossi said, voice hard.

"Then Varda himself," Dom continued. "He might try to go to ground. But we haven't left him many places to hide."

"How long do you need to put it together?"

"Three days, four max, for phase one. I want to give him time to settle somewhere, let him sit on the edge wondering when we're going to strike back."

Matteo nodded. "Do it."

Dom stared at his brother. He hadn't expected it to be that easy. "What about your intelligence about Gallo? The cops?"

"Let me worry about that," Matteo replied. "Gallo and the cops are my concern. Varda is yours. And now you have my permission to kill him."

# Chapter Twenty-Nine

It was dark when she pulled up in front of Varda's mansion, and it sent a chill up her spine. All the times she'd visited this place to pass him whatever tidbit of information Dom wanted to share, she'd never come at night before.

The house loomed over the street, black windows like soulless eyes. Not a single light shone onto the sidewalk, bathing everything in a thick curtain of anonymity. Dom had the go-ahead from Matteo to end it, and she knew he was busy with his meticulous plans.

But he hadn't given her any more information for Varda. What else was there to share? She'd hoped to avoid another meeting with him, hoped he'd be dead before he had a chance to summon her again. But the missive came as she was dropping Antonio and Bella off at school.

*Come tonight after work.*

That was it. That was the command from an unknown number. She didn't need to ask who it was. She'd been embroiled in this long enough to know. Dom knew she was here, not that he liked it. But they were too close to the end of

"

this to make Varda suspicious now. She had to keep playing her part a little while longer. For Bella and Antonio's safety, if nothing else.

When the gate guarding the short driveway didn't swing open, and no one came out to lead her inside, Emilia climbed out of her car and crossed the street at a quick jog. One man stood watch at the gate and eyed her up and down before letting her through.

She wondered where Varda's favorite enforcer might be. He enjoyed leering at her and making her squirm too much to miss one of her trips to Varda's compound. Maybe he was dead. The thought put a little spring into her step.

The courtyard was completely empty, an unusual sight for a man who liked to surround himself with people who would bow and scrape. Dom wouldn't give her any details about the next phase of his plans. Maybe he'd already started to carry them out, and Varda's numbers were dwindling.

If that was true, then all she had to do was get through this meeting with a straight face and the proper amount of deference. Then she could leave Varda for Dom to handle, and this would all be over. Finally.

Ever since Dom had told her Matteo had approved this last phase of his plan, freedom began to feel like a real, tangible thing instead of just a hope for the future. No more payments, no more looming threat of violence and death, no more hiding Dom from her family.

Although now she'd begun to entertain whole new worries. About whether her family would accept Dom knowing he was Mafia. Her mother obviously didn't approve, but Emilia could live with that as long as Bella and Antonio didn't hate him and didn't lump him in with Varda and his thugs.

A man she'd never seen before met her at the back door and led her through the maze of hallways, her soft-soled shoes shuffling across the polished marble floor. The lights were low, and dark curtains were drawn across every window. Varda must be getting paranoid.

Good. She wanted him to feel the icy breath of fate breathing down his neck. His penance had come due, and she was eager for Dom to collect.

Expecting to take the last turn for the study at the end of the dead-end hallway, Emilia was surprised when they veered in the opposite direction and climbed the wide staircase to the second floor. She'd never been taken up here, where she imagined bedrooms were. The idea flooded her system with panic, and she gripped the banister to keep from toppling over backward.

If Varda had no use for her anymore, was he going to rape and kill her? It wasn't out of the realm of possibility. Nothing was where Varda was concerned.

Her heart beat erratically as she followed the lanky man in front of her down a long hallway and around the corner. With each door they passed, her feet dragged and terror clawed at her throat. She was going to die in here. Varda would most definitely have to kill her because she'd rather be dead than let him touch her.

They stopped at an ornately carved door inlaid with gold filigree. It looked oddly French and out of place compared to the rest of the place. The man leading her gripped the large round knob set in the center and gave it a twist. The door swung silently inward, and he motioned her through, giving her shoulder a light shove when she didn't move.

The door closed behind her, and she pressed her back against it. There was a large sleigh bed against the far wall, the dark sheets rumpled, pillows askew. Great. She was going to be raped, and the sheets weren't even clean.

Art hung on the wall over the bed, a Michelangelo if she had to guess, though art history had been her worst class at university. A long, low dresser with a mirror above it dominated the wall opposite the bed, and she wondered if he liked to watch himself. She shook that thought from her head. Her mind was conjuring enough fucked up shit being in what was obviously Varda's bedroom. No need to make it worse.

A noise from the far corner of the room startled her, and she looked up to see Varda watching her from the shadows, the light from the bedside tables barely illuminating the huge space. He was reclining against the wall, arms crossed over his chest.

When he shoved away from it and stalked toward her, she pressed herself as tightly to the door as she could, unable to help the soft whimper that escaped her. He stopped in the middle of the room, an ugly grin spreading across his face before he laughed, quick and cruel.

"Relax, girl. I'm not going to touch you. I have far bigger problems to worry about than what's between your legs."

He summoned her forward with a jerk of his fingers, and she took a deep breath, hands tight on the strap of her purse, as she inched her way across the plush carpet.

"When was the last time you saw Bianchi?"

Emilia swallowed around the lump in her throat. "Not for a few days."

Varda nodded, but he didn't seem angry, more resigned. "It doesn't matter. I finally have the upper hand, and I'm going to end them all."

"You are? How?"

Eyes narrowing on her face, Varda took a step forward. "My battle plans are none of your fucking business. Unless you have something you'd like to share with me."

"I don't have anything to report," she said, heart beating wildly in her chest.

"That's not what I meant."

She tried to keep her voice light. "What then?"

He studied her in silence, dismissing whatever he'd been about to say with a flick of his wrist. "Nothing. With the end so close, I'm no longer in need of your services. I have everything I need from Bianchi to win this."

"Okay." Varda dropped his gaze when his phone vibrated in his hand. "And my mother's loan?"

"Your payments are due until I tell you to stop."

"But you said—"

"I know what I fucking said," Varda snarled, rounding on her. "I know how much you pay and how often and how many times your mother came to me begging for more money in exchange for sexual favors."

Emilia blinked in surprise. "My mother's borrowed more money?"

"Not since you came to Sicily. Though she does like to hang out at a bar my men frequent. The apple doesn't fall far from the fucked up tree, I guess."

Squeezing her eyes shut at the mental image, Emilia grit her teeth. So her mother was more emotionally invested than she should have been. But not with Varda, with one of his men. Christ, she needed this all to be over soon.

"Don't worry, little girl. I'll make good on my promise once I have what I want."

"And what do you want?"

"Domenico Bianchi's head on a stick. And his brothers with him."

Emilia forced herself not to react. Varda couldn't know she was in so deep with Dom, that she was in love with him. He would only use it to hurt them both.

"I hope you get it." The words were sour on her tongue.

"I will," he assured her. "I'll see you on Tuesday for your next payment."

"I have it now." She dug into her purse, flinching when

Varda lurched forward and grabbed the money from her hand. "Can I go?"

"Yes. Emilia," he said when she gripped the knob. "You're tied to me until I loosen the knot. Don't forget that."

Yanking the door open, Emilia ran past the guard and down the hallway, gasping for breath by the time she reached the bottom of the stairs. She retraced her steps to the courtyard and sprinted through the cool night until she was safely locked in her car.

Dropping her forehead against the steering wheel, she fumbled blindly in her purse for her phone, punching in Dom's number and pressing it to her ear.

"It's done. I'm okay," she said when he picked up, unable to keep the tremble from her voice.

"What happened? What did he want?"

"He said he didn't need me to spy on you anymore. Please tell me this is all going to be over soon." Christ, she needed it to be over.

"It is, kitten. I promise. I'm making plans as we speak. Do you want me to come get you?"

"No." She sat upright and started the car, tucking her phone between her ear and her shoulder while she slid her seatbelt into place. "I have to go pick up Bella and Antonio. Dom?"

"Yes, kitten."

She chewed her bottom lip, unsure if she should tell him what Varda said about her mother. "Be safe," she said instead. "If you get yourself killed—"

"You'll never forgive me. I know. Text me when you get home."

She disconnected the call and dropped her phone on the seat beside her. All she had to do was hang on a little longer. And pray every plan Dom was making went off without a hitch.

# Chapter Thirty

"The men are ready."

Dom glanced up at Otto in the doorway of the pool house and nodded. Three days of strategizing were finally going to culminate in phase one of his plan to take down Varda. They couldn't make any mistakes tonight. Everything had to be executed damn near flawlessly if it was going to work.

Grabbing his gun off the table, he followed Otto across the patio and through the house to the front door. The check-in with his men in the security room was all clear, and he stepped outside, where his soldiers gathered at the top of the driveway.

Matteo had sent three dozen men from across the territory to add to the two dozen he already had in residence. Rossi and Otto had been working with them every bit of the three days while Dom plotted, making sure they were ready for tonight. Their form was good, and they understood what was at stake here.

He was leaving a dozen men behind tonight to guard the base. Varda likely didn't have the numbers to attack again, but he'd rather be safe than sorry. The rest of the men he'd spread out into teams. Without Sforza, they'd had to spend some time doing recon to see where Varda's men eventually landed.

Some were at safe houses, some were hunkered down at home like Varda was, windows blacked out to give themselves the illusion of safety. Nothing would spare them tonight.

"This is a coordinated attack," Dom began. "We have to hit all six locations simultaneously to keep them from warning each other. As far as we can tell, these men are the last of Varda's loyal ranks, including his potential heirs."

"And Varda himself?"

"He's currently holed up in his house in Agrigento," Dom explained. "Very few people are allowed in or out."

"You'd think he'd be surrounding himself with men to ward off an attack."

"We're assuming he's keeping his people spread out to give us more targets," Rossi said. "Clearly he's not expecting an assault like this."

"So we're letting Varda get away?"

Dom looked at the man who'd spoken. "Not a fucking chance. Varda's house is huge. I don't want to go after him there. There are too many places for him to hide. And he knows it better than we do."

"But once he hears what happened, he'll run."

"Exactly," Dom replied. "And there are only two, maybe three places he can go. Places that are a lot easier for us to get into and take him out than his house."

"So we're flushing him out."

Dom nodded. "Like a fox in his den. Do all the team leads and seconds have their earpieces? Good. Let's roll out." Clapping Otto on the shoulder, Dom gave it a squeeze. "Thank you for staying behind so Rossi could go."

"He needs to get some blood on his hands to avenge Sforza. I don't mind."

Dom caught Rossi's eye as he climbed into the passenger seat of the waiting SUV. Rossi nodded once, slamming the car door behind him. When the car in front of them pulled away, Dom tapped the dashboard with his fist, and the car lurched into motion.

"Testing comms," Dom said into his earpiece. "Team one."

"Copy."

"Team two."

"Loud and clear."

Dom checked with the other three teams, satisfied with the new tech Luca had been excited to hand off to him. They didn't normally communicate this way, but then again, he'd never pulled off an operation this big. He'd worked and re-worked the plan, going over it in his head again and again.

Taking all of Varda's men by surprise and sending him running and hiding to a known location was their best shot. They'd give him a few days to settle, make sure they could pinpoint his location, let him think he'd successfully escaped, and then attack and end this.

Matteo called this morning to remind Dom he couldn't fuck this up and draw any suspicion from the cops. As if Dom didn't know everything that was at stake here.

They pulled up to the rear of the property he'd assigned his team, and Dom checked his watch. Every team should be in position within the next ten minutes. While he listened to the team check-ins filter through his earpiece, he twisted his silencer into place and studied the house.

It was in a residential neighborhood, a mix of civilians and Mafia, but the civilian presence was strong. Varda liked to do that with his properties—mix them into heavy civilian areas like that would deter an attack. It wouldn't stop him, but it did change the game a little bit.

The goal here was to get in, take out the five men they'd seen coming and going and occasionally smoking on the front porch with silenced weapons, load them into their own cars behind the shelter of the closed garage door, and drive them away. They'd figure out what to do with all the properties once they had complete control of the territory.

When the last team announced their arrival at their location in his ear, he directed his men in the backseat to get out. They'd watch the back of the house for runners. Not a single Varda man was going to make it out of this alive.

"Set up your moves, but wait for my signal," Dom said as they pulled around to the front of the house and parked at the curb.

The vegetation was heavy, hiding the house from the road and the SUV from the house. Dom stepped out of the car and heard his man do the same, following him across the grass as they snaked their way through the shadows, avoiding any patches of light that fell from the windows or nearby street lamps.

Checking with his man, Dom waited for his ready nod. "Now!" he barked into his earpiece.

He darted up the steps and shot out the lock on the front door, forcing it in with his shoulder to break the security chain. Two men were sitting in front of the TV watching soccer. One was dead with a bullet between the eyes before he could even move, and the second one took three to the chest and slumped over in his reach for the gun on the coffee table.

Dom gestured toward the sound of banging pots and pans in the back of the house. The men out back were supposed to wait two minutes and then approach if no one tried to make a break for it. A second later, they heard a grunt and a thud before their men appeared at the end of the hallway.

Pointing up the stairs, his men nodded and followed Dom

silently up to the second level. There should be five men in this house. Three down, two to go.

The hallway was as narrow as the stairs, but there were only three rooms up there. Dom opened the door to the first one and found it empty. The second bedroom was also empty, but the sound of the shower drew him across the room.

Pushing the door in, he fired through the shower curtain, watching the blood splatter against the clear plastic before the guy fell, dragging it with him. That would be handy for cleanup. Water mixed with the blood and curled down the drain as he reached in to shut off the shower head.

"Clear," his men said when they met again at the top of the stairs.

Dom frowned. "We're missing one. Identify the bodies we've already dropped and see who should be here and isn't. Status update," he said as his men split off to do their checks.

"Team four clear. One injury, no casualties."

"Team one clear. Everyone's dead who should be, and our guys are fine," Rossi said.

"Team three took a beating. They were quick to the draw and decided to go out with a bang. Literally. The fucking house is on fire, but I got all my guys out and left them in there to rot."

Dom waited for team two to report, but there was only silence. "Team two, what's your status?" He heard the mutterings of other team leads in his ear but nothing from two. "Who's closest to team two's location?"

"We are," Rossi replied. "We'll head over there now."

"Good. We're missing one guy who should be here. Checking now to see wh—"

The sound of gunfire exploded from the back of the house. Dom took off down the stairs, bypassing the living room and the kitchen and stopping in the hallway outside a bedroom at the back of the house where two naked bodies were bleeding out all over the floor, one slumped against the partially open closet door, the other crammed between the bed and the wall.

"Who the hell is that?" Dom demanded.

"That's Bruno," his man said, gesturing with his gun to the guy leaning against the closet. "And the guy who was blowing him when I walked in here."

Someone whistled from behind him. "Bad night for a booty call."

Dom shook his head. "Let's start cleaning up. How many cars do they have?"

"I found three sets of keys in the kitchen."

"Great. Let's put two in each. I want to clear out of here within an hour."

They wrapped the bodies in shower curtains and blankets and shoved them into the trunk of their cars, then wiped down surfaces and doorknobs. They'd send in a team to do a more thorough clean tomorrow, for right now, he wanted to get the hell out of here before they drew the suspicion of the neighbors.

By the time they were loading the last body into the last car, Rossi's voice crackled over the piece still in his ear. "Team two has been recovered."

Something in Rossi's tone set his teeth on edge. "Tell me."

"Looks like they had more guys here than they were anticipating. They got off some decent return fire."

"Did we lose anyone?"

"They're all still breathing for now," Rossi assured him. "But if we know a doctor in the area, he might want to meet us back at the house."

Dom swore under his breath. "The housekeeper has a son who's a doctor. Let me call her, and I'll have him meet us."

Checking the house one last time, Dom turned off all the lights and the TV and climbed behind the wheel of the SUV. When he pulled away from the curb, his men followed him out. He punched in the number Carina had given him for the housekeeper, and she swore her son would be at the house in less than ten minutes.

He made the turn for the driveway, screeching up to the gate as his men branched away from the compound to take care of the bodies and vehicles. Rossi was already there when he slammed to a stop, helping their man out of the backseat.

Dom shouldered his other side, and they half walked, half carried him into the house. "Get me clean towels and some hot water," he barked at the men waiting in the hall. "The doctor should be here any minute."

They laid him down on one of the couches in the great room. Dom didn't like how pale he was—or how young. When they brought towels in, he pressed them hard into the wound in the kid's side, earning a pained grunt. Better to be in pain than be dead.

The doctor skidded into the room, eyes wide, hair wild, like he'd been roused from sleep. He crossed the space quickly, sinking onto the edge of the cushion and using a pair of scissors he produced from a bag at his feet to cut open the length of the kid's shirt.

He urged Dom's hands away and dropped the blood-soaked towel on the floor with a wet plop, peeling the shirt away from the oozing wound. He prodded around it, pressing on the kid's belly and side, earning disapproving groans.

"It doesn't look like he's got any internal bleeding." He tapped a couple of spots with his fingers and got no reaction. "Exit wound so there's no bullet to retrieve. He's lucky. All he'll really need are some stitches."

Dom's shoulders relaxed. They'd managed to take down all the targets on their list in less than three hours with almost no resistance and zero casualties. The worst they'd have to contend with is the kid who needed a few stitches and would have a wicked scar he'd no doubt use to get laid.

"He should probably go to a hospital." Dom pinned the doctor with a hard stare until the man swallowed and nodded nervously. "But of course, I can stitch him up and give him some pain meds right here. I might need someone to help me hold him down. I don't have anything to numb the area."

Dom gestured to two men standing nearby and got up from the couch. When he saw Rossi motion to him from the hallway, he joined him.

"How'd it go with you?" Rossi asked, eyes fixed on where the doctor was applying pressure to the wound to get it to stop bleeding.

"Fine. We ended up with a sixth body." Rossi slid his gaze to Dom's and raised a brow. "Varda's youngest nephew had a gentleman caller over."

"Tough break," Rossi mumbled. "Was it too easy?"

Dom slanted Rossi a look and crossed his arms over his chest. "Did you want someone to die?"

"No, but—"

Slapping Rossi on the shoulder to silence him, Dom replied, "Take the win, my friend. This is almost over. All we have to do is wait to see what hole Varda decides to burrow into and take him out. And then we're done."

"And you'll control Varda territory."

He liked the idea of it, but the outcome felt bittersweet. Especially with all the animosity that still existed between him and his brother.

"I serve at the pleasure of the Bianchi Don," he said quietly.

# Chapter Thirty-One

Emilia scraped leftover food into the trash and set the plate in the sink. It was a madhouse today. She hadn't heard from Dom in a couple of days, and her nerves had been shot since her run-in with Varda. She needed some kind of update, some hint that forward progress was being made.

She'd tried to convince herself that no news was good news, but the longer she went without hearing anything, the more she worried. Which is why she'd volunteered to work two doubles in a row. Something to keep her hands and her mind busy instead of sitting at home wondering if Dom had gotten himself killed, wondering if anyone would know to tell her if he did.

If she thought about that too hard, she'd spiral into too many what-ifs and maybes, which was a recipe for disaster. Plus, being around her mother had become an excruciating exercise in patience. She was sure she'd bitten her tongue so hard in recent days she was in danger of putting a hole through it.

The revelation from Varda that her mother might be

seeking out one or more of his men chilled her. But then, was it all that different from what she was doing with Dom? She'd fallen for a man just as deadly, just as dangerous, just as mired in this forbidden world as her mother might have. Maybe she was more like her mother than she wanted to believe.

Just because Dom was good to her didn't mean he wasn't a monster to someone else. She hadn't fallen for the man who was extorting and tormenting her family, but she hadn't fallen for a saint either. Something she'd have to reconcile with herself. If it was even possible.

Not having Dom after all this was over had crossed her mind. But the thought caused a deep ache in her chest she couldn't relieve. She didn't want to let him go, and she wasn't quite sure what that said about who she was or what she was willing to overlook for love.

When this was done, when she wasn't walking on eggshells hoping they all survived the night, she'd have to sit down and take a long, hard look at what she really wanted and who she wanted it with. She suspected she already knew the answer, but it didn't hurt to ask the question.

The line cook called up an order for one of her tables, and she pivoted away from the sink, loading the steaming plates onto a wide tray. Hefting the tray onto her shoulder, she pushed into the dining room and carried it out to the patio.

As if she'd conjured him from nothing, there he was. Her heart fluttered a wild rhythm, and she couldn't stop the smile that painted her mouth.

They'd pushed three tables together, a wonder they'd found so many free with as busy as it was, and were settling around it ordering drinks from Alessia while she poured water into their glasses. Dom caught her eye when she passed them to deliver the food to her waiting table, and he grinned, eyes flicking to Alessia.

She shrugged. He wasn't in her section, and Alessia had gotten to him first. Plus, Varda had said she didn't need to see Dom again, and just because she hadn't noticed anyone following her recently didn't mean Varda wasn't still watching her somehow. It was probably best they didn't interact in public anyway.

But she desperately missed the rich, deep tone of his voice in her ear, the touch of his fingers on her skin, the feel of his breath hot on her neck while he kissed her. Shaking the thoughts from her head before she got carried away, she turned toward another table to clear away their empty plates and take their order for the next course.

When she passed by his table, another group got up to leave, forcing her to move back so they could pass. She felt fingers caress her wrist and dance up her forearm, barely swallowing the sigh that threatened to escape her lips. Like that first time, he could still send electricity buzzing along her skin with a simple touch.

She twisted her arm, lightly grazing his palm and finger-tips with her own before stepping away and carrying her tray back into the kitchen. The revolving door of patrons kept her busy for hours, but every time she pushed through the door from the kitchen into the dining room, his eyes would find hers like a magnet and follow her around the room until she disappeared again.

He sat with his friends, talking and laughing, and any time she got close enough, his fingers touched whatever part he could reach. Her elbow, her hip, her wrist, the small of her back. It was its own kind of torture to be touched by him in such a small way and unable to have more.

The second Varda was dead, she was going to keep him in bed for at least a week straight. The only breaks he would get were to eat and sleep, and maybe shower. But the shower in the pool house was big enough for two.

He'd proven that when he'd stepped in behind her, pressed her breasts against the cool tile, and taken her from behind. And too bad it was getting colder. She would've loved to have him finger her in the pool while she tried not to make a sound.

"Earth to Emilia." Alessia snapped her fingers in front of Emilia's face, yanking her out of her daydream.

"Sorry, my head was a million miles away. What's up?"

"Can you close for me tonight?"

Emilia's eyes drifted to the clock hanging over the door to the manager's office. Her manager hadn't so much as looked at her sideways since Dom's threat. It was a nice change of pace.

"Please," Alessia added, poking out her bottom lip. "I'll open for you on your next day."

They had an hour left until closing, and then it would take maybe another thirty to forty-five minutes after that to finish shutting everything down. Antonio and Bella should be fine for an extra couple hours at the neighbor's.

"Okay. Fine. But I open on Saturday. No backing out because you got plastered the night before."

"I swear!" Alessia squealed. "This cute guy from that big party asked me out. He was too hot to say no, and I didn't want to make him wait two hours."

"What cute guy?" Emilia joined Alessia at the kitchen door, peeking through the narrow opening.

"That one. In the red shirt."

"Rossi?"

Alessia's nose wrinkled, and she looked at Emilia over her shoulder. "How do you know his name?"

"Oh, uh, they've been in here before. He's quite the flirt."

"Lucky you didn't snap him up first, then." She untied her apron and hung it on a peg, fluffing out her hair. "How do I look?"

"Fuckable," Emilia decided.

"Perfect. I need to get laid. Thank you again!"

Alessia dashed out through the restaurant, and Emilia followed to watch Rossi sling his arm over her shoulder and whisper something in her ear that had Alessia blushing bright red. Emilia shook her head. Rossi was going to break that girl's heart for sure, but she'd definitely get laid and then some.

Dom caught her eye as the rest of his men threw back the last of their wine and shoved away from the table. The restaurant was mostly empty, just a few stragglers at this time of night, and he crossed to her, sliding his arm around her waist and drawing her against his chest.

"I've been dying to touch you all night," he whispered against her ear, raising goosebumps on her skin.

"All you've been doing is touching me."

"Not in the way I wanted to. Come back to the house with me. Let me show you."

She bit back a groan, pressing a kiss against his jaw. "I can't. I have to close now that Alessia left to get plowed by Rossi."

Dom growled against her neck. "Rossi ruins all my fun."

Chuckling, Emilia gave his shoulder a light shove. "I think you made out okay so far."

"Better than okay," he admitted. "What time will you be done closing?"

"Maybe about ninety minutes, two hours tops. But we probably shouldn't be seen together right now."

His brows were drawn together when he looked down at her. "Why not?"

"Because Varda told me not to see you anymore. If someone's watching me and he finds out—"

"Kitten, there's no one left to watch you."

She captured her bottom lip between her teeth. "So phase one was a success?"

"Completely and utterly, and I want to celebrate with you." His hands slid down to cup her ass and squeeze, and she couldn't stop the groan this time.

"Okay. Come back in ninety minutes. I'll make sure I'm done by then. Worst case scenario, you can always fuck my mouth in your truck again."

He pinched her nipple roughly between his fingers, making her gasp, before stepping back. "That's not even close to the worst-case scenario, kitten. I'll see you soon."

She sighed as she watched him go. And as soon as he was out of sight, she rushed into the kitchen to start her closing duties.

# Chapter Thirty-Two

Facing the back door to the restaurant, Dom reclined against the wall, one foot propped against it, his phone in his hand. He'd handled a little business and made a few calls. Still no news on Varda, but they'd sniff him out soon. Then he'd come back to wait.

He needed inside her, needed to taste her skin and hear her moans, feel her nails scoring his back. When Varda was dead and buried, he fully intended to keep her in bed until she begged him for a break.

The door opened, haloing her in soft light, glinting off the copper in her hair, and he smiled and stepped forward.

"Oh," she said, mouth rounding into a pretty, fuckable O. "I thought you would be waiting by the car."

"I had another idea."

He closed the space between them, easing her back into the kitchen. She'd left only the security lights on, and they cast a pale glow over the spotless stainless steel countertops and appliances.

The door closed with a gentle click, and she looked up at him. "We can't have sex in the restaurant."

He raised a brow in challenge, lifting her into his arms and carrying her into the dining room. "Why not?"

"Because you're going to get me fired."

"You don't need a job. I'll take care of you."

He set her on a table in the corner, and she turned to glance at the front door. He knew the moment she realized anyone who walked close to the far front window could see them when her fingers tightened on his forearms and she drew her bottom lip between her teeth.

Peppering a line of kisses across her jaw, he grazed her earlobe with his lips before whispering, "I know you like the idea of someone catching us, someone watching you take my cock." A soft moan escaped her, and he smiled. "Be my good little slut and take your panties off."

She didn't hesitate, dropping her purse on an empty chair and bracing her foot against the seat to leverage her ass off the table. She shimmied her skirt up and wiggled her panties down, looking up at him as she dangled them off her finger.

Plucking them out of her hand, he stuffed them into his pocket and gripped the back of her neck, tugging her forward for a kiss. She nipped his bottom lip, smiling when she made him moan and slipping her hands under his shirt to stroke her fingers across his back.

Her skirt was still pulled up, but her legs were pressed together from taking her panties off, and he trailed his fingertips up her thigh, squeezing it and forcing them apart. She moaned against his lips when he stepped between her legs, fingernails dragging across his skin as he rocked his hips against hers. Barely touching, but enough for his jeans to create friction against her core.

Capturing her lip between his teeth, he pulled back, letting it slip through until he released it, swollen and red. "I've missed this mouth." He dragged his thumb over her lips.

"I've missed your cock," she replied, running her fingers over his rock-hard length.

"Take it out, then."

Her gray eyes darkened to storm clouds as she flipped the button on his jeans and yanked down the zipper. Easing him back with her hands on his hips, she dropped to her knees and tugged his pants and boxers down.

He ran his fingers through her hair when she looked up at him, wrapping her hand around the base of his shaft and guiding him to her mouth. His fingers tightened in her hair as she swirled her tongue around the tip, teasing him.

He let her set the pace for a while, sliding her mouth down his shaft and back up, her hand following her motions and ending at the base of his cock with a light squeeze every time her tongue wrapped around his tip.

"You look so pretty on your knees with my cock in your mouth, kitten. You can take more."

Emilia looked up at him again, sliding more of his cock into her mouth even as he used his hand on the back of her head to apply pressure, pushing her down until her eyes watered and then releasing her to suck in a deep breath. He slid in again, groaning when he felt the head brush the back of her throat, her lips wrapped tight around him.

"Play with yourself," he ground out, gently rocking his hips to thrust in and out of her mouth. "That's it," he said when she pushed her skirt over her thighs, baring herself to him. "Touch your pussy for me, kitten. Make yourself nice and wet for me."

She groaned around his length as he slid his cock out to the tip to let her catch her breath and then in again, fucking her mouth in short, fast thrusts while her fingers danced over her clit and skimmed down her lips. Dipping them quickly inside her, she brought her hand up to the base of his shaft, stroking it up and down in time with his thrusts in and out of her mouth, and he groaned.

"Fuck," he panted. "You're going to make me come down your throat if you're not careful."

She squeezed lightly in response, working his cock with her hand and her mouth while tears gathered in the corners of her eyes and slipped down her cheeks. Her eyes were intent on his, and he felt the first tether of his control slipping, his thrusts becoming erratic, urgent, primal with need.

She braced her hands on his thighs when he thrust as deep as he dared, shuddering with his release. Fingernails scratching down his thighs, she swallowed every drop, tongue swirling over the tip of his cock when he released her head.

Licking her lips, she sat back on her heels. "That's way better when we're not navigating the tight space of your SUV," she said, voice breathy and a little hoarse.

"Up," he growled, hauling her against him as soon as she was on her feet and shoving her shirt up to expose her breasts.

Tugging the cup of her bra down, he wrapped his lips around her nipple, scraping it with his teeth and making her gasp before dragging the flat of his tongue against it. He pressed against her, guiding her back until her ass hit the table and easing her onto the edge.

"You were supposed to touch yourself while I fucked your mouth, slut," he said against her skin, exposing her other breast and kissing his way to it. "You didn't follow directions."

"I did too," she insisted, breath catching in her throat when he tightened his teeth around her nipple. "You didn't say how long I had to touch myself for."

Dom grinned, dragging his fingers up the inside of her thigh and rubbing them roughly up and down her pussy lips.

"I'll have to be clearer next time. Because I wanted you to come with my cock in your mouth."

He shoved two fingers deep inside her without warning, and she cried out, nails digging into the skin of his biceps as he fucked them in and out of her tight heat. Spreading her legs wide to keep her from rocking her hips, leaving her completely at his mercy, he slipped in a third finger and used his thumb to rub circles over her clit.

"Dom..."

"Hmm?"

"Don't stop," she pleaded, clinging to him as he drove his fingers in and out.

"Of course not. You owe me an orgasm. At least one." She whimpered, and he reveled in the sound. "Come for me, kitten. Then maybe you'll get my cock inside that perfect pussy."

When she began to clench around him, he shoved his fingers deep, massaging against her g-spot until she dropped her head against his chest with a groan and came undone in his arms.

Her breath was hot on his skin as she panted. "Fuck," she breathed, and he chuckled. "Do you feel better now?"

"I do." He pulled his fingers free, smiling when she sighed, and brought them to his lips, licking the sweet taste of her from each one. "But I'm not done with you yet."

"No?" Her voice was deep, needy.

"No. Stand up." She hopped off the table instantly, her legs wobbly. "Turn around."

She frowned but turned so her back was to him. Dom slid his hands up over her shoulders and down her arms, placing her hands on opposite edges of the table and bending her at the waist. A soft moan escaped her when he gathered her skirt in his fingers, easing it up her thighs and over her ass.

Rubbing the head of his cock up and down her slit, he

leaned forward and whispered in her ear. "What does my slut need?"

"I need—" He slipped just the tip inside her, and she groaned low in her throat. "I need you to slide your cock deep inside me."

He slammed inside her to the hilt, grinding his hips against her ass. "Is that it?"

"N-no." She rocked her ass back against him. "I need you to fuck me. Hard. Fast. Deep."

On a growl, he drew his cock out and slammed in again. "That what you need, slut?"

"Yes," she sobbed, squeezing his cock while he ground against her ass.

Standing up, he gripped her hips, pumping his cock in and out of her in hard, deep thrusts. She clutched the table tight in her fingers, making it rattle and scrape across the floor with each punishing surge of his hips.

Her pussy fluttered around him, and without slowing his pace, he snaked a hand down to rub furious circles over her clit, groaning at the way she squeezed him.

"Fuck yes." He rubbed her sensitive clit faster, eager to feel her explode around him. "Come on my cock, kitten."

At his command, she rocked onto her tiptoes and then rammed back against him, forcing his cock deep inside her while her orgasm ripped through her. He slowed his fingers on her clit while her body relaxed, but didn't stop them.

"Hands on the table," he growled when she moved to push his hand from between her thighs.

She whimpered, but obeyed. "I can't."

"You can. You've got one more for me. Give it to me, slut, then I'll come inside you."

"Dom." She shuddered as his hips and fingers picked up the pace again. "Dom."

"Yes, kitten."

"I-I…"

"Mhmm. Give me what I want."

He ached to come inside her, his cock throbbing as her pussy clenched him tight. But he wanted to feel her come one more time before he gave into his own release. Bracketing her clit with his thumb and forefinger, he pinched it roughly, delighting in her scream of pleasure seconds before she gripped him like a vise, forcing his own orgasm as he thrust deep and emptied himself inside her.

Collapsing on top of her, he pressed a kiss to her shoulder. "I can't believe you think you're quiet when you come."

She laughed, deep and throaty, unclenching her hands from the edge of the table and flexing her fingers. "It's your fault. You do crazy things to my body."

"I accept full responsibility." He stood, pulling her up with him and pressing a kiss to the side of her neck. "Are you sure I can't talk you into coming back to the house with me?"

She sighed, turning to look up at him. "No. I need to pick up the twins and get home. But when all this is over with Varda, I want to spend at least a week naked in your bed. What's so funny?" she asked when he laughed, readjusting her skirt and tugging her bra back into place.

He stepped away and pulled his jeans up. "I thought the same thing about you while I was waiting for you to finish your shift." Grabbing the front of her shirt, he pulled her in for a kiss, tilting her head back to take it deeper. "Definitely somewhere soundproof, though. Maybe you'll be even louder."

Laughing, she shoved him away and reached for her purse, digging her phone out when it rang. "Hello? Bella. Slow down. I can't understand what you're saying."

Her knees buckled, her face draining of color, and he wrapped his arm around her waist to hold her upright. "What happened?"

"Don't move," Emilia said to her sister. "We're on our way."

"Emilia. Tell me what's going on," he demanded as she raced to the door.

"Varda was at my house. He attacked my mother."

"Shit." He gripped her hand, ran across the lot, and threw her into his SUV. "Is she okay?"

"I don't know." Her breath hitched on a sob, and she pressed her fingertips to her lips. "Before he left, he set the house on fire."

Dom floored it, peeling out of the parking lot and speeding toward her house. She couldn't lose her family. He wouldn't let that happen. She needed them as much as he needed her, and he couldn't lose her now.

# Chapter Thirty-Three

Dom shouted orders into his phone, but she had no idea what he said over the blood pounding in her ears. They circled increasingly closer to her house, and she saw the hazy orange smoke before anything else, billowing over the tops of other homes and the trees. Then Dom took the last turn onto her street in a squeal of tires, and everything came into view.

Flames danced behind the windows on the second floor, and terror clawed at her throat as they lurched to a stop. Shoving out of the car, she sprinted up the front walk, Dom right on her heels. She was almost to the door when a strong arm wrapped around her waist and hauled her back.

"No, kitten," Dom said in her ear over the roar of the fire. "I can't let you go in there."

"My family's in there! I can't leave them," she sobbed, struggling against his grip.

"I'll go." He pressed a kiss to her temple. "Stay here. Back-up's on the way."

She watched as he shoved open the door, covering his mouth and nose with his t-shirt, and pushed through the thick curtain of smoke until he disappeared. The smell of burning wood and plastic curled into the night, and a wave of nausea rolled over her. Everyone she loved in the world was inside that house.

It was impossible to make out any shapes through the swirling gray smoke thickened and backlit by the fire beyond. She couldn't let him go in there alone. He couldn't bring out all three of them. Not without getting hurt himself.

There was a back entrance near the kitchen. They didn't use it often, but it was there, and it didn't look like the flames had reached that side of the house yet. Dom could be mad at her later. She wasn't going to stand here and do nothing.

Movement caught her eye just over the threshold before she turned for the side of the house, and she rushed forward into the smoke, blinking against the sting. But it wasn't Dom. It was Antonio, face streaked with soot and sweat. Gripping his arm, she pulled him out into the fresh air.

"Oh, thank God you're okay." Relief warred with fear in her chest.

She wrapped him in a hug, patting his back while he coughed and sputtered the smoke from his lungs. When she pulled back to look at him, her shirt came away heavy and wet. She brushed at it, nearly collapsing when she realized her hand was slick with blood.

"Antonio. You're bleeding. Where are you hurt?" She grappled for his shirt, lifting it to inspect his stomach and chest, her hands roaming around his back.

"Not...mine," he rasped, and her heart plummeted into her belly.

"Whose?" she demanded, glancing toward the house and willing Dom to appear with Bella and her mother.

"Mama's."

"No." She pivoted toward the house again, but Antonio gripped her arm to hold her back.

"Don't. It's not safe."

"I can't just leave them in there," she said, voice breaking.

"I told him where Mama was. He'll get her."

Her eyes darted from window to window, trying to catch some glimpse of them, a shadow, a body part, something to reassure herself they were okay. That everything would be okay.

"What about Bella?"

Antonio's head jerked up. "She's not out here? I told her to wait outside and call you." His gaze darted over the empty yard. "Maybe she ran inside to help. I have to go find her."

Hacking coughs rang out behind them, and Emilia spun at the sound, stumbling toward Dom, who carried her mother over his shoulder. His face was dirty, and his shirt was plastered to his body, but he was alive; he was breathing. Thank Christ.

He laid her mother gently on the ground and glanced toward the street as three more SUVs screeched to a halt and men poured out. She recognized Rossi and some of the other men who'd eaten at the restaurant tonight. Rossi's gaze was a mix of sympathy and rage when he joined them on the grass.

"We can't find Bella," Emilia said, fighting her rising panic. "Antonio thinks she might have gone inside after she called me."

"The upstairs is completely engulfed, but we can search the first floor before it spreads downstairs," Dom said, voice hoarse. "You three inside with me. The rest of you guard them and deal with the cops and fire service when they get here. No one talks to or touches them but me."

"Dom." She gripped his shirt and hauled him in for an urgent kiss. "Be careful."

He claimed one more, squeezing her waist before disappearing back into the smoke. The remaining men formed a circle around them, hiding them from view, and Emilia sank down to her knees next to her mother.

"Mama." She brushed a strand of sweat-soaked hair off Maria's forehead, eyes traveling down over her mother's body until she found a growing patch of blood soaking through the shirt at her stomach.

Shoving the fabric up, she groaned at the deep, jagged knife wound in her mother's side. She met Antonio's pained gaze before tapping the man closest to her on the leg. Her mother wasn't moving, but Emilia could make out the subtle rise and fall of her chest in the orange glow of the fire.

"I need a towel, a rag, something to stop the bleeding."

He stripped off his shirt and handed it to her, and two other men did the same. Balling them up, she pressed them tight against her mother's side, gagging at the squelching sound they made. When she applied more pressure, her mother's eyes fluttered open, and she moaned low in her throat.

"Mama!" Emilia inched closer on her knees. "What the hell happened? Can you tell me?"

Maria's lips moved, but Emilia couldn't make out what she was saying. Leaning forward, she brought her ear close to her mother's face.

"You killed him."

Emilia jerked back. "What? Killed who? Mama, what are you talking about?"

"None of this would have happened if not for you," Maria said, her voice rough. "You should have stayed in Rome. We didn't need you. You ruined…everything."

"I…I didn't…" Emilia said, tears spilling down her cheeks. "I was helping you."

"I didn't want your help. I wanted him."

"Who?" She looked up when Antonio scooted forward,

and there was something in the look on his face. "What the fuck is she talking about, Antonio?"

"Varda's enforcer."

"The guy I was making payments to?"

The one who'd been tasked with following her, who was probably dead now. Antonio nodded.

She looked down at her mother, and the horror of it washed over her, chilling her down to the bone. Her mother was in love with the man who'd beaten her? Raped her? Threatened to kill her? No. That couldn't be it. She had to mean something else, someone else.

Maria's eyes were cold, but her grip was strong when she wrapped her hand around Emilia's wrist.

"What did you do, Mama?"

"I told him. I told Varda you were spreading your legs for a Bianchi soldier. That you'd fallen in love with him. That you were betraying Varda to the Bianchis."

Emilia tried to jerk away, but Maria's nails dug into her skin. "You wouldn't do that. Why would you do that?" she asked on a choked sob.

"I wanted you to know how it felt to lose someone you loved," Maria spat. "But I got punished instead. Isn't that always the way? Paying for your mistakes."

"You did this," Emilia insisted, wrenching her arm from her mother's grasp. "You knew what he would do. You knew he would attack me, kill me, and you told him anyway."

Maria's smile was cruel. "You were always a burden I didn't want. You ruined my life from the moment you were born."

Her mother's words knifed into her, ripping her to shreds. "I didn't ask to be."

"And I didn't have a choice," Maria shot back, eyes glazing over when she shifted to look up at her daughter. "I tried to be the best mother I could."

"That was you trying?" Emilia demanded, clenching her fists against her thighs. "You were my mother. All I wanted was for you to love me."

"I couldn't. You looked too much like your father, and you're the reason he left me. You took two men I loved from me just by existing. How could I ever forgive you for that?"

Maria coughed, wincing at the movement. "I hope my death sits heavy on your conscience for the rest of your life. It's no less than what you deserve."

Emilia shoved to her feet as her mother took one last rattling breath and went still. Tears blurred her vision as she spun, desperate to run as far away from her as she could. But someone caught her before she could move, locking their arms around her even as she struggled.

"It's me," Dom murmured against her ear. "It's me, kitten."

Collapsing into his arms, Emilia sobbed against his chest. "It's all my fault. I shouldn't have… I never should have…"

"Stop." Dom ran a hand down her hair, his voice hard, angry. "You did nothing wrong. You tried to help. You tried to love her, to save her. In the end, she killed herself."

Emilia wasn't so sure. Maybe all she'd done since coming down to Sicily was make things worse for the very people she was trying to help. Maybe her family really would have been better off without her. Her family. Bella. She jerked back, eyes searching Dom's.

"Where's my sister?"

He shared a look with Rossi, and her legs gave out, forcing him to scoop her into his arms. Bella couldn't be dead. Emilia couldn't lose her. Not sweet Bella, who was supposed to go to that concert Theo had finally asked her to. Bella, who was so excited over her plans for what to wear and how to do her makeup.

Dom sat on the open tailgate of his SUV and settled her on

his lap. "She wasn't in the house. We couldn't find her anywhere. The firefighters will look for a body, but I don't think she's here."

Emilia glanced up, noticing the flashing lights of the fire trucks and police cars for the first time. "If she's not here, where is she?"

The car jostled when Antonio sank down beside them, and Emilia reached out to rub his back and shoulders when he dropped his head into his hands. "What if Varda took her?" he whispered.

Dom twitched underneath her, and the look on his face said he'd been thinking the same. "No," Emilia breathed. "Why would he do that? What would he want Bella for?"

"I don't know," Antonio said. "Because he came here looking for you."

# Chapter Thirty-Four

Emilia slapped a hand over her mouth, but it barely muffled the sob. She hadn't been here because she'd stayed late at the restaurant with Dom. And since he couldn't have Emilia, Varda had taken her sister instead.

She started to ease herself off Dom's lap, but he tightened his hold, his fingers digging into the skin of her hip.

"You did not do this," he murmured in her ear over and over until she relaxed against him.

"He wanted me. And now he has her. How do we…" She choked out a sob. "How do we get her back?"

"I don't know. But we will. I swear it."

"Maria Sagona?" Emilia jumped at the sound of her mother's name, turning toward the man in a bright yellow firefighter's jacket standing just beyond the perimeter of the men who'd formed a wall in front of them.

"That was my mother." Her throat constricted on the word. *Was.* "I'm her oldest daughter, Emilia." She rose, grateful when Dom stood behind her, supporting her body with his.

"We didn't find anyone else in the house. Was that your

mother on the lawn?" She nodded, not trusting her voice. "She appears to be the only casualty. Do you know what caused the fire?" he asked, but that question was directed at Dom.

"Varda," Dom confirmed, and the man's mouth set into a hard line.

"What are you doing?" Emilia hissed, twisting to look up at his face. Dom gave her shoulders a gentle squeeze.

"We'll mark it down as accidental. It looks like it might have started in a bedroom upstairs. We can say a candle got knocked over."

They gripped forearms before the man nodded at her and wandered away. Emilia watched him go, her gaze catching on the burned-out husk of her mother's home, tendrils of smoke drifting up into the starless black sky. The place had never been hers, but everything she owned had been inside.

What were they supposed to do now? Where were they supposed to go? And did any of that really matter until Bella was back in her arms?

"Who was that?" Emilia spun, jabbing her finger into Dom's chest. "And why did you tell him the truth? Are you trying to get my sister killed?"

Dom's eyes darkened at the accusation, and he captured her hand in his before she could poke him again, lacing their fingers together and jerking her forward. "He's one of our men. And we need his help if we don't want the police poking around."

She looked out over the yard and saw the same firefighter talking with a police officer, gesturing toward the house while the officer nodded. "Now they won't investigate because they think it's an accident."

"Exactly."

Emilia sagged against him, wrapping her free arm around

his neck. "I'm sorry." Her breath hitched, but she swallowed the tears. "I just want her back."

Dom rubbed a hand up and down her back. "I know. I'm going to get her back for you." He turned to Antonio. "Can you take me through everything that happened?"

Antonio looked back and forth between them before his gaze settled on Dom. "Bella and I were across the street with friends." He shot a look at his sister. "Emilia asked us not to be home without her and said she had to work late, so we stayed over to watch a movie."

Dom squeezed her fingers when she shifted on her feet. "Then why were you in the house?"

"Mama called Bella. She sounded scared. She thought someone had broken in and wanted help."

Her temper flared, and Emilia tried unsuccessfully to stamp it out. "She thought someone dangerous was in the house, and she called her two teenage children to help?" she gritted out.

Antonio shoved a hand through his hair so it stuck out at odd angles and blew out a breath. "Yeah. We looked out the window, and we didn't see anyone, didn't see any doors open. But we were worried, so we wanted to check."

"Then what?" Emilia prompted when he didn't continue.

"When we pushed open the front door, we heard screams." He shook his head as if he was trying to clear the sound from his memory. "I told Bella to go back outside and call you. So you could call him." He gestured at Dom.

"I went looking for Mama. I didn't realize she was upstairs until I heard him running down them. I only saw him for a split second, but it looked like Varda. I yelled Mama's name and ran upstairs to find her."

He shuddered, curling in on himself as he remembered. "Your room was on fire, and when I went into Mama's, I found her on the floor. There was blood. So much blood."

"Antonio," Emilia breathed, throat tight.

She sank down next to him on the tailgate and wrapped her arms around him. She expected him to brush her away, to hate her for not being there, but he surprised her by leaning into her instead. They waited for him to tell the rest of it.

"The fire was so hot. It was moving into the hallway by the time I dragged her onto the landing. I got her down the back stairs, but the smoke was so thick I couldn't see anything. Then he was there." He gestured at Dom. "And you know the rest."

"Did Varda say anything to you?"

Antonio looked up at Dom, brows knit together. "No. Why?"

"Then how do you know he came here for Emilia?"

Antonio opened his mouth and shook his head. "I don't know. Mama kept talking about Emilia. 'It was supposed to be Emilia. She's the one.' She said that over and over."

Dom's grip tightened on her shoulder, and she fought back a fresh wave of tears. What good would it do to cry over a woman who'd never cared about her own daughter past what Emilia could do for her? A woman who'd tried to sacrifice her in the end.

"I should have done more," Antonio whispered. "I could have saved her."

"No," Emilia assured him. "You did everything you could. This isn't your fault."

"We have to find Bella," Antonio said, voice thick with unshed tears. "She has to be okay. She's my other half."

"We will." Emilia looked up at Dom, who nodded. "We're going to find her, Antonio. I promise you we will."

Rossi stepped up next to the SUV, motioning Dom over, and Emilia joined them. "They think they found him. No confirmation on whether he has the girl with him, though."

"You found him already?" Emilia asked. "Where is he?"

Rossi waited for Dom's nod of approval before speaking. "We think he's here." Rossi held up a photo of a map with a red circle on it. "It's closer to a populated area than I assumed he'd go for, but we've staked it out before. It doesn't have much surveillance, so he wouldn't see us coming."

"This is one we suspected had tunnels under it, though, right?"

"Yeah," Rossi confirmed. "He could be hiding her anywhere."

Emilia didn't like the way Franco said hiding. Like Bella might already be dead. Dom laid a reassuring hand on the small of her back.

"Send a team to scope it out. I want confirmation they're in there, but I don't want them to engage. I'm going to take Emilia and Antonio to the compound. Meet me there when you're done."

Once Rossi left, Dom cupped her face in his hands and pressed a kiss to her forehead. "I'm going to fix it, kitten."

She blew out a long breath and nodded. "Are you sure you want us at the compound? We could probably stay with the neighbors."

Dom looked offended at the idea. "The only place I trust you're safe is under my roof with my men. No arguments," he said when she opened her mouth to speak. "I won't risk you. Come on, let me get you settled. You can shower and get something to eat."

Antonio climbed woodenly into the backseat of Dom's SUV, and Emilia climbed in beside him, reaching out to take his hand in the dark. They drove in silence, and each mile away from the house made her stomach tighten. Bella was out there. With him. Alone, scared, maybe hurt.

Emilia pressed the back of her hand to her mouth to stifle a sob. It was her job to keep her brother and sister safe, and she'd failed them. She'd been so wrapped up in Dom that she'd neglected them. She was no better than her mother. Putting her own fleeting happiness above the safety of the people she loved.

Dom watched her in the rearview mirror. She felt the heaviness of his gaze, even though she refused to meet it. How could she? Whatever he wanted to say to try and make her feel better, this was her fault. If she'd been there, she could have done something. Or at least spared Bella by presenting Varda with his real target. Her.

They pulled up to the compound and through the gate, Antonio's hand tightening on hers when the house came into view. As soon as Dom parked at the top of the driveway, half a dozen men rushed out to greet him, and he barked orders as he led them inside.

She'd never been inside the main house before. For those few days she was here, she never left the pool house. When they were hungry, someone brought food and then came back to collect the dishes. She'd had everything she needed in that little house, Dom included.

But as nice as it was, it was nothing compared to the main house with its white stone and wall of windows and soaring ceilings. Antonio took in everything in awed silence, wrapping a protective arm around her even though she was the one who was supposed to be protecting him.

They stopped in the doorway to a living room. A man with dark blond hair reclined on one of the sofas, a knife twisting around and around his fingers. He looked cold, dangerous, and his piercing green gaze sent a shiver down her spine.

"Alexei," Dom said, reaching for Emilia's hand. "This is Emilia. And her brother Antonio."

"The infamous Emilia." Alexei shoved off the couch and stalked across the room to stop in front of her. "You drive our Dom to do such wicked things in the name of love."

"Shut up, you asshole," Dom said, tightening his grip when Emilia's hand jerked in his. "You look over the property map I sent you?"

"I did. Hard to say where exactly the tunnels would dump out, if there are any. Makes me lean toward the tunnels being a rumor. Unless he was dumb enough to build them so he crawled out of the ground in the city square."

Dom nodded. "I thought the same. We'll leave as soon as Rossi gets back."

"You really should have the doctor look at you before you go."

Emilia turned at the sound of a woman's voice. She was gorgeous, with subtle hourglass curves and dark brown hair swinging to her shoulders. Alexei's eyes softened when he saw her, and he wrapped his arm around her, pulling her against his side.

"What are you doing here, Carina?"

"You almost died in a fire, I'm told." She turned to Emilia with a curious look. "And I've been dying to meet the mysterious Emilia. I brought you some clothes."

"That's very…" Emilia swallowed around the lump in her throat. "Thank you. That's very kind."

"I'm sure we can find something for you," Carina said to Antonio. "But first, the doctor. Smoke inhalation isn't good for you. I should know." Alexei frowned and gave Carina's neck a quick kiss.

An older gentleman appeared in the doorway with a stethoscope draped around his neck, and Emilia nudged Antonio forward.

"I don't need a doctor," Dom grumbled as the doctor listened to Antonio's lungs.

"Yes, you do," Emilia insisted before Carina could speak, earning an approving nod from the woman.

Dom sighed but didn't argue again, letting the doctor listen to his lungs and check his eyes and throat.

"Lungs and hearts sound good. Everyone seems healthy. But I'd suggest food if you can stomach it, lots of water, and plenty of rest. I'll be back to do another check tomorrow."

"Thank you," Carina said, dismissing the doctor before Dom could protest again. "There's food on the stove reheating whenever you're hungry. Otto can show you where the kitchen is," Carina said to Antonio.

Emilia hesitated. The idea of ever letting Antonio out of her sight again made her uneasy. But they were safe here. She knew that. She nodded, and he followed Otto around the corner, shoulders slumped.

"He won't survive it if we lose her. He feels responsible for Mama already."

"Your mother's death wasn't any more his fault than it was yours," Dom said, voice laced with anger. "I won't have you blaming yourself for it, Emilia."

"It's not that simple. I—"

"It is that simple. You did not put them in danger. Your mother did when she called them. They weren't home already because of you."

"If I'd been there…"

Panic flashed in his eyes, and his hold on her tightened. "You weren't, and because of that, you're safe."

"I'm safe." Tears gathered in her eyes, and she blinked them back. "But Bella isn't. What's he going to do to her?"

"Nothing," Dom said, glaring at Alexei when he scoffed. "He doesn't want Bella. He wants you. He won't get you if he hurts her."

"But he hasn't even asked for me. We haven't—"

The shrill ring of her cell phone sliced through her words, and she jumped.

"Answer it," Dom said, and she dug the phone out of her pocket. Unknown number. "Put it on speaker."

Emilia swiped her thumb across the screen to accept the call. "Hello?"

"Emilia. I think I have something you want."

# Chapter Thirty-Five

Dom grabbed Emilia when she swayed on her feet, pulling her in tight against his chest. Varda. Finally making his move.

"I went to your house tonight to have a little chat, but you weren't there. So I took the next best thing."

"If you hurt her—"

"She's fine," Varda insisted. "And she'll stay that way if you follow my directions exactly."

"What do you want?"

"I want you."

Emilia squeezed her eyes shut, and Dom felt her tremble in his arms.

"And if you get me, you'll let her go?"

"That's right," Varda confirmed, though his tone told Dom he was lying. Varda wanted something else, something only Emilia could get for him.

"Why don't you cut to the fucking chase and say what you really want, Varda," Dom growled.

"Oh, Domenico. There you are. I figured you wouldn't be far once Maria told me you managed to turn my spy into your little double-crossing whore. Be careful with cunts like that. They're quick to stab you in the back."

Dom grit his teeth, fighting to keep his voice as even as he could. "Where are you?"

"I suspect you already know. I've seen two black sedans drive by at least three times now. There's a bar near here called Vito's. Meet me there in an hour, and we'll discuss the next steps."

Emilia turned to Dom, eyebrows raised. He was just as surprised. Why would Varda want to meet in public, even at this hour? If he thought Dom wouldn't shoot him in the face unless they were behind closed doors, he was sorely mistaken.

"Don't get any wild ideas, Dom," Varda warned. "Come alone, just the two of you. No weapons. If you don't, there will be consequences."

The line disconnected, and Emilia hurled her phone at the couch. "It can't be that simple. He's toying with us."

"You're right," Alexei agreed. "And Dom was wrong."

"Wrong about what?" Emilia wondered.

"You're not his real target either. Dom is."

Dom nodded. He'd considered the possibility ever since he listened to Maria say those ugly things to her daughter. Varda had no use for Emilia. She'd been a pawn to get to him the entire time.

"He wanted you so he could draw me out. Now he's using your sister to draw us both."

"He wants to kill you," Emilia breathed. "We can't let him do that." She turned to Alexei and Carina, then back to Dom. "I won't let him do that. I can go by myself. Or we can call back and renegotiate."

"Hey." Dom wrapped his arms around her when tears spilled over her cheeks. "He's not going to kill me. Or you or Bella."

"I can't lose you. I can't lose anyone else today, Dom." Her voice was muffled and hoarse against his chest, and he ran a comforting hand down her back.

"If he's drawing you out into public, he must think he has the advantage there," Carina said. "What edge does he think he's got?"

Dom pulled his phone from his pocket and brought up the map Rossi had sent him. The realization hit him all at once.

"He's close to the Gallo border."

"The what?"

"Nero Gallo controls this part of the island," Dom said to Emilia, indicating the borders with his finger.

"Exactly how many Mafia families are there in Sicily?"

"Dozens," Alexei said.

"Five," Dom corrected when Emilia blanched, shoving Alexei back a step. "Five ruling families. Bianchi, Romano, Varda, Gallo, and Antonetti."

Emilia stepped away, rubbing her temple, and Dom's heart sank. He might be in very real danger of losing her when this was said and done.

"And what does Nero Gallo have to do with any of this?"

"He was donating weapons to Varda's cause in the war. Not that it did much good. He won't escape what Matteo has planned for him."

"But Varda might think he can make a run for it," Alexei said. "Use Dom as a bargaining chip and hold off the inevitable for a little while."

"He's mistaken," Dom replied.

The front door opened and closed, and Rossi appeared in the doorway a moment later. "They spotted them."

"We're way ahead of you."

Dom brought Rossi up to speed, keeping a close eye on Emilia, when Carina pulled her to the side of the room. Varda was alone and desperate. They could rush him and take him down, and the entire thing would be over in less than five minutes, but Dom wouldn't risk Bella. He couldn't let Varda take someone else from Emilia. He had to save her sister if he hoped to keep her.

"I don't want anyone close enough to be spotted. If he is in league with Gallo, then Gallo's just as likely to have men stationed as lookouts now that Varda's loyal soldiers are dead. And send men out into the territory to keep an eye on things. I don't want petty skirmishes to pop up as a distraction."

Rossi nodded. "You're really going in without a gun?"

Dom stared at Emilia for a long minute before he answered. "Yeah. I am." He checked his watch. "We need to get going, or we'll miss his deadline."

"Don't do anything stupid," Rossi said, gripping Dom's forearm. "You either," he added to Emilia. "This guy will be a pain in the ass for the rest of his life if you get yourself killed."

Color flooded Emilia's cheeks, and she nodded. Dom turned to Alexei as Carina pulled Emilia in for a hug.

"Brief Matteo on what's going on."

"He's going to hate this."

"Yes," Dom agreed, holding out his hand for Emilia's when she stepped up beside them. "He is."

She laid her palm in his, lacing their fingers together. Dom brought her hand to his lips and pressed a kiss to the back of it. Whatever he had to do, whatever he had to sacrifice. He would make sure Emilia and her sister walked out of this alive.

They drove in silence, hands clasped over the center console and Emilia's thumb drawing circles over his knuckles. He circled the bar twice before finally seeing Varda sitting at a table on the edge of the outdoor patio. He could only see the girl Varda was sitting with from behind, her hair gathered in a messy ponytail.

"Is that her?" He made another loop, trying to give Emilia as good a glimpse of the girl's face as he could with the way they were sitting at the table.

"Yes. I think so. Who else would it be?"

He wouldn't put anything past Varda at this rate.

Parking at the front of the bar, Dom took Emilia's hand, pulling her back against him when she moved toward where Varda was waiting.

"Whatever happens, you need to make sure Bella is okay."

"Dom—"

"She is your priority," he insisted. "You get her out first. And you don't put yourself in harm's way for me. Understand?"

"You expect me to stand there and watch him kill you?"

"No." He grazed her cheek with his thumb and pressed a lingering kiss to her lips. "I expect you to take your sister and get the fuck out of here."

Before she could argue, he stepped away and led her around the side of the patio. He swept the area around them. It was empty of civilians at this hour, the windows dark, but it was hard to tell if people were watching them from the shadows, if anyone was waiting to pounce.

Varda shoved to his feet when he saw them, grabbing the girl by the shoulder and hauling her out of the chair. When she turned, it was obvious she and Emilia were sisters. They had the same heart-shaped face and red hair.

"Bella." Emilia's voice broke, and tears shone in Bella's eyes.

"You actually listened. Isn't that surprising."

"Let her go," Emilia pleaded. "You want me. Take me."

"Tempting," Varda said, bringing his gun up and pressing it against Bella's temple. The girl cringed away, but Varda held her fast. "First let's make sure you followed all the directions. Bella darling, go pat them both down for weapons. If you lie, I'll know."

Varda gave Bella a shove forward, and she stumbled before catching herself on the table's edge. She hesitated in front of Dom, but he raised his arms out to the side and nodded in encouragement. Her hands moved quickly, patting his arms and down his sides.

"Don't forget the legs," Varda barked, and Bella squatted, patting down the length of his legs to his ankles. "Good. Now your sister. And hurry up," he snapped. "I don't have all fucking night."

Emilia mirrored Dom's pose. "It's going to be okay, Bells. I promise. Did he hurt you?"

Bella shook her head as she patted her sister down, tears shimmering in her eyes. She ran her hands down each of her sister's legs before standing again.

"Come here, girl," Varda commanded.

"No," Emilia said, taking a step forward and pushing Bella behind her. "Me for my sister. That was the deal."

"I told you, bitch," Varda sneered. "I can change the rules whenever I want. And if not for you stabbing me in the fucking back, I'd be winning this war. So maybe I'll kill her to punish you, kill you to punish him, and then kill him to give Gallo what he wants."

Dom shifted when Varda took a menacing step closer, positioning his body in front of Emilia's. "Gallo wants me dead? Why?"

"Your brother has become a thorn in his side. I guess Gallo thinks taking out the Bianchi general will buy him some time. Not that I care much. I just need Gallo to float me a loan and keep me alive until I can get off this island."

"Running with your tail tucked firmly between your legs. I always assumed you were a coward."

Varda snarled, aiming the barrel of his gun squarely at Emilia's chest. "Careful, Bianchi. I might get so mad my finger slips."

"Let's stop playing games." Dom gave Emilia a long look, and she shook her head ever so slightly when he closed the gap between him and Varda.

"Dom, don't—"

"We all know I'm the one he really wants," Dom said, raising his arms again. "Come on. Shoot me. I'm right here. Even a piss poor shot like you should be able to hit a mark this close."

Dom took another step forward, a smirk spreading across his lips when Varda hesitated. "See, you've got me right where you want me, and you're still too weak to take the shot. That's why you were never going to be able to hold on to this territory, no matter how hard you tried. And now a better man than you will step in to run things."

"Matteo? He's hardly a better ma—"

"No," Dom said with a dark laugh. "Me. I'll sit on your throne. I'll command your men. I'll make sure they all know what a weak bastard you were until your last fucking breath."

On a strangled snarl, Varda took aim. But Dom anticipated the move, darting forward to grip Varda's wrist and shove it into the air as he fired. Varda lashed out with his free hand, catching Dom in the jaw and snapping his head to the side.

When he took aim again, it wasn't at Dom but at one of the women behind him. Dom dove for the gun, wrapping his fingers around Varda's arm and wrenching it at an unnatural angle until something snapped, and Varda screamed. The gun fell from his limp fingers, and Dom made a grab for it, grunting when Varda recovered fast enough to kick it away.

"I'm going to kill you," Varda panted, cradling his arm

against his chest as he circled, inching closer to where Emilia stood with her sister.

"Not a fucking chance. Emilia," Dom said without turning around. "Take Bella to the car."

"But—"

"Now, Emilia."

He waited until the sound of their footsteps quickly receded, studying Varda as his eyes darted from place to place, searching for the best escape.

"You're not leaving here breathing," Dom said.

"I've been defending myself with my fists longer than you've been alive, boy. You don't scare me."

"That's because you're stupid. But you have some crimes to pay for. And I'm here to collect."

Bringing his foot up into Varda's gut, Dom grinned when Varda doubled over with a groan. He would pay for every penny he took from Emilia, every time he laid a hand on her, every time he scared her or threatened her.

He'd pay for taking Bella. And even though Emilia's mother had seemingly brought this all on herself, Varda would pay for her death too. Just because Dom would enjoy making it hurt.

Varda landed a solid punch to Dom's stomach and had him stumbling back a step. He used the opportunity to scan the ground for the gun he'd kicked away. Unable to find it, he pulled a knife from his jacket pocket and flicked out the blade with his good hand, the other hanging limp at his side.

When Varda lunged, Dom feinted, narrowly missing a slice to his chest but catching Varda in his injured arm. Hissing in pain, Varda dropped back and scanned for the gun again.

Dom seized on the momentary distraction, yanking Varda forward by his shoulders and driving his knee into the bastard's chest, knocking the breath from his lungs. When

Varda fell back against the side of the building, Dom rushed him, grabbing for the knife. But Varda anticipated him, rolling to the side and slashing at Dom's stomach.

Spinning away from the blade only managed to change the knife's trajectory as it dragged along his skin, rending a deep gash from his belly button to his hip. Blood immediately soaked his shirt and the waistband of his pants, and he braced a hand against the brick wall of the bar to steady himself.

"Looks like I might leave here breathing after all," Varda said, voice thin.

Dom wiped his bloody hand on the thigh of his jeans. "You got in one good blow. I'm hardly in a body bag."

"Not yet." Varda grinned. "But you're losing blood pretty fast. Must have nicked something important."

"I've never felt better," Dom lied, swaying on his feet.

Varda's blow might have been lucky, but that didn't make it any less lethal. He needed to find that fucking gun.

"Maybe I should just watch you slowly bleed out," Varda taunted. "Then I'll take your bitch and her sister. They can entertain me."

"In your fucking dreams."

Dom looked up to see Emilia leveling a gun at Varda's back. Varda spun, a predatory grin on his face. But when he lunged for her, Emilia fired as if she'd been born with a gun in her hand. Varda pitched face-first onto the stone and went still. Emilia stood over him, firing one shot into the back of his head.

Moving to her side, he pried the gun from her fingers and tucked it into the waistband of his jeans. "Where the hell did you learn to use a gun?"

"A camera wasn't the only thing my grandfather taught me how to shoot." She gripped his face in her hands and pulled him in for a desperate kiss. "I thought he was going to kill you."

"He was trying."

She stepped back enough to lift his shirt up and tug it off over his head. "Fuck. We need to get you back to the house. To the doctor. Don't tell me you're fine, Domenico," she snapped when he opened his mouth to speak. "I've already watched one person bleed out tonight. I won't watch you too."

Dom let her shoulder some of his weight as she led him back to the car. Bella's face peeked out from the back, eyes wide, while Emilia helped Dom into the passenger seat. He slumped against it, holding his shirt to the wound in his side as his vision blurred.

Varda was right. He was losing a lot of blood.

Emilia jumped behind the wheel and peeled out of the parking spot. "Don't you dare die on me, Domenico Bianchi," Emilia said, voice tight. "If you do, I'll—"

"Never forgive me," Dom finished. "I know."

# Chapter Thirty-Six

Grabbing her robe from the end of the bed, Emilia crossed to the door and quietly eased it open, checking to make sure she hadn't woken Dom before closing it behind her.

The house was dark and silent as she padded down the stairs. Stopping by the patio doors overlooking the pool and the sea beyond, she drew her robe tighter around her and sighed.

With Varda dead, Dom had spent the last two weeks strategically placing his men throughout the territory to maintain tight control over anyone left on Varda's payroll. He spent most days in meetings or on patrol. He was the leader of this territory now, holding it for his brother as they set their sights on their next target.

While Dom finished security updates on Varda's old mansion, he'd moved out of the pool house and into the compound's massive owner's suite with its stunning views. It hadn't even been a question that Emilia and the twins would move in here with him.

They'd seemed to fit themselves seamlessly together, as if

they'd been destined to be a family all along. But everything felt so different between them now. This wasn't the future she'd envisioned when this thing with Varda was finally finished.

Everything was gone. Their home, their security. Every possession they had left in the world burnt to a crisp. She was now responsible for seeing two confused and scared teenagers through this nightmare. And people kept calling to offer condolences for the death of a woman who'd confessed to hating her own child.

Emilia felt shattered. She didn't know how to come back from this, how to pick up all the pieces of herself again. Dom was beginning to sense something was wrong, but she hardly knew how to tell him she'd started to wonder if this was all a mistake.

Her mother had fallen in love with a Mafioso and ended up dead. Maybe it was better to step away. Before she became so consumed by Dom that she was blind to everything else. She couldn't—wouldn't—put Bella and Antonio in danger the way their mother had. And this life was dangerous. Dom had said it himself.

It was easy to love him when she was in his arms, to let everything fall away with the heat of him pressed against her back or when he moved inside her or when he whispered how he would never let anything bad happen to her ever again. But it wasn't only her happiness at stake here. Not anymore.

She had Bella and Antonio to think of now. They had to finish the rest of the school year, maybe look at universities, get jobs, and be normal, adjusted, healthy, happy human beings. They had to be her only focus. Even if it meant sacrificing her own happiness for a little longer.

Turning from the window, she made her way to the

kitchen, surprised to see the golden glow from the light over the stove illuminating a single silhouette.

"What are you doing up at this time of night?" Her eyes darted to the clock over the stove.

Bella turned and offered Emilia a tired smile, hands cupped around a steaming mug. "I couldn't sleep, so I made some hot chocolate. Like Mama used to make." Her voice caught, and she stared down at her mug. "There's more in the pot if you want some."

Crossing to the stove, Emilia pulled a mug from the glass-fronted cabinet and poured in the rest of the thick chocolate drink, setting the pan in the sink.

"Want to talk about it?" she asked Bella, claiming the stool next to her and blowing across the surface of her hot chocolate.

"I finally made Antonio tell me what Mama said to you."

Emilia sighed. "I asked him not to do that."

"I know. But I have more secrets over him than you do. So don't be mad at him."

Shaking her head, Emilia chuckled, then sobered. "It doesn't matter what she said."

"It does," Bella insisted. "It matters because I know you."

"Bella, I—"

"I'm glad she's dead." Bella sniffled, swiping her fingers across her cheeks. "A part of me is sad. She was my mother, and now she's gone. But a bigger part of me is so angry. Angry for how she treated us, for this mess she got us into, for what she said to you."

"This is why I didn't want Antonio to tell you." Emilia reached out to squeeze Bella's hand. "We've had enough taken from us already. I didn't want to steal your good memories of Mama too."

"You think I didn't know what she was like? We were

stuck alone with her for two years after Papa died. It didn't take long to figure it out. Good riddance."

Emilia rubbed at her forehead. This is why she couldn't afford to be distracted now. Bella and Antonio needed all of her attention if they were going to get through this. Her own happiness would have to wait.

"I've been looking at apartments."

Bella went still beside her before slowly lifting her mug to her lips and taking a sip. "Is Dom kicking us out already?"

"What? Of course not. He wants us to move into Varda's old mansion when it's ready."

"Then I don't understand."

"I just want to make sure my focus is on you and Antonio." Emilia took a deep breath and willed the ache in her chest to go away. "You are more important to me than any relationship."

Bella nodded slowly. "So you're breaking your promise to me."

"What? What promise?"

Pushing away from the counter, Bella carried her mug to the sink and ran water into it. "You promised me when this was all over, you would figure out how to be happy. But now you want to walk away from it."

Emilia blinked in surprise. She'd forgotten about that conversation. It seemed like lifetimes ago. And too much had transpired since then.

"Making sure you and Antonio are safe and happy will make me happy."

Bella snorted, turning for the door. "We both know that isn't true. At least not completely." She paused in the doorway, crossing her arms over her chest and squeezing herself tightly. "If that's the choice you want to make, fine. But don't lie to yourself about it."

Bella disappeared down the hall, and Emilia dropped her

head to the counter. It wasn't nearly as simple as Bella made it out to be. Emilia could not—would not—turn into their mother and put her own happiness above the people she was supposed to love and protect.

Easing back from the counter, she crossed to the sink and carefully washed and dried the dishes they'd used, storing them back in the cabinets. Her feet felt heavy as she climbed the stairs. Bella might not understand her choice right now, but she would one day.

Dom, on the other hand, wouldn't understand at all. But she couldn't put the conversation off for much longer. It would be better to make a clean break. He could move into Varda's place and set it up as his command center, and she could move into an apartment with the twins.

She could probably get her old job back. Or Carina might be able to help her find something else. Either way, they would land on their feet, and everything would be fine.

Turning the doorknob slowly, Emilia slipped into the bedroom, stopping short when she saw Dom sitting up in bed. He was reclined against the headboard, sheet pooled around his waist to reveal the stark white bandage stretched over his tan skin.

"I didn't mean to wake you."

"I was awake the minute I felt you slide out of bed." He held his hand out to her, and she went to him. Like a moth to a flame. "Are they okay?"

Shedding her robe, she crawled under the covers and waited for him to scoot down so she could lay her head against his chest. She listened for the steady, reassuring thump of his heartbeat before responding.

"They're okay. Bella couldn't sleep either, so she was in the kitchen making hot chocolate."

"My mother used to make that for me when I had nightmares."

Emilia's smile was sad. "Mine used to make it for Bella and Antonio too."

Dom lay his hand over hers when she rested it on his chest and twirled a strand of her hair around his finger. "What's bothering you?"

"How do you know something is bothering me?" He didn't answer, just waited for her to explain. "I was thinking we should move out."

"The house in Agrigento isn't ready yet. It should be by next week. Then I would really love for you to redecorate. The place is fucking hideous."

"No, I mean." She swallowed hard, willing her voice not to betray her nerves. She'd been practicing this for days, but it never felt quite right. Probably because she didn't want to have to say it. "Me and Bella and Antonio. Maybe we should get our own place. Somewhere we can start over."

His hand stilled in her hair, and she heard his heartbeat quicken under her ear. "Why do you insist on pushing me away when all I want to do is take care of you?"

"That's not what this is. I—"

"Then what is it?"

"Bella and Antonio are my priority right now. I have to make sure they're okay, make sure they're safe, provide for them."

"And you don't think I can do that for them, for you? You don't think I want to?"

She squeezed her eyes shut at the hurt in his voice. "This is more than you bargained for, Dom. You didn't ask for me and two teenagers. And the last thing I need is to end up like my mother and—"

Dom knifed off the bed and hauled her into his lap, gripping her chin in his hand and forcing her to meet his gaze. "You are not your mother, Emilia. How many times and how many ways do I have to say that to you before you believe me?"

The heat in his tone and the sincerity in his eyes almost made her believe him. Almost.

"My mother fell in love with one of Varda's men, and it destroyed her. I don't want loving you to destroy me. The thought of giving you up is hard enough already."

When a tear slipped down her cheek, he caught it with his thumb, cupping her face in his hands. "Then don't, kitten. Let me love you. Let me take care of you, take care of all of you."

"What if she and I are the same? What if—"

"You aren't. You aren't," he said again when she started to protest. "When was the last time your mother quit a job she loved to take care of you? When was the last time she sold everything she had to make sure you were safe? When was the last time she put herself in danger to protect you?"

He pressed a soft kiss to her lips. "When has she ever had less so you could have more? So Bella and Antonio could have more?"

"Never," Emilia whispered. "She's never been that way, never been capable of those things. She was always selfish, cold. But I never thought..." Her breath hitched, and she pressed her lips into a hard line. "I never thought she was all of those things because she hated me."

Dom pulled her closer and pressed a kiss against her temple. "You gave up everything to keep your family safe. Your job, your friends, your freedom. You stole moments of happiness, and now you feel guilty about it. You are nothing like her, Emilia."

Emilia's gaze drifted to the window and the slowly lightening sky beyond it. Soon the gulls would wake and call to each other and boats would fly across the water and fishing trolleys would honk their horns. All of that felt full of promise, of hope, of new beginnings. It felt so out of reach.

"I don't know how to do this part. This isn't how this was supposed to end. Everything is broken. It's not right."

"No, it's not. But you don't have to pick up the pieces alone." He leaned in to press a kiss to her jaw. "Let me help you."

"Why?"

His lips trailed a path to her earlobe, where he whispered against her ear, "Because I love you." He shifted her until she was straddling him, reaching up to tuck a strand of hair behind her ear. "Let me love you, Emilia. You're mine. That's the only thing that matters."

"Yes." She dropped her forehead against his, cupping his face in her hands.

"Say it."

"I'm yours, Dom."

He skimmed his hands down her sides and around to the small of her back, pulling her closer. "That's right. And I'm going to prove to you every day what that means."

Wrapping her arms around his neck, she brushed her lips against his. "Promise me something."

"Anything," he replied, slipping his fingers under the hem of her nightgown and tracing circles over the backs of her thighs.

"Don't ever let me lose myself. I never want to become so lost in something else I forget who I am."

"I promise, kitten. And if you get lost, I'll always come find you."

# A Note for the Reader

Dear Reader,

From the very bottom of my heart, thank you. Out of all the billions of books available to read you choose mine. I had so much fun diving into the dark side of Mafia life in this book and I'm so excited for what comes next for the Bianchi family. I hope you enjoyed Emilia and Dom's story and I'm deeply grateful that you took the time out of your life to come along on their journey.

If you enjoyed this book, I would really appreciate a little more of your time in the form of a review on Goodreads or Amazon or wherever you purchased it.

I couldn't do this writing thing I love so much without you. This is the first book in the Sicilian Mafia Wars Series but I'm not done telling stories yet. Head to Amazon to purchase the next book in the series, The Secrets We Keep featuring Luca, the third Bianchi son, and his forbidden love, Sienna.

For exclusive sneak peeks, updates, release dates, and more, sign up for my newsletter at https://meaghanpierce. com/newsletter or follow me on TikTok.

All my love,
Meaghan

tiktok.com/@meaghanpierceauthor

# Also by Meaghan Pierce

*Callahan Syndicate Series*

Sweet Revenge

Bitter Betrayal

Deadly Obsession

Dark Secrets

www.ingramcontent.com/pod-product-compliance
Lightning Source LLC
Chambersburg PA
CBHW051136190726
48290CB00006B/1876